"BUFFALO STAMPEDE!"

the voice rang out. "We're right in their line and there must be a million in that herd."

Directions were shouted.

"Form a wedge with the wagons, two of the oldest at the point. Have buckets of oil ready to throw on them. Send men to the front with rifles and plenty of shells. You know the rest. Rustle!"

A strange low incessant rumble, a heart-stopping sound, like the rolling of distant thunder, resounded in the air. The ground shook. The din was deafening.

"Hear that?" Shaw asked. "They're running wild, stampeding full tilt! Scared half to death!"

Out there was a mass of brutal life on the rampage. The oil-soaked wagons burst into flames, illuminating the scene with an eerie light.

If the herd split around the obstacle, the buffalo would pass on each side of the wedge. If not—!

Books by Zane Grey

Published by POCKET BOOKS

ZANE GREY

WESTERN UNION

PUBLISHED BY POCKET BOOKS NEW YORK

POCKET BOOKS, a division of Simon & Schuster, Inc.
1230 Avenue of the Americas, New York, N.Y. 10020

Published by arrangement with Harper & Row, Publishers, Inc.

ISBN: 0-671-83537-8

First Pocket Books printing December, 1974

15   14   13   12   11   10   9   8

Printed in the U.S.A.

DEDICATED
TO
A SINGLE STRAND
OF IRON WIRE

It Can Be Done!

Not so long ago President Abraham Lincoln lifted deep cavernous eyes to his friend and visitor, Hiram Sibley, head of the Western Union Telegraph Company.

"Sibley, wonderful as your idea is, its consummation sounds fantastic and visionary. However, I shall ask Congress for an appropriation."

Sibley's idea was to stretch a telegraph wire across the Great Plains and the Rocky Mountains to the Pacific. Long before he knew whether or not Congress would help or if his associates would approve such a project, Sibley sent for his chief engineer, Edward Creighton, who had just returned from a year-long trip to California.

"Here. Look at this map," Creighton said. "There! That line is the Oregon Trail. We'll follow it. I've talked to ranchers, soldiers, buffalo hunters, Pony Express riders. I've talked to the Mormons. There are thousands of hostile savages, millions of buffalo, hundreds of miles of prairie with no trees for telegraph poles. The job figures impracticable and impossible, but *it can be done*."

Congress appropriated only $400,000 toward the building of this telegraph line, which was a tremendous disappointment to Sibley and Creighton.

But the building of a telegraph to connect the East and the West is going forward. To-day marks the beginning of the stringing of that tiny iron wire westward out of Omaha, with Creighton himself in charge.

Chapter One

IT WAS a summer day in 1861, when I boarded a west-bound stage-coach in Omaha, Nebraska, at the end of my resources and the end of my rope.

I put back in my pocket the newspaper clipping which had been responsible for giving me inspiration at a time when I needed it most. At twenty-four years, everything I had tried had somehow failed to hold me. I had long been in doubt whether or not there was anything really in me.

My father wanted me to try law, so I went to Harvard for a year, then gave that up. Then I tried medicine for a year. No good. I had interest in medicine, but I could not stay indoors and study. Those two frustrated years, however, revealed to me what was the matter. The ambition of my parents and relatives to put me in a profession or if not that, into business, had influenced me against what I really wanted.

I needed to get away from Boston and New England, out somewhere in the open country, preferably the West, where I would be free. My mother was Scotch and she said that I was like one of her brothers who was a Highlander and loved the hills and the rivers and the fights of his own country.

Outside of being big and strong and active on my feet, I had no qualifications that I knew of for pioneer life in the West. Nevertheless, it was the West that called increasingly to me.

Then I had been troubled about the rumblings of war between the North and the South. Now it was a fact. My father was a Southerner by birth and strong in his feelings against the Yankees.

I did not feel that I would not have made a good soldier because there was something about a soldier's free life for adventure and danger that appealed to me.

Still, with my parents split on the issues of a Civil War, I seemed between the devil and the deep sea. So altogether my dissatisfaction and unhappiness drove me to undertake the long journey to the West.

As I looked around me, I suddenly noticed that I was the first person aboard the stage. In fact, even the driver himself was nowhere about. But finally the other passengers began to arrive.

There were two soldiers, one a sergeant; weather-beaten, hard young men, who were evidently recovering from too close an intimacy with the bottle. There was a keen-eyed man whom I took to be a rancher, and a buxom woman who was evidently his wife. Another passenger had climbed to the driver's seat. The last one, to judge from his garb and florid face, might have been a well-to-do merchant. He took the seat beside me.

As we were about to roll into the open country a clamor of friendly voices arose, bidding us good-by; no doubt some of our well-wishers actually knew some of the passengers, but from the wave of sound that arose, I could see that the departure of this creaking vehicle was an event for the townspeople; and I seemed to feel that some of the good-bys ringing in my ears were for me.

The Platte River ran to our left. The channel was wide and was composed of two swift muddy streams separated by sand bars and flats. The low banks were lined with willow and cottonwoods just beginning to be clothed with bright green. I had my second glimpse of the great wide Missouri River running bank full, its strong swirling current showing numerous bits of driftwood. I saw a stern wheel steamboat in the distance.

Soon we were out of sight of the river and the town, rolling along at a good clip over a hard packed road which seemed to run in the center of a number of roads. In fact, there was a wide space of perhaps a hundred yards which had been cut several feet deep by the endless stream of wheels that had passed. There were old wheel tracks and fresh wheel tracks on each side of our hard packed road.

I gathered, presently, that we were bound out on a

branch of the Overland Trail, which was the Oregon Trail, for years the thoroughfare from Independence, Missouri, to Oregon. We would come into the main Oregon Trail at Grand Island.

My seat was next to the open window through which I gazed at the winding stream and the level gray plain extending into what appeared to be infinitude. At intervals we passed ranches and scattered cattle, but we were on the edge of wild country. I saw wild ducks on the stream, blue heron standing in the shallows, muskrat houses sticking out of the water, an increasing number of jackrabbits and cottontails, and an occasional gray bushytailed animal of distinctly wolfish aspect.

I gazed and gazed, without tiring of the gray monotony of the scenery. I did not miss any of the scant conversation of the passengers. Presently the gentleman sitting next to me made several affable remarks as to the weather and the pleasant ride, and finally inquired where I was bound.

"I'm going out to work on the Western Union," I replied.

"Indeed! That is very interesting. I'm on my way out to take a look at the work myself. My name is Williamson."

"I'm glad to meet you, sir. My name is Wayne Cameron, from Boston."

"I thought as much," replied the other, with a laugh. "New Englanders are rather easy to tab. Myself, I'm from New York. What sort of a job have you got with the telegraph company?"

"I haven't any—yet . . . but I hope to get one."

"You won't find much trouble on that score—what—with the war and all, they're finding it hard to get men anyway."

We struck up a conversation, and I tried to make myself as agreeable as possible. One thing Williamson said was that construction work had already started from the Pacific coast under an engineer named Gamble who was to build the telegraph line East to meet Edward Creighton's crew, who, by this time, had almost strung their threadlike iron wire to Gothenburg.

Presently Williamson resumed conversation. "Cameron, are you familiar with Creighton's trip across the plains and the mountains to study the land and conditions?"

"Yes, I read about it," I replied. "I think it was heroic."

"It was that and more. I have never met Creighton and I'm very glad that I am going to meet him shortly. From all accounts, he is a wonderful character. Some of the lines he built in the East were not easy jobs by a long ways, but this western idea is beyond conjecture. I heard Hiram Sibley tell about Creighton's trip across the divide to the coast. It really beggared description. He rode six or seven hundred miles via horseback over some of the wildest country. All alone and not sure of his direction. Part of that journey was accomplished in mid-winter through the Humboldt Valley. The hard winds drove sand and alkali dust and snow into the eyes of the lone rider until he was almost blind. Three times the skin peeled from Creighton's face. When he arrived in Carson City he was more dead than alive. Marvelous indeed that he did not perish! But his superb constitution and indomitable will enabled him to carry on to the end."

I turned often to glance at the telegraph line to which Williamson had long since called my attention. The shining yellow peeled poles, the single thread of wire stretching away westward—these seemed somehow to be so little, so insignificant, so frail, to carry the tremendous weight and importance of rapid communication between the East and West. But it was all there in that thin wire —the magic message of Hiram Sibley's friend, the inventor Morse.

By sundown we arrived at a commodious ranch house where we were to spend the night.

In the morning, we were soon away again rolling westward along the Oregon Trail, sometimes within sight of the Platte River and always with wide and increasing stretches of prairie land from ranch to ranch. By and by, somebody told me, there would not be any ranches at all.

That night when we made our stop, this time at a hamlet where there were a store and a saloon and a few shacks, I made overtures to the stage-coach driver. I asked him to have a drink with me, and presently found him to be affable enough and most intensely interesting. The passenger who had ridden on the seat with him departed at this station and I eagerly asked to have his place.

Jim Hawkins (that was the driver's name) had been driving stage-coaches for ten years, and I simply reveled in the thought of what a mine of information he was and what opportunity I would have while I was with him through the long hours on the driver's seat.

In the middle of the night, while I lay awake, I heard the strange and melodious honk-honk of wild geese flying north.

I faced the next day's drive high on the driver's seat in the bright sunlight. The prairie stretched out westward just as gray and hazy as it had been on former days, but it was almost imperceptibly growing to be wild and uninhabitable country. I called the driver's attention to dust clouds on the horizon and a long irregular line low down along the ground that was new to me.

"Wal, young man," he replied, "I reckon there ain't nothin' the matter with your eyesight. Them sharp eyes of yours, when they learn to know what they see, are gonna save your life some day. Thet's your first wagon-train. An' it's a purty big one. You'll see plenty of wagon-trains from now on an' beyond Ft. Kearney; unless it's a thumpin' big one, you'll see they hev an escort of soldiers."

"That sergeant riding with us told me that the telegraph construction work would have to go on under the guardianship of dragoons. Is that necessary altogether on account of the Indians?"

"Mostly, I'd say," returned the driver. "The Cheyennes air gettin' mean again, but they ain't a marker for the Sioux. You'll meet them west of Ft. Laramie an' along the Sweetwater, an' up toward South Pass. Them Indians ride down out of the Wind River mountains, raid like Comanches, an' ride back into their hills where no soldiers could find them. All the tribes of redskins hev a grievance against the whites an' it ain't no wonder. An' some day, mebbe in ten years or more, when the whites begin killin' off the buffalo fer their hides, all the Indians from the Dakotas to the Rio Grande will rise up to fight like the devils they air. Fer the buffalo air their living."

"But I've read that there are millions of buffalo," I said. "Surely the hunting of buffalo for their meat and hides would not make enough difference in their numbers to inflame the savages."

"I reckon it would," rejoined Hawkins, shaking his grizzled head. "Buffalo an' deer an' all game would last forever if they were hunted only by the Indians. White men are mostly wasters, as well as bein' greedy and unscrupulous. I know an old Indian onct who said white men were heap hogs."

"But there is such a thing as progress," I protested. "America has to expand. The tide of empire has set toward the West. First came the Spanish missionaries, then the fur traders, then the explorers, then the pioneers and the gold seekers—and now we have the telegraph wire. Just as surely as that is successful there will be railroads crossing the continent."

"Shore, son, shore you're right," replied Hawkins. "Thet's as true as we're sittin' here. But it doesn't do 'way with the fact thet this was the red man's country, thet he was depraved by liquor, thet he has been robbed, an' will go on bein' robbed until he rebels an' fights against overwhelmin' odds until what's left of him will be driven back into the waste places of the West. Jest how it is in the sight of God, I cain't reckon. But in mine it shore ain't a purty picture."

That dissertation of the old stage-coach driver gave me an entirely new idea of the American Indian.

We rapidly rolled on to catch up with the wagon-train. Before we reached it I took advantage of a bend in the road ahead and counted the big prairie schooners. There were sixty-three of them. They were hauled by yokes of oxen. Along each side men on horseback rode with them. These large prairie schooners seemed alive, and rolled along with the spirit that dominated these pioneers. They looked like big boats mounted on huge wheels and with wide brown canvas tops. Here and there, however, were wagons that did not have a canvas cover. Some were on one side of the wide Oregon Trail and some on the other.

As we caught up with them Hawkins slackened somewhat the brisk gait of his teams. Still that was fast enough to pass by the prairie schooners as if they were stationary. The huge oxen wagged to and fro with their heads bent; the drivers' seats, beside the driver himself, were usually loaded with children and young people, and here and there a woman.

As we went by with Hawkins and some of the passengers in the coach cheerily calling, the pioneers returned the expressions of good will and good luck. The round aperture under the canvas hood was almost in every case enlivened by one or more young women. The riders on horseback, mostly traveling alone, were sturdy men in the crude habiliments of pioneers. I waved my hat at the youngsters.

As we drove by one of the big prairie schooners, I espied a pretty girl sitting beside a stalwart, gray-headed driver. Her eyes met mine as we drove alongside for a moment and I felt that I should not soon forget them or the luster of her rippling hair. I waved my sombrero at her and she smiled and raised a gauntleted hand. Then she was gone back out of sight and wagon by wagon took the place of the one she had ridden in. I looked and looked but somehow the great zest for me did not continue. I would have liked to have the stage-coach drive alongside that particular prairie schooner all the rest of the day. But we rolled on.

I felt a pang when I realized that there was a girl that I could have liked and would surely never see again.

Toward the front end of the wagon-train the horsemen were more numerous, and half a dozen or more with long rifles over their saddles led the caravan.

We passed on ahead of the wagon-train and again faced the endless plain. Occasionally I still looked back and finally, when the wagon-train disappeared in the distance, I sighed and looked no more. That girl had interested me. I would not soon forget the flash of her eyes, the flush that came to her cheeks, the shine of her chestnut hair, and that friendly wave of hand.

Chapter Two

NOTHING IN the next several days took the thrilling place of that wagon-train. Grand Island, where we arrived one night after dark, seemed like all the other Nebraska stops, only there were more buildings, more lights and more people. Here we joined the main Oregon Trail which was deeper and broader.

Our next stop was Ft. Kearney where we lost our soldier passengers. It appeared to be just a barracks and I was disappointed.

We rolled on west of Kearney. One day I saw a moving dot away along the road and thin puffs of dust so far away that I could not make out what they were.

"Driver, what's that coming?" I asked.

"Wal, if I'm kerrect," he replied, after a long squint down the road, "thet'll be Jed Schwartz. Along here is where he usually passes me. He's a Pony Express rider."

My curiosity mounted in proportion. I had heard of the heroism of the Pony Express riders and now I saw one, swiftly bearing down upon us. In this rarefied western atmosphere, objects looked very much closer than they actually were. It was amazing how that moving black spot enlarged until it stood out in the outline of a horse and rider. As he drew closer I saw that the house was stretched out, running low and level, his mane and tail flying, and the rider's scarf burned in the sunlight and waved out behind him.

Hawkins guided his teams to the right and gave the Express rider an open road. He bore down on us like the wind and as he flashed by, too swiftly for me to see anything clearly, he waved his gloved hand at Hawkins and yelled a greeting. The driver answered just as lustily.

I turned to watch the horse running down the road. It was a big lean animal, swift and strong, and the way he spread distance between him and the stage-coach was something remarkable to see. It was my first experience with a fast running horse in the West where horses were of cardinal importance. Then in response to my eager inquiries Hawkins said:

"I reckon this here telegraph line you're goin' to help build will spell the end of the Pony Express. Some mighty fine fellers will be out of jobs, but I reckon they'll be glad to quit with their scalps still on. They carry the mail. It costs five dollars an ounce. The riders change horses every ten miles or so an' they keep their horses on a dead run from one station to another. It takes them eight days to ride from Saint Jo, Missouri, to the Coast. I've known some mighty fine fellers on the Pony Express. Jed Schwartz is about the best of the lot. He's a hard, fearless rider. He packs two guns an' say, can he use 'em!"

"I'd like to be a Pony Express rider," I said almost to myself.

"Wal, it's sort of late in the day now," replied the driver, who had evidently heard me. "But you'll get your belly full of ridin' an' shootin' on this Western Union, if I don't miss my guess."

Hawkins was loquacious enough to satisfy even an insatiable tenderfoot like me. I asked him a thousand questions and I reserved one to ask him when he got better acquainted with me. That question was—how to comport myself when I once got out on the frontier. I didn't have courage enough to ask him yet.

Next day we caught up with a small wagon-train hauling telegraph poles. I was thrilled because I knew at last we were approaching our destination. We reached Gothenburg quite a while after dark. The same dull yellow lights, the same dusty road, the same shacks and tents, and high board fronts with which I had become familiar, appeared to compose this town of Gothenburg.

"Son, this is a purty hot place," admonished Hawkins, with a chuckle. "I wouldn't advise you to miss seein' what's goin' on, but mind your p's and q's. I reckon the construction camp is here or close by and the burg will be lively. You're shore likely to be taken fer a tenderfoot. Wal, don't take no backtalk from nobody. When you go into Red Pierce's gamblin' hell, if you've got any money, look out fer the painted ladies an' steer clear of the gamin' tables."

The tavern which took care of the travelers was unprepossessing from the outside, but inside it proved to be comfortable with a clean room and bed and a supper to which I certainly did ample justice. There were two girls waiting on tables and one of them was decidedly pretty. She had a pair of roguish eyes that she was not afraid to use. She recalled to me the girl of the wagon-train who had smiled and waved at me. I began to grasp that the farther I got away from her the stronger my regret would be.

After supper I thought I would stroll down the street and look things over. As I went out, Williamson accosted me and said with hearty satisfaction:

"Well, Cameron, we've arrived. The construction work and Creighton's traveling camp are only a few miles from here. The town is full of workers. I'll keep a look-out for Creighton and I'll tell him about you if he comes into town."

I thanked him and then went outside on the plank walk and tried to accustom my eyes to the opaque darkness dimly lighted by yellow lamps. There were saddle horses tied to hitching rails in front of the tavern and several vehicles, one of which was a buckboard. I saw a few pedestrians but not enough to account for the noise that seemed to come from the main square down the street.

Presently I walked in that direction and began to encounter a motley string of men, a score or more in all. There were cattlemen and cowboys, but, for the most part, the pedestrians appeared to be laborers.

A little farther on I came to a large, crude-looking edifice constructed of boards and made emphatic by reason of the wide-open door from which bright lights streamed and men were passing in and out. I saw a painted sign above this door with the rude letters spelling "Red Pierce."

With a decided acceleration of my pulse, I entered my first gambling hall in the West. Whatever I had anticipated was somewhat different from the reality, but I was in no wise disappointed. The place was an enormous hall with three huge lamps strung down the middle and a long bar at the left where men stood two or three deep, drinking and laughing and talking.

To the right, opposite the bar, were a number of tables around which the gamblers were sitting and standing. I heard the rattle of the roulette wheel and the musical clink of coins, but if there were any voices among these players, they were silenced by the louder clamor of those at the bar.

At that juncture there burst out a lively flare of music and I looked down the hall to see a number of men standing around an open space on the floor where several couples were dancing. At that distance the girls appeared to be attractive and showed white faces and scarlet lips and bare arms.

There were spectators at the gambling tables and I joined them to look on for a while. When I tired of this I walked back to the lower end of the hall and watched the dancers. It did not occur to me until one of the girls took particular notice of me, flashing sharp eyes from my boots to my head, that I was surely conspicuous in that crowd. It annoyed me, but remembering Hawkins' advice, I decided to stand my ground. I regretted that decision presently when the dance ended and one of the girls came up to me. I certainly did not remember ever being looked over as I was then.

"Would you like to dance?" inquired the girl, smiling up at me. She had a nice voice and she did not look at all like a dance-hall girl to me.

"Yes," I replied diffidently, "but I'm an utter stranger, just got in, and I feel——"

As I hesitated she took my arm and interrupted.

"You're a stranger all right, but that's nothing. Strangers come every day. Let's dance. I'll soon make you feel at home."

I was about to surrender to her suggestion, not without pleasurable sensations, when she was rudely torn away from me by a tall dark young man, a rowdy in appearance and certainly under the influence of drink.

"Come on, Ruby," he said, in a thick voice. "What d'ye mean grabbin' that tenderfoot? You promised this dance to me."

He whirled her away, though hardly before I became aware that it was much to the girl's distaste. She flashed me another smile which was reassuring, to say the least. I did not mind the interruption so much because I really would rather not have danced, but the coarse allusion to my being a tenderfoot rubbed me the wrong way and I thought I'd better make tracks out of that place. And I was going out when something halted me as I said to myself, "No, I'll be damned if I will! It's coming to me and I may as well take it and get used to it."

So I watched the gamblers for a while. I was approached by several men, certainly not workmen, who looked me over with sharp eyes as if they could pierce through my clothes into my pockets. They asked me to participate in this game and that. I declined.

I changed my position to one behind some spectators beside the roulette table and I was unmolested for a while. Then I watched the poker game at another table where there were gold double eagles and rolls of greenbacks in front of each gambler. This was a big game. And the three men sitting with the two black-garbed gamblers certainly were not laborers.

Then my attention was distracted, and so was that of everyone in the hall, by a fight outside on the walk. There were loud voices, scuffling boots, and a gun shot—after which there was silence. The players resumed their gambling and a few men left the bar to peer out the door to see what had caused the excitement. I joined them but could not discover any signs of what had surely been a fight.

Manifestly such commotions as this were commonplace in Gothenburg. Just as commonplace, I observed, was the fact that most of the men present packed guns. I asked a bystander if there were any officers of the law in that town and he laughed at me. That was not so pleasant. I wondered if I should have taken the advice which that driver, Hawkins, had given me about purchasing a gun.

At this juncture, as I was moving away from the gambling tables, I was accosted by three men, one of whom was the rowdy who had snatched the girl off of my arm. He said something to the man in the middle about me being the fellow. This central figure in the trio was a short, low-browed man with prominent eyes and a leering look.

"Stranger hereabouts, huh?" he asked. "What's your business here?"

"That's my business," I replied, tersely.

"Say, stranger, it don't pay newcomers, specially tenderfeet, to be impolite in these diggin's."

"I did not mean to be impolite. I answered you in the tone in which you addressed me."

"Well, Yankee sticks out all over you, young fella. And if it didn't stick out, we sure could hear it."

"Certainly I'm a Yankee," I replied, beginning to feel heat in my veins.

"Suppose you set up the drinks," he suggested, insolently.

"I won't do anything of the kind, and if I buy drinks I'll choose those with whom I want to drink."

"See hyar, tenderfoot," interposed the dark-faced rowdy. "I take that as an insult. And it's too much comin' after your gettin' fresh with my girl."

"You're drunk or crazy," I returned hotly. "I didn't get fresh with your girl."

Then without more ado he slapped my face and not by any means lightly. The blow amazed me and, suddenly infuriated, I lunged out and knocked him sprawling to the floor. Some of the gamblers noticed the incident, then reverted to their game, while some watching bystanders laughed. Out of the corner of my eye, as I watched my assailant slowly get up from the floor, I saw two figures come in the door and move around sideways. One figure was tall and slim and the other was short and bowlegged. They passed out of range of my sight, but I had a feeling that they were interested in my encounter with this trio and it worried me to have them pass behind me. But I could not turn then because the center man who had been the first to accost me pulled his gun and extended it low down, almost pointed at my feet.

"Tenderfoot, you'll order drinks for us and dance a little to boot."

"Mister, I won't do anything of the kind," I rang out at him.

"Aw, yes, you will. Do some fancy steppin' now or I might hit your leg."

"You go to hell! Isn't this a free country out here? What kind of a man are you to threaten me with a gun just because I won't make myself ridiculous?"

"Dance, tenderfoot," he howled in fiendish glee, and his gun spouted red and banged at my feet.

I felt the burn of a bullet grazing me above my ankle. I was stunned and suddenly divided between fury and terror. He had attracted the attention of everybody and it was plain he was going to shoot at my feet again. I did not know what to do.

I had no idea how I would have further reacted to that situation but I was spared the painful decision by the cutting in of a cold voice in a single ringing word which in my agitation I could not distinguish. Then a sharp gunshot rang out behind me. With a loud yell the bully dropped his gun clattering to the floor and clapped a hand to his shoulder. I saw blood spurt out between his fingers. He was suddenly transformed into a different man, his face showing an agony of pain and extreme fright.

Then into my sight from one side strode the two figures I had before caught out of the corner of my eye. The tall one held a smoking gun extended and as he stepped, he moved it slightly indicating the door.

"Hombre, thet's the second time to-day you've bothered me," he drawled in cool, easy, soft speech, with an accent peculiarly southern. "Beware of the third time!"

And again the smoking gun made that slight unmistakable move toward the door. The three desperadoes, if they really were such, were quick to take the hint. One of them picked up the gun from the floor and the three of them hurriedly left the saloon. At that the sudden silence was broken again by the sound of voices and the rattle of the roulette wheel.

I turned away from that last sight of my assailants to confront my rescuer. He was in the act of sheathing the long gun and his peculiarly light eyes were fastened on the men at the bar, some of whom had protested at the fracas.

"Much obliged—you did me a might good turn," I burst out, as he turned to face me. He had a young, still smooth face, tanned to a gold hue, and I thought it was almost girlish in its singular charm. Then his companion addressed me.

"Thet hombre must hev hit you," he said. "Yore laig is kinda quiverin'. 'Spose you let me take a look." And he went down on one knee and ran his hands over my left leg. "Ahuh, hyar's a hole in yore pants. . . . But I don't feel any blood. . . . Wal, he jest burned you an' you shore air plum lucky. He might've busted a bone." He arose to his feet, his ruddy homely face wreathed in a grin. "Reckon thet is the fust time you've ever felt hot lead?"

"Indeed it is," I replied, in great relief.

"Purty close shave," he went on. "Most times a tenderfoot has to pay a damn sight more than thet to git by the bad place."

"Fellows, I knew I was a tenderfoot all right, but I just didn't know how to react to that situation."

"You didn't do so bad," returned the little fellow with friendliness. "We was listenin' an' watchin'. You shore socked thet mean hombre an' I was tickled to death to see him git it. He reckons he owns thet dance-hall gurl, Ruby, an' he's diad wrong. She was nice to me an' particular nice to Vance hyar."

"Stranger, mebbe you will drink with us?" asked the tall fellow.

"I will—I certainly do need a bracer."

He led the way to the bar where at one end the customers were obviously eager to give him room and presently we were lined up facing each other with glasses in hand. I thought it about time to introduce myself.

23

"My name's Wayne Cameron, from Boston. I'm out here to go to work on the telegraph line."

"Wal, Cameron, you shore didn't need to tell us you were a Yankee," returned the little fellow, with a laugh. "Thet ain't so good out hyar. My pard hyar, Vance Shaw, is a dyed-in-the-wool rebel an' I'm from Missouri. But mebbe we kin git along together. I most forgot. My name is Jack Lowden."

I shook hands with him and then with Shaw. There was a great similarity in their handshakes, but a potent difference in their hands. Lowden's was coarse and calloused and the grip was strong and friendly. Shaw's hand was slim and soft, almost like a girl's, but he had a grip as if his hand were steel covered with velvet. Then we proceeded to take our drinks.

"I take it you're cowboys?" I queried.

"Yep, jest plain cowhands, so far as shootin' an' ridin' air concerned."

"Will you have a drink on me?" I asked.

"No thanks. One's enough," replied Shaw. "Let's get out of here. Ruby's spotted me an' I've a hunch she'll edge this way. If she gets another dance with me I'll have to bore thet mean hombre proper."

"Wal, hell!" exclaimed Lowden. "You oughta hev done thet last night. Why for do you want to turn the girl down 'cause of thet jealous geezer? You liked her, didn't you?"

"I reckon," rejoined Shaw, thoughtfully. "More'n a fellow ought to like a dance-hall girl. But she's only sixteen years old—kinda fresh an' innocent yet, an' I feel sorry for her. I told you, Jack, I didn't like the set-up. There's a nigger in the woodpile about this dance-hall situation. If I hang around here any longer—you know me, pard. I just cain't keep out of things."

"Mebbe this is the deal thet you oughtn't to stay out of," said Lowden tersely. "Come on, let's mosey."

We went outside and stood in the bright light to the right of the wide doorway. I asked my new acquaintances to come down to the tavern with me and have a smoke and a talk.

"Shore'd like to," returned Shaw. "But let's hang here for a little. I'm lookin' for someone."

"Hell, pard, you've been lookin' fer thet Texas hombre since we left the Rio Grande," said Lowden with disdain. "We'll never run into him way up hyar around the north pole."

We lounged at ease outside the gambling hall, and while my cowboy friends scrutinized the pedestrians passing to and fro, I took advantage of the opportunity to size them up with a keenness I never remembered applying to anyone I had ever met before.

Shaw was tall and slim but on close scrutiny he appeared to me a magnificently built horseman, broadshouldered, small-hipped, round-limbed, and when he moved, the muscles of his arms and legs showed through his clothes. He wore dark blue jeans much the worse for wear and dusty in places. He smelled of leather and horse-flesh and smoke. He wore high-topped, high-heeled boots, practically worn out.

His gun belt was dark except where the shiny tips of shells showed, and the sheath, also dark, hid all but the black butt of the big gun. That gun sheath and gun hung inconspicuously quite far below his right hip, and I noticed his gun belt crossed the front of him somewhat below the belt that held up his trousers. Over his blouse he wore a thin vest of some kind, also dark, and his broken-rimmed sombrero was dusty and full of holes. The wide brim, however, did not hide his fair clustering hair.

Despite his striking get-up, his face fascinated me most. From side view it was clear cut as a cameo, dark, cold, at once a youthful face, yet in shadow seeming to show under the smooth skin the lines and ravages of havoc. I remarked again that he had the most extraordinary eyes I had ever looked into. He must be as grand as he appeared, I decided, and I warmed to him with the most unusual emotion.

Lowden was also remarkable in his appearance, though he presented a vivid contrast in every way to his comrade. He was small of stature, sturdy and powerful, with arms too long for his body and legs markedly bowed from living much on horses. In repose his ugly face was hard and lined. His eyes were blue and possessed the same look that characterized Shaw's, only not so intent.

As I studied these Westerners, more and more resolved to try to make friends with them, Shaw kept silent while his partner, watching just as sharply, made caustic remarks about the pedestrians. Suddenly Lowden's tone showed more than casual interest.

"Pard, look hyar. See thet cowboy edgin' closer? He's gonna brace us. Gosh, he looks down on his luck. Ragged, worn out, beard uncut, an' he's been sleepin' in the brush all right."

I was quick to turn my attention to the individual so strikingly indicated. He was now coming toward us, hesitatingly at first, and then, as if finding our scrutiny favorable, with more assurance. He might have been about our age, but his haggard face permitted of no accurate judgment about it. He had fierce dark eyes in which I detected a shadow of hope. He stopped abreast of us.

"Howdy, cowboys," he said. " 'Scuse me for bracin' you, but you're the first approachable riders I've seen."

"Howdy yourself," returned Jack, friendly enough. "Shore we're approachable."

"I wanta ask if you'll buy a grand hoss?"

"What's wrong with the cowboy who'll sell his grand hoss?" returned Shaw, curtly.

"Why do you suppose, man?" flashed the cowboy with spirit, as if nettled at the implication. "I've been ridin' the grub line for days, an' believe me, camps an' ranches are few and far between along this old trail. I'm most starved to death."

"Wal, thet's reason enough," returned Shaw, thoughtfully. "We won't buy yore grand hoss, but we'll see thet you eat. Is thet all yo're lookin' for?"

"Thank you, cowboy. . . . Good Lord, it's so long since I looked for anythin' else that I've forgotten what there might be to look for."

While these two men, about equal in height, locked glances, Lowden took a step forward and interposed.

"Cowboy, you could hev struck wuss fellers then us,

if I do say it myself. You kin talk or not as you like. My pard hyar is from Texas an' I'm his ridin' hand. This big gazabo with us is a Yankee from down East, but we reckon he's all right."

"I wouldn't mind talkin' after I get somethin' to eat an' a drink," returned the stranger.

"Hyar, 'scuse us fer bein' so thick. Take this money. There's a purty good eatin' place next door. Go in there and fill up. We'll be hyar a while—*if* you want to come back."

The cowboy took the money with a grateful look, and without a word, hurried to the door of the restaurant and went in.

"Vance, what do you know about thet?" queried Lowden, with strong interest.

"About what?" asked his comrade.

"Why, you dern fool, is the milk of human kindness soured in yore breast?"

"No, Jack, I reckon not, but it's gettin' kind of a bitter taste."

"Dawg-gone you, yo're a-lyin'," returned Lowden. "Cameron, what did you think about thet hombre who jest braced us?"

Thus appealed to, I frankly unburdened myself of my impressions of the fellow. Lowden replied with a snort of satisfaction.

"See there, pard. Our Yankee tenderfoot is purty durn keen. Thet feller is a purty sad case. Wouldn't you say he's on the dodge?"

"Reckon I got thet hunch. Thet cowboy has killed somebody an' not very long ago. But I wouldn't take him for crooked."

"Neither would I, pard, but you know us tender-hearted cowhands hev made mistakes before. Howsomever, let's take a chance an' wait fer him an' see how he stacks up."

No more was said at the moment and the cowboys resumed their watching of the passers-by and I fell to doing likewise. I found difficulty in being what I thought rational in my attitude toward my new comrades and the time and place. My intense interest was not consistent with New England aloofness and judgment, but it was as if I had suddenly discovered in myself instincts and feelings that I never knew I possessed. I tried to place each individual that came along and to identify him as workman, cattleman, teamster, gambler, and so on. There were not so many pedestrians now as there had been earlier in the evening.

Presently it afforded me great pleasure to espy a couple of Indians approaching. They were far from the dignified romantic specimens that my imagination had conjured up. Their short bulky forms were blanketed, their black hair fell over their shoulders, and their swarthy features were interesting but not attractive. They shuffled along on moccasined feet and their short bowlegs showed beneath the blankets. As they passed us, Lowden remarked under his breath, "Lousy redskins!"

I did not see a single woman on the street during that half hour we stood there. Probably there were but few women in the town. I felt curious to see the dance-hall girl, Ruby, again, and then suddenly my mind was stirred by memory of the wagon-train girl whose unforgettable face intrigued me more and more. At this juncture the luckless cowboy came out of the restaurant and approached us directly.

"Fellers, I'm glad you waited. I shore feel a different man."

"Wal, when a starved man gits his belly full again, it does make a difference. I've been there."

Here I suggested that we all go down to my quarters where we could have a drink and a smoke and talk.

"Where's yore hoss?" queried Shaw of the cowboy.

"I staked him out of town a ways. Only a patch of grass, but it'll do for him to-night. I'll go back to him by and by."

My attention was given more to my companions as we walked down the crowded street to my lodging than to the men we passed and to my surroundings. The big hall in the barn-like tavern was crowded so I took my acquaintances to my quarters. It was a large room, bare, with four bunks and very little furniture, and the lamp gave a rather inadequate light. I told the fellows to make themselves at home while I tried to find another lamp and something to drink and smoke. The proprietor told me there was not anybody else to occupy that room but myself and I replied that I might have my friends stay there that night. I returned with the articles, and the new lamp gave a more cheerful atmosphere if anything could have done so.

"Now, fellows," I said cheerfully, "here's some smokes and drinks. I hope we can get acquainted."

"What you want fer two-bits?" inquired Lowden, dryly. "If you knowed Westerners you'd hev seen we got acquainted long ago."

By way of introducing the subject, I told them briefly about myself and ended up by mentioning how glad I was to meet them, not to say thankful for their help.

"Wal, Wayne," drawled the cowboy Shaw, and smiled for the first time. It was an illuminating transformation and it seemed to give him another character. "If I can just get around yore bein' a Yankee, I reckon we'll get along tip-top."

"Hell, pard, there ain't any war out hyar yet," said Jack Lowden, "an' mebbe there never will be."

"Aw, it's as shore as death. If you were from Texas instead of Missouri you'd have seen thet long ago."

"Listen, Shaw," I interposed. "I forgot to mention in my little story about myself that my house is one divided against itself. My mother is a Yankee and my father is a Southerner. His business keeps him in the North, but his heart is in his homeland."

"Holy Moses!" ejaculated Lowden. "Thet makes you half a rebel anyhow."

"Wal, fellers, thet puts a different complexion on Cameron," said Shaw. "An' I reckon we'll get along just about fine. Now, Jack, you tell him an' our new comrade here who we are an' what we're doin' here."

"Thet's easy," returned Jack, puffing a huge cloud of smoke. "And I kin do it short an' sweet. We're jest a couple of no-good cowboys from the Rio Grande. No homes an' no kin folks to speak of, no money an' no sweethearts, jest the clothes we got on our back an' the guns, an' I mustn't forget, two of the finest hosses any cowboy ever forked. It got kinda hot fer us down there an' as there were no jobs to be had with wages, we reckoned we'd do well to ride a grub line north. It was months ago when we started an' I fergit about what happened on the way. Down in the Panhandle we heared a rumor about this telegraph line goin' to be built across the plains an' what a hell of a job it was goin' to be so we made north an' hyar we air."

"Fellers, Jack was always slick at leavin' things out," interposed Shaw. "He should have said we got chased out of Texas. But all we did was shoot a couple of bad hombres who had a lot of tough relatives."

"How long have you been here, Vance, and what do you know about this Western Union work?" I inquired.

"We've only been here a coupla days, but thet was a long enough time to get in bad with some mean hombres on account of the girl, Ruby. An' to find out thet the laying of this telegraph line will beat any deal ever made in the West, *if* it can be done. I've seen this man Creighton. I've heard him talk. An' I just figure thet he rings like steel. Creighton is about as big as all outdoors an' the kind of a man thet can influence men to go to hell for him."

"I had the same opinion," I replied. "Maybe we can all get work with him."

"Thet will be easy," added Jack. "We found out what a hard time Creighton has in gettin' men an' a wuss time keepin' them on the job. I hev my doubts about Vance an' me. We jest hate work, thet is, diggin' fence-holes, workin' on yore feet, cuttin' an' sawin' wood an' all such work as thet."

"Don't worry, pard," rejoined Vance. "Creighton will never build this line without riders and hunters an' Injun fighters. There's where we qualify an' I can make him see it pronto."

"That accounts for three of us," I said, and I looked inquiringly at the fourth member of our party.

He had been sitting a little in the background and had not entered into our conversation. At this juncture he got up and came into the light. His movements were restless and nervous and his haggard face betrayed agitation. It was my opinion that he would have been a good-looking fellow if his beard and the stains of travel and the havoc of trouble and hardship were removed. He gazed at each one of us with dark speculative eyes, as if to show that he could face anybody. This glance of his added to my sympathy.

"Fellers," he began huskily, "you hit me kinda deep down below the belt. I've had a hunch ever since I met you. But I can't tell whether or not I ought to come clean about myself . . . or whether or not I should jest keep on ridin'."

"Cowboy, tell us or not, jest as you like," spoke up Shaw. "I reckon I can speak up for Cameron an' for my pard, Jack, here, an' shore for myself. Throw in with us an' let's help this grand gazabo Creighton to beat the hell he's up against."

"Much—obliged, Shaw," returned the cowboy, haltingly, struggling against his emotion. I could see his face work and the constriction of his throat. "That's what I feared. I'm so damned wretched that I'm not proof against a few kind words. My Gawd, how I'd like to throw in with you! . . . If I only dared——"

"I reckon you've got the hunch you need," interrupted Shaw, his voice ringing; and the look of him then made me feel what it would be like to have him for a friend.

"Look here," burst out the cowboy, almost violently, and facing us in the lamplight he threw off his coat, and unbuttoning his ragged and soiled shirt he removed it in one swift action. It showed him to have a wonderful muscular development, but he was trained down too thin for his size. Then with tragic and shamed eyes he added, hoarsely, "This ain't so damn easy to do."

Turning abruptly he showed us his back. It was a mass of black and blue welts and cuts, some of them not altogether yet healed. I drew my breath sharply with the shock of realizing that this young man had received a terrible beating from somebody and that the shame of it and the reason for it must have accounted for the tragedy that he expressed.

My eyes were riveted on these great stripes, some of which were swollen and stood out at least an inch from his back. Not one of us spoke. Then he turned around with a deep long breath and swiftly got into his shirt again.

"Hell an' blazes, man!" exclaimed Jack, almost stridently. "No wonder you was queer. How in hell kin we help askin' you where you got that?"

"Cowboy, hangin' could be no wuss," added Shaw, poignantly.

Questions rushed to my lips, but I could not voice one of them.

"Fellers, I'm glad I had the guts to show you," spoke up the cowboy in relief, "an' I can see from your faces that you jest bet I did not deserve that beatin' or I wouldn't have showed you."

"Strikes me thet way," said Lowden. "But, hell, feller, you'd never hev showed us if you didn't intend to tell."

"Reckon that's so," admitted the cowboy. "But I didn't know it fust off. There's a terrible relief in tellin'. Sometimes I felt that I'd croak if I couldn't get this off my chest. Now I'll do it. Then we'll see afterward. I reckon I oughta ride as far as ever I can ride. All the same, right or wrong, I'd like to make a halt where I can work an' eat an' sleep again."

"Wal, what you showed us an' what you said so far makes me want to have you stop heah with us more than ever," said Shaw earnestly.

"Four or five hundred miles is a long way in this country. Mebbe it is far enough to be safe," returned the cowboy. "Mebbe I've showed yella to ride so far away. . . . All right. Listen. I'll bet you Texans never heard the beat of this. My name is Darnell. I've only been in Wyomin' a few years, at the head of the Sweetwater River in the western part of the territory. Best cattle range in all the West, an' that minin' town of South Pass, which you shore have heard about, has lately got to be the richest, wildest, bloodiest town ever. I'll tell you about that later.

"The Sweetwater range was first settled by wagon-train pioneers who saw its possibilities an' settled there to develop them. Cattlemen an' ranchers followed until the Sweetwater range was taken up for a hundred miles.

They have jest come to be prosperous. But that country will be as rich in cattle as South Pass is in gold. Only one Texan among those cattlemen that I know of. He is a fine rancher but tough on the cowboys an' in the war that's comin' between cowboys an' cattlemen I see that he is goin' to get shot. Cattle thieves have jest begun to work the Sweetwater. Rustlin' will be a big thing there some day, but not soon.

"All the cowboys I knew of stole mavericks. It got to be a bad habit. It made the cattlemen madder than hell. But I was ketched red-handed in the act. They made me a prisoner an' kept me tied an' locked up for days. I didn't have anythin' to eat but bread an' water. I wouldn't tell what they wanted to know because that involved the honor of a woman. So finally the two heads of the cattle outfits on our range took me at night out into the willows along the river an' tied me up an' stripped me. They built a big bonfire so they could see.

"The half a dozen or more men who were hired to do the dirty work wore masks an' they didn't talk, so I never recognized them. But the two ranchers didn't hide their faces. They had my arms stretched up with ropes an' they told me that if I didn't give away what they wanted to know, they'd beat me half to death. I laughed in their faces an' cussed them out. Then they beat me, all right. One man after another beat me until the inch thick willows broke in their hands. But I never opened my mouth. They called a halt in the beatin' an' gave me another chance to squeal. All I spit out was that as shore as God made little apples, I'd kill those two cattlemen.

"Then they had me beaten again until my blood splattered in the faces of the fellers who were doin' it an' finally they got so sick they wouldn't beat me any more. I was taken back to the cellar where they held me an' three days later I made my escape. I stole a hoss an' rode bareback up out of the valley to South Pass. It was morning when I got there. People seen me as I rode through town with my bleedin' back like a red flag.

"I run into the two cowboys I knew an' they lent me this gun I'm packin' an' these clothes I'm wearin'. An' they told me there was a cattleman convention in town right then. An' I asked if the two ranchers I'd sworn to kill were with them. They were. The cowboys told me where to go an' wished me good luck. I rode down into town an' scattered a crowd in front of the place an' busted in to brace these two cattlemen. I didn't say much but it was plenty. I killed them both an' I rode out of town an' I've been ridin' ever since.

"I'd never stopped at all if it hadn't been for my hoss. I forgot to say those two cowboys gave me a saddle. I don't know how many days it is since I left South Pass, but I could tell you the few times I've had any grub. . . . That's my story, fellers, an' I swear it's the truth."

After a moment of intense silence Vance Shaw spoke coolly. "I reckon thet calls for a drink." We followed his suggestion and presently the situation seemed to grow easier.

Lowden said, "I need a little fresh air as much as I did a drink. Darnell, what say to my goin' out with you an' hevin' a look at yore hoss? There's a livery stable hyar at this place an' thet hoss shore deserves to be fed proper an' be bedded down."

"He shore does," returned Darnell. "I'd forgot about him. You're welcome to go."

Then I spoke up to say, "There are four bunks here. Why not all of you or some of you stay here with me to-night?"

They all agreed readily enough and I was pleased. Shaw and I went out with them to the street and watched the two out of sight. Then we returned to my room.

"I shore knew somethin' turrible had happened to thet cowboy," said Shaw, thoughtfully. "I never seen such a lot of bruises an' welts on one human bein'. He must have suffered a great deal. An' mentally just as bad. Cowboys are funny people. Mebbe you wouldn't think it, but they have pride an' spirit." Without waiting for any comment from me, he went on. "If we can get thet feller to stick here with us, we'll be doin' him a good turn an' mebbe ourselves, too. He's been alone too much. He's been shamed to feel every man is against him."

"It puzzles me. Of course I can't figure western things.

He said he was caught red-handed stealing—what was that he said?"

"Mavericks. A maverick is an unbranded calf thet you find on the range, an' if you find one without its mother yo're not stealing when you take charge of it yoreself. We cowboys never regard ropin' mavericks for ourselves as actually stealing."

"But to beat him that way! He said he wouldn't give someone away—thát it involved the honor of a woman. What is your angle on that?"

"Lord knows. I haven't any yet. But I've a hunch there's a hell of a mess out there in the Sweetwater Valley an' we're goin' to run plumb into it. Thet's a long ways, though. Mebbe we'll not last thet long."

"We will last," I replied decidedly. "I have a prophetic feeling—what you fellows call a hunch—that we'll go through with it."

"Wal, thet's the way to feel," responded Shaw. "I see you tryin' to roll a cigarette cowboy fashion. You make an awful job of it. Let me show you how. If there's one thing thet brands a tenderfoot, it's the way he rolls a cigarette."

Whereupon Shaw began seriously and laboriously to teach me the art of rolling a cigarette with my left hand. I flattered myself that I was not in the least awkward. But I spoiled a dozen cigarettes before I actually caught the trick. The cowboy was good enough to say that I would do. I asked a lot of questions about the construction work, most of which he was able to answer. And presently Jack Lowden returned with Darnell.

"Say, pard," blurted out Jack, "this Wyomin' cow-puncher has got a hoss thet's every bit as good as mine an' I'll bet he'll give yore hoss Range a run fer yore money."

"Jack, are you out of yore haid? Range is the best hoss on the plains," returned Shaw with spirit. "Did you bring him back to town?"

"We put him in the barn here," replied Darnell, "and believe me, Wingfoot acted like he appreciated it."

"Wingfoot? Thet's shore a flatterin' name. Wal, we'll see."

"Uh-huh," responded Darnell. "I ain't gonna risk havin' Wingfoot beat, not to say startin' any argument with you fellers."

Shaw responded quickly to that. "You mean yo're goin' to throw in with us?"

"I'd be a fool if I didn't."

"Say, pard, what do you think I said to him to win him over?" asked Jack, beaming.

"I haven't the least notion. I'll bet it was some exaggerated idees."

"I told him it was all wrong to ride on forever. I told him thet if it had been you who got thet beatin', you'd hev stayed up there an' hev killed every damn one of them fellers. I told him thet in the natural course of events he's bound to buck up against trouble. Wal, hyar air three pards to tie to. I told him thet it was somethin' to see our tenderfoot slug a man. I told him I was the most damn-handy man to hev around in a fight. An' last I told him you was the slickest man with a gun an' the best shot that ever came out of Texas."

"Wal, is thet all?" drawled Shaw, dryly. "I was afraid you might have bragged some."

Even Darnell's grim expression changed at that. "Fellers, I'm throwin' in with you an' I swear to heaven you'll never be sorry."

"We'll gamble on thet," responded Shaw, with another of his inspiring smiles. "Now let's all turn in. We're all tired, an' Darnell is about daid on his feet. To-morrow is another day with a hell of a lot to look forward to."

Little more was said after that. Before both lamps were extinguished I observed that the cowboys' preparations for bed were to remove their boots, spurs and all. However, true to old habit, I undressed, and blowing out the last lamp, I crawled into my bunk between the blankets. I had hardly stretched out comfortably when I made the remarkable discovery that those three cowboys were already asleep. They lay like logs, breathing slowly and regularly. Lowden began to snore a little. But I was too excited to sleep.

I lay there in the cool darkness, snug and warm under the blankets, and listened to the sounds faintly coming to me from outside. Now that all was silent in the room I could hear the click of coins and glasses, the rattle of the roulette wheel, the hum of voices into which rang a woman's low sweet laugh. That started my whirling mind on another turn.

In my calculations of future western life I had omitted women, but this was not to be expected. There was something fascinating about that dance-hall girl, Ruby. It wasn't because she was so young and so pretty. It must have been because she was unfortunate and bad. Then I thought of the wagon-trail girl and I recalled her intent look, her rippling chestnut hair, the sweep of her arm as she waved to me, and I decided that if I ever happened to meet her, I was done for.

It was hard to realize the actuality of my presence there. Now out on the frontier, already in contact with wild characters, and soon to meet Indians and buffalo, and to have my mettle tried. I thought about these three comrades of mine sleeping there in the darkness.

I was a New Englander, from a family of high character and religious principles, and I could not all in a moment repress my shrinking at so suddenly making friends of men who had killed their fellow men. I wondered if I would ever be called upon to shoot a human being. The experience in the dance-hall showed me that I would not have to go much farther in quick anger than I had gone when I struck out at that lout. From that I realized that the men and women I met out here would make the situation. There would be more need of friendship, stronger ties, and the unleashing of a pent-up spirit.

I meant to win and hold these three cowboys, no matter what it cost. I vowed I would anticipate things and try to be prepared. And at last as my eyelids closed and drowsiness stole over me, my fading thoughts merged into sleep.

Chapter Three

IT SEEMED that my slumbers were rudely interrupted by a strange voice piercing them.

"Wake up, Wayne, old boy, the day's busted an' what we gotta do is aplenty."

This was Lowden's cheery voice and it roused me almost instantly. I sat up and threw the blankets back. A bright sun was flooding through the window and the keen cool air had that sweet strange tang that I could not get used to. Shaw was pulling on his boots with considerable effort.

"Dawg-gone-it," he muttered. "I've gotta have some socks an' another pair of boots."

Lowden in his stocking feet was in the act of awakening Darnell and he was pretty gentle and quiet about it. I jumped out and hastily threw on my clothes.

"Jack," spoke up Shaw, "now thet we're stoppin' at a luxurious hotel the first time for months, if ever, 'spose you rustle out an' fetch some hot water. You an' me gotta shave. An' it wouldn't hurt our new pard none to clean up a bit. We're goin' to ask for jobs. An' our spick an' span Yankee pard will have too much the best of us."

"I'll fetch the water, Jack," I said. And I hurried out. In the kitchen I was given a metal pitcher so hot I could hardly hold it. When I returned to my room the cowboys were all up and two of them smoking cigarettes. Darnell sat on his bunk. He said good morning to me and inquired if I might have an extra shirt to lend him.

"I surely have, and socks, too," I replied, and hastened to open my bag to procure them.

"Say, pard, I could use one of them shirts, too," spoke up Lowden, in cheerful brazenness.

"You're welcome, Jack. And here's a pair of socks for you, Vance," I replied. "I'm sorry I have only one

38

pair of boots. As you see, they are laced boots with low heels and I don't suppose you cowboys could wear this kind."

"Hell, yes, I could wear them but I wouldn't," replied Jack. "What d'ye 'spose would happen to me if I forked a hoss in sech boots?"

"Jack, it's just dawned on my mind thet we cain't go out on thet construction job without boots an' gloves an' a lot of things," observed Shaw.

"Yo're shore brighi all of a sudden," replied Jack. "I've known thet ever since we got hyar. How much money hev we got?"

"I've been scared to look."

"Darnell, I reckon you dropped in on us plumb busted, too?" queried Lowden.

"You would have knowed shore, if you could have seen me eat last night," replied Darnell, ruefully.

"Fellows, I've some money left," I spoke up. "Not a great deal, but it ought to be enough to stake us until we get some wages."

"Wayne, you shore hev one cowboy characteristic," said Lowden. "An' I bet my spurs thet it won't be long till you get some more."

I dug down in my coat, and taking out my wallet, I divided my money equally among the four of us. The action had a markedly cheering effect upon my friends. Lowden was funny. Shaw briefly thanked me, and Darnell appeared too affected for words. Whereupon they went about their ablutions and I was to learn how quickly cowboys could do things when they started. In a few moments they were clean-shaven and presented a vastly better appearance. I would not have known Darnell to be the same person.

After breakfast we made our way outside and I for one felt like a boy bound on an entrancing adventure. Hailing the driver of one of the big wagons, we asked him about a ride out to the work camp.

"Boys, if you're looking for jobs you better see Creighton here. He's in town and rarin' as usual. He had to fire a no-good bunch last night and if you youngsters really want work, and I mean *work*, you'll sure get it."

"Where will we find Mr. Creighton?" I asked.

"I seen him just now in that big merchandise store."

I led the way to the store with my companions trailing behind me, and looked eagerly around for Mr. Creighton. In the back of the store several men were talking. I recognized one of them as Mr. Williamson. He shook hands with me.

"Glad to see you, Cameron. We've been looking for you. I told Mr. Creighton I had the pleasure of riding out with you and here he is. . . . Creighton, let me introduce the young New Englander, Cameron, about whom I spoke to you."

I turned from him to confront a stalwart man, still young, with a leonine head and flashing eyes quite different from Shaw's, but which had almost the same effect upon me as they pierced through me. Judged by his garb he might have been a miner. His grip was strong and rough as he greeted me.

"How do you do, Cameron," he said. "Williamson has recommended you, and judging by what I've heard, you couldn't have a better recommendation."

I was surprised that on such short acquaintance Williamson would vouch for me.

"Are these boys with you?" Mr. Creighton continued.

"Yes, sir. Looking for a job, the same as I am."

"Come inside, all of you," he returned, and excusing himself to Williamson and the other men, he led us into a small room that was evidently an office. "Cameron," he continued, turning to me, "Williamson says you were part way toward becoming a doctor before you left Harvard. That's good. I haven't a man in my outfit who has any technique of medicine or surgery. And you bet we'll need the last. You're hired. Now let me meet these boys you have with you. Cowboys, if I know my West. Call them here one at a time."

I beckoned to Shaw standing just outside the door and he came in with his slow musical step. I liked to look at him always, but at this moment with his clear intent gaze fastened upon Creighton, he was singularly striking. I introduced him.

"Glad to meet you, Shaw, and hope I can use you.

What can you do that would be of value to a hard-pressed construction boss?"

"Reckon no work atall thet would be the regular line of yore laborers," returned Shaw, easily. "But I've a hunch of what yo're up against on this job an' I can show you thet you will need me an' my pards."

"Have you been a plainsman?"

"Born on a hoss. Used to the ranges all my life. Handled cattle every way. I know the buffalo. Reckon I'd be valuable in the tight places yore outfit will meet."

"Have you ever fought Indians?"

"Yes. Ever since I was knee-high to a grasshopper. I take it, Mr. Creighton, thet my value to yore outfit would be as scout an' hunter. You'll need men on hosses, rangin' all around, keepin' an eye open for Indians, findin' water in dry country, fetchin' in meat, an' in particular, the way I figure yore work, I'd know where to find timber."

"Ha! Timber? You mean for telegraph poles? You hit me square in the midriff. You're hired. We'll talk wages later. Call in your friends."

In another moment the sturdy little bow-legged Lowden entered with his clinking step and following him, the erect, dark-faced Darnell, intense and fire-eyed. Creighton shook hands with both of them and appeared to absorb them in a glance.

"What can you do?" he asked of Lowden.

"I'm used to ridin' with Shaw an' thet's the job I'd like. Handy with a gun, though sure I cain't compare with my pard Shaw. He wouldn't tell you he was about the slickest shot in Texas. Outside of thet I reckon I'm no good."

"Well," returned Creighton, with a laugh, "you're hired. And now," he turned to Darnell, "tell me why I'm not going to build this Western Union telegraph line without you."

"Mr. Creighton, I reckon I need not tell you any more than this," replied Darnell earnestly. "I have jest ridden east over the Oregon Trail. I know the Sweetwater Valley, the South Pass country, an' the high range on toward Bridger, as well as any rider in Wyomin'. As a range man I figger that your worst job will come along between

41

Julesburg an' the Sweetwater River an' westward up to South Pass."

"What do you mean—my worst job?" inquired Creighton.

"Indians. They won't take kindly to this work. The Shoshones, under that great chief Washakie who is a real friend of the white man. like as not will help you, but the Sioux, Cheyennes. and Arapahoes, and probably other hostile tribes will make hell on earth for your outfit."

"You're on, too," returned this man we suddenly knew as our boss, his teeth clicking. "All of you, hunt up Ben Liligh, my foreman. He's in town somewhere, I think at the blacksmith's shop. He's got an empty wagon that will be just the thing for you boys. You'll go with my wagon-train directly on the line of the construction work. Cameron, I have a couple of medical kits in my wagon and you can take charge of them. I'll expect you all on the job in the morning. I had hoped to run the line as far west as here by to-night or to-morrow, but one thing and another has held us up. I'm expecting a wagon-train with poles. Poles, poles, poles' They haunt me in my sleep."

Whereupon Creighton left us, and if my comrades felt as I felt, we were all left profoundly elated, and yet awed with the force that had swept over us. As we left the store to hunt for Liligh, gradually we awoke to the realization that we had been favorably received by Creighton.

"Wal, we're lucky," said Shaw. "It calls for a drink. What say, Wayne?"

"I guess one might steady me a little," I replied. We went in the nearest saloon and had our drink and then, returning to the street, we made tracks for the blacksmith's shop. We heard a clanking sound of metal and saw a burst of sparks, and presently came in sight of the smith, a huge bearded man wearing a leather apron.

As we approached, I noticed a little wiry man, gray-faced and gray-haired, coming from one of the wagons. He wore a soiled buckskin shirt, fringed and beaded, and that made him stand apart from the laborers we had seen. His old slouch hat was cocked on one side of his head and he was smoking a pipe.

"We have been sent by Mr. Creighton to report to his foreman, Liligh," I announced.

When this buckskin clad individual turned to us, it required no perspicuity to grasp that here was another remarkable personality. His face was sallow and thin and lighted by piercing eyes. I thought that if a few more men looked at me like this I would find myself shrunk to most insignificant size.

"I'm Liligh," he replied, in a dry crisp voice, as he removed his pipe. "What'cha reportin' to me about?"

I burst out into hurried explanation.

"Ahuh. So thet's it. Wal, I reckon there ain't no help fer it. I've already hed hell'n damnation with every kind of workman on this hyar damn job, but I haven't tried a Yank yet, an' sure, no cowboys. Reckon it won't hurt to try yu, but I ain't dead set on Yankees an' powerful skeptical about cowboys."

"All we want is a chance to make good," I said curtly.

Shaw drawled in cool easy insolence, "Say, Mista Liligh, ain't thet scar above yore ear a mark of where some Injun tried to lift yore hair?"

The old frontiersman, easily recognizable as such, jerked up as if he had been struck. And he yelled angrily, "Yer damn right, cowboy, an' I'll say yer eyes are purty sharp. But what'cha make a crack like thet fer?"

"Wal, old timer, if you had me an' my pard with you when thet happened, like as not you wouldn't have got it."

"Ho, ho! Indian fighters, heh?" Liligh retorted, yet his keen scrutiny took second and more shrewd stock of the cowboy. "Yu sound like business. Come over hyar an' see yer wagon. It's such a damn good wagon thet I wanted it myself. It was built to float like a boat. Yu can lift it off the wheels an' pack yer load across a river. The wheels air made of Osage orange an' white oak an' oughta last forever. The tongue is good stout wood an' double-jointed. There air no nuts in this wagon to work loose. You see she's rifted all through. New canvas an' I'll bet redskins cain't shoot an arrow through this plankin'. A grand prairie schooner, boys, not too big or heavy! . . . The galoots who hed this wagon stole everything but the bunks an' the blankets. Yu'll hev to hev a complete new outfit."

"Will we have to pack grub an' do our own cooking?" asked Shaw.

"No. Not with Creighton's wagon-train. We hev a good cook. Yu can pick out yer bunks an' put yer personal belongin's under each one, an' then go to the store an' get the things yu need an' charge to Creighton. Cameron, I see yu've got a pencil an' an envelope already. Take down this list. Rifles an' plenty of shells, plenty of shells fer yer six guns, workin' outfit of clothes, an' don't fergit some warm, heavy things. But fust, is any one of yu a teamster?"

"Hell, I kin drive a coupla teams," answered Lowden in answer to a look from Shaw.

"Boss, that drivin' will be my job," spoke up Darnell. "I've done a lot of freightin'. Hosses or mules—it makes no difference to me."

"All right. We're gettin' somewhere," returned Liligh. "Take down this list an' pack the stuff over hyar. An' yer private possessions, if yu hev any. Fix up the wagon to suit yerselves an' make it comfortable. Tools, buckets, basins, towels and soap, plenty of bandages, canvas waterbags, an extra blanket apiece, an' I reckon thet oughta be all 'cept what yu wanta buy on yer own hook."

We hurried over to the merchandise store to get the things Liligh had told us to order. My comrades insisted that the first thing to do was to fit me to a rifle and gun belt and gun. When they buckled a big cartridge-filled gun belt around me, I rather ridiculously asked if I should keep the gun and belt on.

"Hell yes!" ejaculated Lowden. "What'cha think—thet it's an ornament to wear to parties? Yo're gonna need this gun, Yankee! Savvy thet?"

"Wal, I hope he won't need it before I teach him a quick draw an' how to shoot," interposed Shaw.

"Yeah? I'll betcha he'll need it before you learn him."

"Listen, pard, our friend Cameron wasn't born on a hoss an' been looked up by gunmen ever since he was a kid. Don't make no more funny cracks about this gun business."

The parcel of shells they bought for me was about as heavy a load as I ever carried. While the boys went on selecting more rifles and ammunition I got another clerk and proceeded to buy a list of things I thought I'd need. When this was done, I told the boys I would go to the tavern and pack my belongings and take them down to our wagon.

Half a block down toward my tavern, I came to another store which I had not noticed. As I was about to pass, a slim young girl, bare-headed, came out and accosted me. I stopped and spoke and wondered where I had seen her. It didn't take more than a second glance to notice how pretty she was. She had auburn hair, almost red, dark blue eyes, and her white face, despite being a little too thin, was very attractive.

"You appear to know me, Miss."

"I am Ruby. You saw me at Red Pierce's."

"Oh!" I replied, in surprise. "You look so—so different this morning—and younger. How did you know my name?"

"I know all about you," she said, with a smile that made her brighter. "Facts and gossip travel fast out here. I was interested in you, and then, when you slugged Hand Radford, I was so glad I—I wanted to meet you."

"Then you are not his girl?" I asked, gazing hard at her.

"I am any man's girl—that is, so far as dancing and drinking and all the rest of my job is concerned," she said, wistfully and bitterly, "but I hate some of these men and that Radford is mean. He's brutal and he thinks he owns me. He's 'most as bad as the man I work for."

"Who is that?" I queried, intensely interested.

"Red Pierce, who runs the saloon and gambling hall."

"I seem to grasp that you dislike this job."

"Of course I do. You may be a tenderfoot, but you look like you have intelligence."

"I'm finding out that I'm not so bright as I thought I was. Ruby, aren't you very young?"

"I'm sixteen but I feel as old as the hills."

"How long have you been on this job?"

"Only a few months, but they seem like years."

"Where's your home?"

"I haven't any," she replied.

"Oh, that's too bad. Haven't you parents—relatives?"

"I had, not so long ago," she returned, mournfully.

"They were all killed in the massacre of Scot's Wagon-Train. Didn't you hear about that? The Cheyennes attacked us outside of Grand Island. I was one of the few rescued by soldiers."

"No, I hadn't heard of it. I am very sorry indeed. That is the second tragedy I have run into and I've only just got here! . . . Let's step inside the store here for a minute," I suggested. "You don't talk like the regular Westerners."

"I'm from Iowa. We moved there from Illinois, where I was born and went to school."

"Well," I asked, thinking fast, "how did you ever get into Red Pierce's saloon?"

"I just fell into it. I was hungry and had no place to go."

"Do you intend to stay there?"

"No longer than I have to."

"What do you mean by that? Does Pierce have some hold on you?"

"He beats me. If we were alone now in my room I could show you how bad."

"No, I'll take your word for it," I responded hastily, shuddering as I thought of Darnell's back.

"Pierce would beat me again if he found out I told you," she said earnestly. "He'd kill any man who tried to take me away from him. He's already killed one man."

"Well," I replied, "I don't know much about shooting and less about killing, being a tenderfoot, but you've met my friends Vance Shaw and Lowden . . . so if you really want to leave I doubt that Red Pierce could stop Vance Shaw."

"Vance—he's really grand! He was to come to see me last night at the dance-hall but didn't. Guess it's just as well because Pierce saw him dancing with me the night before and was more jealous than he'd ever been of any man I'd ever danced with."

"I don't mind telling you that Shaw said he liked you

better than a man should and that if Pierce made any trouble while he was dancing with you he'd probably kill him."

"I saw Shaw early last night on the street and he wouldn't even look at me," she replied hotly. "If he likes me as well as you say he does, why doesn't he go after Pierce!"

"I don't know, Ruby," I returned. "It certainly isn't from fear—that cowboy is not afraid of anyone. I'm pretty certain that he's killed men before. Despite that I'm for him. I never met anyone just like him."

"Yes, I like him too. Maybe because he's a Southerner. They respect girls no matter who they are. Or maybe it's not just because he's a Southerner. Maybe it's because he's him. Anyway—and don't tell him—I'm in love with him."

"Ruby," I interposed hastily, "please don't say any more. I must hurry about my work now, but before I go please tell me some more about this man, Pierce."

"He's a bad man, and has some bad partners," she said quickly. "One of them, Black Thornton, is his right-hand man. He's the one that shot at your foot. The third man I didn't know. Pierce is running a saloon and a gambling hall, but the point is he has moved his business right along with the construction work all the way from Grand Island. So I suspect that he and his men have some other irons in the fire. They're in some kind of shady business. From what I hear, they're going to move west with the telegraph line as far as South Pass. And they have big plans for that gold diggings."

"Thanks, Ruby, for telling me all this," I replied. "Unless I miss my guess, you're going to see four friends at the dance-hall to-night. Good-by till then."

It was indicative of my excitement that as I strode toward the tavern I did not take any particular notice of the sound and bustle in the street. When I got to my quarters I sat down upon my bunk to ponder a little.

Ruby had roused my deepest sympathy. What is more, I liked the girl, which fact, I reflected, would raise the hair of some of my home town folks. If that cool drawling Southerner Shaw could be moved to think more of

Ruby than he had already confessed, I resolved to speak to him as soon as I could get him alone.

I had my packing about finished when Darnell came in, knocking his jingling spurs against the floor. He said: "I reckoned I had better come back an' help you pack your bags to the wagon."

As I looked up at his dark impassive face, I received an intimation that this cowboy had been drawn toward me. It raised a warm glow deep within me. I said:

"Much obliged, pard. These bags are pretty heavy. Did you get all the stuff?"

"Yes, an' already at the wagon. I had time to hunt up Liligh an' take a look at our oxen. We have four young beasts that shore took my eye. I used to freight a good deal an' I know oxen. On a long hard trip, when you can take your time, there are no critters that can beat 'em."

"I remember now, you're going to drive us. Shaw and Lowden will, of course, ride their horses. That leaves me to ride with you, doesn't it?"

"It shore does. On the front seat with a rifle acrost your knees, practicin' shootin' at jackrabbits, so you can get good enough to hit Injuns ridin' their ponies like mad an' shootin' at us from under their hosses' necks. Take a hunch from me. That won't be very long."

"*Whoopee!*" I yelled, yielding to an uncontrollable impulse. That hoarse bawl I let out surprised me as much as it did Darnell. Ordinarily I would have been ashamed of such an outburst, but this time it seemed natural enough.

"Say, air you loco, or just plumb crazy?" Darnell smiled.

"Grab that bag, Darnell," I said. "Take a look and see if the fellows left anything here, and come along after me. I'll go pay the bill."

Upon leaving the tavern, Darnell led down an alley to a back street, which was really the open plain, and from there we made directly to the blacksmith's shop. I found the wagon much more attractive to me than when I had first seen it, and that had been enough to thrill me. These cowboys knew what to do with a prairie schooner to make it a home on wheels.

Inside they had put some boxes up back of the driver's seat on each side which would do very well as cupboards. A small mirror had been hung over each one. The two bunks on each side had been moved back a little and in front of them had been placed a box for a seat. Upon one improvised bureau was a lamp with a shade. The blankets and articles were distributed upon the four bunks. In the back were the buckets, basins, and other things, and a movable stairway with three steps led from the wagon to the ground.

"Boys, this is why I left home," I said, highly elated. "Which bunk do I get?"

"Wal, you can have any one you pick," replied Shaw. "Or mebbe you would want us to move them around so you could sleep in between us all."

"Don't worry about him none, Vance. He wants to fight Injuns already," Darnell sallied.

"I'll take my chances, Vance Shaw, and my medicine," I said. "I'll pick the bunk on the right side next to the driver's seat."

"I've got an idea," said Darnell. "Let's buy one of them big wooden buckets an' some things to cook in. There's room for half a dozen shelves on this side back of the bunks where we can keep grub. I've a hunch we're gonna have times when we'll be far away from the camp chuck-wagon."

"Slick," responded Shaw. "Then all we'll have to do will be to kill meat an' am I hankerin' for a good old juicy piece of buffalo rump steak!"

By this time it was getting along well in the afternoon. Shaw and Lowden went back to the store to make the final purchases. While we were waiting for the boys to return, I had further indication that Darnell had sort of gravitated to being friendly and helpful. He told me that just aiming a rifle was as good practice as actual shooting.

"Take a fly on the tent or wagon cover, for example," Darnell advised. "Follow him with the bead when he crawls. Then freeze on him and squeeze the trigger."

Presently I heard the loud creaking of wagon wheels.

"Here comes Liligh," said Darnell.

"Boys, it ain't all bad news," Liligh greeted us. "The boss says yu don't need to hurry out to the line to-morrow. Take it easy an' go along with me. We got as far west to-day as we had telegraph poles. An' then we dug post holes all the way almost to this burg. This is the fust time thet Creighton has been held up. He expected two wagon-trains of poles to-day but they didn't come. One o' them ought to be comin' up from the South any time now. He'll be shore to hev poles, but he had a long way to go for them."

"Held up?" I repeated, reflectively, thinking of our leader's absolute intolerance of delay. And I thought, How would it be with him when we got out on the plains where there weren't any poles? and I voiced that query to Liligh.

"What'll the boss do?" cracked Liligh. "Hell, he'll do a lot. Yu kin bet yer life on thet. He'll make us git telegraph poles where there ain't any. Cameron, how did yu fellers git along with yer wagon?"

"Come and see."

Liligh inspected our wagon. "Wal, where yu gonna put the clothes press an' the pianer?"

"We'll have to dispense with those, Liligh," I replied with a smile.

"Thet's the all-firedest, nicest fixed-up wagon we hev."

At this juncture Shaw and Lowden returned laden with bundles and packs which they dropped with relief at the tail of our wagon.

"Boss," spoke up Darnell, "how about a small barrel or keg to fasten outside the wagon?"

"What'cha want thet fer?" asked the boss. "Do yu wanta carry thet full of rum?"

"Say, Liligh, we'll want it for water," returned Darnell. "There are stretches between here and the Sweetwater where you gotta make dry camp. An' for that matter, there's no timber for telegraph poles nor wood to burn nor any game to shoot for Lord knows how many miles."

"So I've heared about nine million times," replied Liligh, testily, "but thanks fer yer idee. We'll put small water barrels on all the wagons."

Liligh spat tobacco juice at a stone a good ten feet

away and he hit it. Then he fixed his narrow slits of eyes upon Shaw and looked him up and down again. I knew something was coming.

"Shaw, did you run agin anybody in perticular up town?" he queried.

The cowboy looked intently at the plainsman as if his tone and question were significant in some way or other. "Cain't say thet I did, boss."

"Wal, where were yer eyes? Ain't yu one of them Texans thet's always lookin' fer some man?"

"Not any more. I quit lookin' way down on the other side of the Red River."

"Thet's good fer yu an' probably not so good fer him. Now all you gotta watch out for is someone lookin' fer yu. Hev yu ever heared of Joe Slade?"

"Nope," replied Shaw, laconically. "I never did." But I was inclined to think that the cowboy prevaricated about this for some reason or other. "Who in hell is Joe Slade? The *name* sounds kinda tough."

"Wal, I reckon thet, jedged by yer Texas standards, Slade would not rate as a gunman, but he's a killer all right. He's got about a dozen men to his credit or discredit already. Some of them bad hombres thet ought to be killed, I reckon, but on the other hand, some of them were decent fellers. Funny, Slade 'pears to be a pleasant enough feller on occasions. If yu wasn't wise yu'd never take him for a killer. But when he gits a grudge agin someone, he's shore bad medicine. I'm tippin' yu off Shaw, an' yer pard, too, not to step on Slade's toes or in any way excite his queer nature."

"Thanks for the advice, Liligh," returned Shaw, without warmth. "I'm wonderin' just why you picked on me?"

"Shaw, no offense meant. I know my West an' I know Westerners whether they're from the South or some where else. Jest naturally, Shaw, yu'd be bound to be picked out fer notice by most anybody 'cept an old-timer like me who knows the frontier. Savvy?"

"Yes, I savvy, an' I reckon I'm not insulted."

"Slade rolled in this afternoon with sixteen wagons," went on Liligh. "He's been workin' fer the Overland

Company. Some kind of official job or other an' I heard him say thet he wanted to git on this Western Union job. I'll bet he wants to git on all right, but not fer any job. . . . Wal, I've got to go back to the wagons an' show Smitty about the repairs to be made."

I was quick to see the glance exchanged between Shaw and Lowden. "Pard, what the hell you make of thet?" queried Lowden, testily. "I reckon Liligh was purty decent. Shore didn't want to offend, but thet was a kinda pointed hunch he gave you."

"Damned if I know, Jack," drawled Shaw, "an' I care less. But I reckon Liligh has run into somebody from Texas who knows me."

After a while I said: "Boys, it's getting along late and I'm as hungry as a bear. What do you say to unpacking this stuff you just brought, stow it away in the wagon, and then go eat?"

"Jest dandy," agreed Lowden, with his cheerful grin. "An' thet reminds me, pards, who'n hell is gonna be the boss of our outfit?"

"Thet's right, Jack, who? We cain't all be bosses."

"If that is necessary, of course you should be the leader," I said, designating Shaw.

"Me? Why the hell me?" protested Shaw.

"You just seem to be the leader, that's all."

"He means you jest talk all the time," Lowden put in.

"Nix. I tell you what we'll do—we'll cut the cairds," replied Shaw, ignoring Lowden's sally.

Shaw produced a dingy pack of cards and squatting, he began to shuffle with remarkable dexterity. "Set down, pards. We want it understood thet this cut is to be strictly on the level. There. They're shuffled all right. Now you cut the cairds, pard. . . . There. Now we can draw. You pull the fust caird, Cameron."

"Why me? I shouldn't be included. I'm a tenderfoot. I wouldn't know what to do."

"Ump-umm. Well, you gotta draw anyhow," returned Vance.

I carefully drew a card from the inside of the pack and turning it over found it to be an ace. That drew pleasing comments from my comrades. Shaw drew a deuce, Darnell got a jack, and Lowden with a ten spot.

"Wal, that's settled," said Lowden. "Cameron, yo're the boss of our quartet, an' it's a damn good thing. You'll be conscientious if nothin' else. Darnell, here, has too many moody spells to be boss. Pard Vance hates work an' if he was boss, would be gettin' out of it, an' I jest ain't no good atall. But we know what's comin' an' you can decide things fairly after siftin' over our advice."

So there I suddenly found myself, elected leader over our little unit, and I was both thrilled and frightened. These Westerners were hard to understand. Why they should be satisfied with me as any sort of boss, or squad leader as it were, was more than I could fathom. How could I possibly live up to the trust they placed in me? Did they see in me something I had never before discovered myself? Was this the beginning of what I had come West to find after fruitless and wasted years? Had I possibly stumbled into the niche for which I was meant?

As I fought to overcome emotion with reason, my talk with the dance-hall girl, Ruby, returned vividly to mind and I knew I must somehow broach that subject to Shaw as quickly as possible. But when the opportunity offered and I told him I had something to discuss with him he called the boys, even though I had intimated it was a private matter.

"Wayne has somethin' he wants to say. Wal, there ain't anythin' where it concerns the well-bein' of any of us that we cain't all hear, at least as far as I'm concerned."

In a short while then, I found myself sitting on my bunk with the three cowboys across from me. I supposed my face was serious and I knew my voice was unsteady as I began.

"Listen, boys, when I left you a while back to go uptown, I ran into the little dance-hall girl, Ruby."

I went on to tell the boys Ruby's story and at the end of my recital I found myself vaguely suggesting that we do something about her. When I finished, their reaction did not seem to be forthcoming soon.

Shaw leaned back against the canvas, a cigarette between his lips, his eyes like daggers piercing into mine.

His face was impassive otherwise, and I could not make anything of his reactions. Darnell gave a queer little laugh and dropping his dark head muttered to himself something about women making all the trouble in the world. Jack Lowden was the first to speak.

"Two days on the frontier an' you break out. Gonna rescue a dance-hall girl! Gonna brace a tough outfit an' git the hell shot out of you! Dawg-gone! Now I'm wonderin' what the hell you'll do when you grow out of bein' a tenderfoot."

"Jack, perhaps I've suggested something terrible from your point of view," I protested, "but what *could* I do?"

My distress was so evident that it silenced Lowden.

Shaw blew a great cloud of smoke out of which he drawled, "Fellers, I knowed he'd pull some trick like thet. Let's go have a drink an' then eat on it."

We climbed down out of the wagon and started for the street with Darnell and Lowden somewhat in advance. I took Shaw's arm and held him back until quite a little distance separated us from the other couple.

"Listen, Vance, I didn't tell you all," I broke out, hurriedly. "I couldn't give Ruby away in front of our pards until you knew. The poor kid is in love with you, Vance!"

"How'd you know thet?" he drawled in his cool, easy voice.

"I guessed it from her talk even before she confessed it. She said she fell in love with you because . . . well, never mind what she said. But I believed it."

"Pard, did it occur to you thet these gold-diggin' dance-hall girls are as slick as hell?"

"I humbly admit to being a tenderfoot, Vance, but I am no fool in regard to human nature. Life and tragedy and agony are the same whether here on this frontier or down East. That girl was tragic. Pierce may have forced her to be a gold-digger, but to *me*, she was honest. Do you get that, my Texas cowboy friend?"

"Aw, hell, I figured thet myself," drawled Shaw, flinging his cigarette aside. The action was swift and passionate. "I just knowed all the time thet I'd have to shoot the daylights out of thet Red Pierce. But let's go eat first."

Chapter Four

WHAT PLANS Shaw was formulating, if any, to get Ruby away from the dance-hall, I did not know. But I was determined that she must leave.

I had split up my money among the four of us and my share was not enough to send her East on the stage-coach and keep her for any length of time until she found a home. Out here the only safe place I knew for Ruby was with the four of us. But how could a girl ride West in a covered wagon with three wild cowboys and a tenderfoot engaged in building a telegraph line?

The four of us were lined up in a row of seats before the counter of a dingy little restaurant. Vance was sitting next to me. The other boys did all the talking. Vance had not spoken at all since he had made that cool biting assertion about shooting the daylights out of Red Pierce, which I was surprised to find had not shocked me at all.

I knew he meant it. There was something about the fellow that made doubting him impossible. If I had not been to blame for his enmity toward Pierce, at least I had precipitated it. I could not take it back. I did not want to. I was not shocked at the thought that he was going to kill Pierce, but rather because I would have liked to do it myself.

When the Chinaman placed our supper before us, conversation ceased, and all fell to heartily except myself. I had been hungry but now I was not. How Shaw could eat with apparent relish before the crisis which must inevitably arise, I just could not understand. I fussed with my food and made pretense of eating and finally did drink half a cup of coffee.

Upon going out into the street again, I found it was dusk and the usual bustle had quieted down. We walked up the street as far as the tavern.

"Fellers," spoke up Shaw, "spread out and listen for a while. I want to find out what's goin' on."

With that we separated and I made my way to the tavern fireplace and, turning my back to the genial warmth, I pondered Shaw's suggestion. I supposed I looked nonchalant standing there appraising the crowd. My outward appearance certainly must have belied my feelings.

Presently I left the proximity of the hot fire and sat down on a long bench which was occupied by two other men talking to one standing.

"Pierce left on the afternoon stage for Omaha," said the man standing. "He can't get back for some time and the cattle deal we had in mind is out for the present."

"Bartlett, I never had any faith in Pierce's buying cattle," returned one of my neighbors on the bench.

"He could afford it because he's raking in the coin in that joint of his," replied the man addressed as Bartlett.

"But what would he do with a big bunch of cattle?"

"Well, he could do the same as we want to do," returned the first speaker. "Cattle prices are going up. You know there are but few cattle between here and Ogallala and none at all that I know of across that barren range to Ft. Laramie. This construction work has boosted the cattle deals. Pierce's plan, I understood, was to travel along with the telegraph line, living off the construction workers until he gets to western Wyoming. As long as he is going by slow stages, it would be easy to take a herd of cattle with him and sell out for big money out there on the Sweetwater."

"It's the coming cattle country, I tell you," exclaimed one of the others. "I can figure Pierce rustling cattle but that's all."

"Well, rustlers are working west these days and rustlers steal cattle and sell them, don't they? Let's wait till Pierce comes back. We don't care who or what he is, as long as he pays cash."

"Right," assented the first. "Let's go have a drink on it."

I suddenly experienced extreme relief at the certainty that there would be no gunplay between Pierce and

Shaw in the immediate present. My next thought, at variance with the former, was keen regret that Pierce might get off. And my third was sincere gladness that during Pierce's absence something could be done to get Ruby away from that place. My immediate impulse was to hurry in search of Shaw; then I reconsidered and thought I would wait for him to find me. There was no hurry about his learning Pierce was gone.

I kept my seat, gazing into the fire, and occasionally glancing around. The news that there was a big wagon-train moving west along the Trail and that it had a large herd of cattle with it returned to mind and intrigued me greatly. Could it be that the girl of the waving hand and flashing smile was with that wagon-train? I wondered who she might be and why she was traveling westward. Was she going out to Oregon to marry some stalwart and lonely pioneer youth?

It now seemed certain that, owing to the delay caused by the shortage in telegraph poles, we would be hung up at or near Gothenburg, which might enable the big wagon-train to catch up with us. With that girl in mind, a total stranger to me and one I had never been closer to than several yards, I nevertheless seemed to lose myself in building up a romance. I had certainly not delayed in succumbing to the suddenness of western ways, I reflected. But an answering voice told me I had seen great emotional gulfs spanned in less time than it took to tell it. All in a few days I had seen superlative hate, love, friendship. Two of them I had already experienced. Where I had come from it took years to develop what happened here on this raw frontier in a matter of minutes.

I resolved to make every attempt to meet that girl, if ever the chance offered.

Under the spell of my mental aberrations, I took little heed of time. And presently along came Darnell and, espying me, seated himself beside me.

"Howdy, pard," he said, cheerfully. "I've been watchin' you from back there an' you 'peared to be more interested in dreamin' over that fire than seein' what's goin' on."

"I was, for the moment," I replied, with a laugh. "But I'll bet you two-bits I've got more news for Vance than you have."

"Gosh, you're a bettin' feller. Here comes Shaw and Lowden probably lookin' for us."

I lost no time imparting the news of Pierce's departure. Shaw did not make any comment and his face did not show whether he was relieved or not. Lowden, however, gave us distinctly to understand that so long as a job of killing some hombre had to be done, it was best to get it over with.

"Wal, pards, I reckon we have to go see Ruby anyhow," spoke up Vance casually.

We left the tavern and made our way toward the bright yellow flare which indicated Pierce's Gambling Hall. Shaw strode ahead and as Tom and Jack dropped behind, I hastened to catch up with the tall cowboy.

"Vance," I said, "now would be a good time to get Ruby away."

"Hell's fire, Wayne. I seen thet as soon as you told me Pierce was gone," Shaw snapped.

"Have you any plan, where to take her, what to do?" I asked.

"We'll get her out of that hole first an' worry about what to do later. You stick close to me an' keep yore eyes peeled. Pierce is away but the town is full of ugly fellers. Pierce has friends. Anythin' can happen."

When we entered Pierce's there did not appear to be as much smoke as usual or noise, although the hum of voices from the crowded bar and the discordant music were not by any means quiet. The roulette wheel was idle on the moment and there were only three gambling games going on at the tables. In the rear of the hall, toward which we wended our way, two couples were dancing, and a number of men were sitting along the wall; and there were two men standing talking to a girl whom I could not see plainly until she moved from behind the taller of the two. It was Ruby. If she had looked flashy the preceding night and pretty that afternoon when I met her, she now appeared beautiful.

She was quick to see us reach the dance floor. She

gave a perceptible start, her dark eyes flashed. I seemed to see something in them that had not been there before. Quickly she smiled and waved to us.

Vance had halted a step or two in front of me with Lowden on his right. Darnell was behind me. Instantly I sensed something in the air but I had no idea what it was.

"Vance, thet's the gazabo all right," whispered Lowden, "an' he don't look very tough to me, but you know how some fellers fool you."

"Shore, thet's him," drawled Shaw, coolly, "an' he just had to be makin' up to Ruby. Wal, let's see if Ruby introduces us. . . . Spread out a little from behind me, you geezers!"

That last order was intended for Darnell and me, but I did not yet know what to make of the situation. I realized, however, that the individual Shaw had intimated was making up to Ruby might be in for a bad moment. He was well dressed, not at all roughly, and he was a pleasant, mild-appearing man around thirty. He had a smooth face, deep-set eyes, and a rather odd conformation of chin and lips that denoted the opposite of weakness. As Ruby spoke to him in a nervous, hasty manner, he turned to watch us slowly approach. It was then I observed he wore a gun belt from which new brass shells glittered, and the gun sheath swung at his right side under his coat almost out of sight.

Shaw halted in his slow stride a couple of paces from this group and we followed suit. I with my heart in my throat and wondering what on earth was going to happen.

"Oh, here you are, boys," cried Ruby, in a rather high-pitched, nervous voice.

"Evenin', Ruby," returned Shaw, quietly, and the rest of us spoke to her, and removed our sombreros as Shaw had done, quite gallantly.

"These—are my cowboy friends working for the Western Union," spoke up Ruby to the two men with her. "I want you to meet them. . . . Boys, this is Mr. Joe Slade —and Mr. Hall. And my friends are Vance Shaw, Mr. Cameron—and—and——"

"Howdy, gents," drawled Vance, with his easy southern accent marked more than usually. He took a slow step forward but he did not offer his hand. I could not see where Vance was looking because I was obsessed with the expression on Ruby's face and the fact that here we were, face to face with the notorious killer, Joe Slade.

I felt my mouth grow dry and my tongue tried to cling to the roof of my mouth. I broke out into a cold sweat. It was not fear that possessed me, rather that here was another situation that might bring sudden and violent death, the shattering of hope. I realized that I had not the slightest idea how to cope with it, but I watched Vance. He surveyed the group coolly, evidently waiting to see which way things would go.

"Good evening, gentlemen," Slade returned, affably. "I have engaged Miss Ruby for the next dance."

His pleasant smile and his gracious, gentlemanly air seemed momentarily to relieve the tension, at least to me.

"I reckon I savvied thet," said Shaw, quiet matching Slade's pleasant voice and manner. "Shore, go ahaid. I don't mind my girl dancin' with gentlemen."

"Thanks for the compliment, Shaw," returned Slade, with a slight laugh. He was not acting. He really felt pleasure in the moment. "Come, Ruby, I'm sure I'll enjoy the dance even if you are his girl."

Ruby had stood there like a lovely statue from the instant of Shaw's cool assertion of his claim on her. She saw no one but Vance on the moment. Her eyes were strained and looked unnaturally bright and dark out of her white face. They held, too, something wistful and wondering.

She was still staring at Vance when Slade put his arm around her and whirled her on the floor. He proved to be a graceful dancer and Ruby appeared as light on her feet as thistledown. As I watched them glide away I heard Lowden say, "Pard, what'n'ell do you know about thet?"

"Jack, you can never tell about some fellers. Maybe Slade ain't a bad feller atall. An' you bet we cain't let him go us one better in courtesy to a lady."

At that fascinating moment a hand touched my arm

and a husky voice spoke at my elbow: "Hello, handsome. I'm Flo. Don't you want to dance with me?"

I turned abruptly to see one of the other girls standing beside me. She appeared about twenty years old. She was dressed in a gown which revealed much of her full body. She struck me as very handsome, except for her eyes which were not smiling as was her mouth.

"Yes, thank you. I'd like to," I replied, and I was glad that I had exchanged my boots for a pair of shoes. In a moment I found myself whirling around that dance-hall floor with a girl whose business it was to be seductive to men. It would not have been any use to try to get away from her. In fact, I returned the pressure she exercised upon me. And I must say it was not entirely the western influence upon me.

Soon we circled close to Ruby and her partner and I watched them. Slade was making the best of his opportunities. I wondered how Vance was going to like seeing Ruby so obviously hugged, particularly after his courteous reception of Slade's request. I was afraid to look around to see how he was taking it, but I felt it in my bones that something was going to happen out of this meeting with Slade.

Once I caught Ruby's eyes. They flashed a look of intelligence at me which signified that she understood somewhat how I felt. Her smile momentarily softened the hard but sad look of her face.

"Say, stranger, you may be a tenderfoot, but you're a darn good dancer," was my partner's first remark.

"Thanks for the compliment, Flo," I replied. "I'm glad somebody appreciates some of the Yankee in me— you see, I went for dancing in a big way down East."

"What did you say your name was? Oh, thanks, all right—you didn't say, and I didn't ask you."

"Wayne Cameron. I'm from Boston and I came West to work on the telegraph lines."

"We don't have the luck to have many Easterners like you drift out here."

"What do you mean by luck, Flo?"

"Well, most of the Easterners were sent out here by their parents, or somebody for some good reason—if you know what I mean. They didn't want to keep them back East."

"By the way, I wonder if you know where Pierce is."

"Sure, he went to Omaha after some more girls. You see, his business is growing and he figures he can use more girls as he follows the telegraph construction gang. Say, don't you like me better than Ruby?"

I evaded the bald question by answering. "It's Shaw that likes Ruby—in fact, I think they like each other."

"Well, let me give you a tip. Pierce likes her too, and he doesn't like Shaw. I heard him say so. Shaw better watch his step."

"Do you have to watch your step too with Pierce? Does he beat you up the way he does Ruby?" I asked.

"Me! Like hell he does! If he ever hit me, I'd fill him full of lead," she said fiercely.

After a couple more rounds of the hall, the dance ended and we came to a stop right where we had started. Before we joined the others, however, Flo buttonholed me and looked up with a bold glance.

"Wouldn't you like to come up to my room later? It isn't much of a room but it's warm because the chimney almost runs through it."

"Thanks, Flo," I replied, as easily as I could manage, "I—I—we've some particular work to do to-night." I reached in my pocket for some money and pressed it into her hand.

"You mean you're giving me this—without coming up to my room?"

"Forget it," I answered.

"It was a nice dance, Wayne. You're a prince. I think I'll give that cowboy friend of yours, the little fellow with the bold eyes, a fling around the hall—and, say, if you should need any help about Ruby, call on me."

As we joined the others I looked expectantly at Shaw who stood before Ruby and Slade. We exchanged commonplace remarks about the dance, and the girl, Flo, shot a battery from her eyes at Lowden with the remark, "Say, cowboy, I'd like to take you on next. Can you straighten out those bowlegs of yours enough to keep your spurs from tearing my stocking to pieces?"

"Lady, I kin dance rings around our Yankee friend," said Jack, banteringly. "Shore I reckon my bowlegs ain't very handsome, but they kin hold a girl on my lap without lettin' her slip through."

"Well, you don't say?" she asked, flippantly. "You'll have to buy me a drink before I can risk myself with you, cowboy."

Slade faced Shaw with his pleasant enigmatical smile. "Your girl is a grand dancer. Thanks for allowing me the privilege."

"Wal, yo're shore welcome," replied Shaw. "I never seen her beat an' I've danced with a lot of girls."

With that Slade bowed and went his way toward the bar where he was joined by the stockily built man I recognized as Black Thornton. Thornton flashed a meaning glance in our direction.

"Ruby, you look sort of fagged," said Shaw, solicitously.

"I'm dead on my feet, Vance. I had hell with Pierce to-day before he left and I was just about ready to die."

"Aw, thet's too bad. I wanted to dance with you myself, an' I reckon pard Wayne heah wanted to. But we'll cut it out. Take me somewhere private. I've got lots to say to you," Shaw replied looking casually around. His eyes nevertheless seemed to miss nothing.

"Come to my room."

"Okay, thet'll be fine. Wayne, you tag along with us, an' Darnell, you keep yore eye on Jack. Keep him from drinkin' too much, an' thet means you'll have to get him away from thet girl."

Ruby led us out of the hall to a dark narrow stairway. Shaw assisted her, and I groped after them. There was a dim light burning somewhere on the landing above, and my observation was that the upper story of that building had been a loft, partitioned off into rooms.

The room Ruby led us into proved to be, when Shaw lighted a lamp, almost as bare and comfortless as the rest of the quarters in Pierce's establishment. The floor was rough board, there was a bed with a red coverlet, a rude washstand and a mirror, and a curtain across one corner

63

where evidently Ruby hung her few clothes. Shaw wasted no time in coming to the point of our visit.

"Ruby, I'm goin' to take you out of this place," he said as he rose from lighting the lamp and approached her.

"Oh!" gasped the girl, and she fell weakly against him, her nerveless hands clutching at his coat. "Take me away? . . . Oh, where—and how?"

"I don't know exactly where, but I'll show you how."

"Oh—how wonderful! But—what about when Pierce comes back—he'll never give me up."

"To hell with Pierce. We'll be out on the Trail before he comes back an' if he hunts you up, wal, thet'll be too bad for him."

"Vance! . . . You'll kill Pierce?"

"Looks like thet was slated, Ruby. I'm kinda sorry Pierce went away."

"He's bad and he's treacherous. He has a tough gang."

"Ruby, stop worryin' about thet outfit," responded Shaw, a little impatiently. "I told you I was takin' you away, didn't I? Wal, I can look out for you an' we can match Pierce an' his gang any day."

"Oh! I—I don't know what to say," she whispered, huskily. "Wayne has told you what I said? He was sorry for me. Is it that way with you? Are you going to send me back East? I've no home, no friends, no money. Or are you going to keep me as your girl?"

"Ruby, I'll marry you as soon as a parson comes along."

"You can't—you can't do that, Vance," she cried, wildly. "I'm not—fit to be your wife. I'll live with you—work my fingers to the bone for you—but I won't marry you—no, no!"

"Say, girl, maybe I figured you wrong. Don't you love me?"

"I do—I do."

"Wal, thet makes it okay, for I fell turrible hard for you the minute I laid eyes on you. Ruby, I've been in love with lots of girls, a couple of dance-hall girls long ago, more than one Mexican señorita, an Indian girl once, an' I had it awful bad for a rancher's daughter whose feller I had to shoot, but thinkin' it over these two days an' layin' awake nights, I know I never loved any girl like I do you. So, of course, honey, I cain't do any other way but marry you."

Ruby's response to that was the most beautiful and touching thing I ever saw in the relations of man and woman. She fell against Vance and would have slid to her knees if he had not caught her. She couldn't speak. She leaned back, her arms falling to her sides, and she looked up at him with amazement and worship that erased the havoc from her face.

I found myself asking what I knew about love and tragedy. This waif of the plains had for me then an exquisite pathos and supreme beauty. The look in her eyes hurt me and I thanked God if I had been instrumental in helping her. An instant later Ruby burst into tears and buried her face in the cowboy's breast.

"Pard," spoke to Shaw, "we gotta rustle out of here an' make up our minds what to do."

Ruby was transformed, awe-struck yet radiant, unable to keep her eyes from the cowboy's face.

"Ruby, have you got any belongin's? Any clothes you would want to take? To hell with them dance-hall duds thet you wore!"

"I haven't very much," she replied. "A couple of plain dresses. When I was saved from the Indians, I had nothing but the clothes on my back."

"Ahuh. Did you keep them?" asked Shaw.

"Yes, I have them still."

"And what are they?"

"A boy's blue jean overalls, a blouse, an old slouch hat, and a pair of boots. I wore those on the wagon-train."

"Good!" exclaimed the cowboy. "We can disguise you with thet outfit. I see there's yore bag. Now pack them things you want pronto, an' let's rustle out of here."

In a couple of moments more we were going down the stairs. Ruby showed us a back door that led from the hall to the rear of the building, and we were soon out under the starry sky in the cold night air. It was as easy as that. I carried Ruby's bag and Shaw helped the girl as we made our way along the rear of the buildings toward the lower part of town.

I walked a little way ahead of them, heard Shaw's murmuring voice and Ruby's excited reply, but I could not distinguish what they said. I racked my brain wondering what to do. I was positive that Shaw would not give up his job and that reduced the matter to taking Ruby with us. And that seemed practically impossible. I was revolving these unsolvable questions in my mind when we got back to our wagon, which stood some little distance from the blacksmith's shop. There was a dying camp fire near, but not anyone in sight. The low hum of the town's revelry came to my ears.

"Strike a light, pard," said Vance, "an' hand down thet heavy coat I just bought. It's above my bunk. . . . Here, Ruby, slip into this an' go sit by thet fire while Wayne an' I fix up a place for you."

"Place?" echoed Ruby. "Where on earth? I'd be scared to sleep outdoors and I'd freeze to death."

"Wal, it's shore goin' to be a little irregular," drawled Shaw, "but we have to do the best we can until somethin' better offers."

He led her over to the smoldering fire and fixed a seat for her beside the red embers. Then he returned to me. We looked at each other in the starlight. His eyes were audacious and he let out his easy laugh, no doubt at the bewilderment in my face. He glanced toward the slight figure drooped over the fire, then turned back to me.

"Pard Wayne, you shore got me into one hell of a fix," he drawled.

"My word, Vance, I certainly have. But somehow I just *can't* be sorry."

"All same chivalrous Yankee galoot, huh?" went on Shaw. "What the hell will Jack an' Darnell say? What will thet old geezer foreman Liligh say? An' what will Creighton *do?*"

"Lord only knows, Vance. I'm simply stumped. But if ever I did something I'm proud of, it's to help you save that girl. But what will we do now?"

"Pard, we're goin' to take Ruby with us," Shaw answered simply.

Chapter Five

"SHORE, PARD, I was only teasin' about you gettin' me in this fix. If you hadn't got to me deep before, you shore have this night. Now I have an idee. Lucky we've a big wagon. We'll shove all but one bunk an' a couple of them boxes back toward the rear an' fix up the front end for Ruby. I'll give her my bunk an' I'll sleep on the floor here at the end. There's some extra blankets an' a buffalo robe. Thet new tarp will come handy because we'll cut a piece off of it an' hang up a curtain between our quarters an' Ruby's. Thet's simple enough. Let's pitch in an' do it an' all the time figure on the things thet ain't so damn simple."

In short order Shaw effected the needed changes, with what help I was able to give him. I was too nonplused to say anything. I had no idea how long we would be able to conceal Ruby. But by the time she was discovered, she would be far from Gothenburg and Red Pierce. And I was glad.

I suspected that both Shaw and I felt like boys at a game as we fixed the wagon, and we were certainly pleased with the result. Then we joined Ruby and sat down by the glowing red embers. Her eyes were raptly eloquent in the ruddy glow. She watched the imperturbable cowboy, and so did I, and perhaps our marvelings were alike.

He rolled a cigarette and put it in his mouth. He lifted a red ember on a chip and lighted it. He gave several little puffs on the cigarette, then took a long draw to expel a huge cloud of smoke which momentarily hid his fine dark face.

"Listen, kid," presently he began, "it's goin' to work out fine. You haven't a thing to fear. Get it into yore little haid now—I'll take *care* of you. An' I'll bet a lot thet my pards will go the limit for me. We gotta disguise you. In the mawnin' you get into those boy's clothes. I happened to think of somethin' I used to be pretty handy in when I was about a million years younger. An' thet is thet I used to know how to make a white boy look like a Mexican. I'll fix you up as dark as any Mexican ever was.

"I wouldn't have you cut them pretty curls for all the Pierces an' all the bosses in the West. You'll have to gather them up an' hide them under yore slouch hat. I'll coach you on talkin' Mexican which I can speak like a book. You'll stick pretty close to the wagon for a while except to get out a little at night after dark; an' when we have to tell anybody who you are, we'll say you are a poor Mexican orphan thet was throwed off from the last wagon-train. What you think of thet, honey?"

"It's like a story," murmured Ruby, dreamily.

"Pard Wayne, what do you think about it?"

"It's all right," I said, although I was a bit skeptical. "We'll be way out of this town before Pierce comes back and maybe we'll never see him again. . . . Now, I'll leave you two alone for a while. I'll keep a lookout for the boys."

I walked away out of earshot of the couple by the camp fire and patrolled a beat along a line of trees at the edge of the prairie, and every now and then I would glance back at the dark figures sitting in the glow. There was something so big about Shaw that it made me swell inwardly to think about it. In my association with him and our companions, I must necessarily assimilate some of the character of these cowboys, and that was what I needed. I certainly would have worthy examples to look up to.

When I returned to the camp fire, I found that Tom Darnell had come back from town and that Ruby had disappeared. I caught the last few words of Shaw's story about the girl and then he asked Darnell what he thought about it.

"Women make trouble for men, especially it seems for us poor cowboys," returned Tom, thoughtfully. "I don't know if or why cowboys fall wuss in love than any other men but it shore looks like it. No cowboy ever suffered more through love than I have, but I wouldn't change it if I could. I reckon the outdoor life—the long lonely days an' nights in the open—make a feller more susceptible to women an' more in need of them.

"Vance, I think what you're doin' for this girl is great. I'm all for you. I reckon we couldn't do any different. I'm sort of a queer feller, Vance, when it comes to hunches. I've had two since I've been in this burg. One, the first time I seen you fellers standin' in front of Pierce's saloon. It was a queer thought that I would get on with you fellers. The second hunch came to me jest now. This deal of yours for Ruby is okay an' it will turn out to your good."

"Wal, listen to him, Wayne," returned Shaw, in droll humor that did not hide his strong impression, "he's a cowboy philosopher. Did you ever hear the beat of thet? . . . I'm shore grateful, Tom. . . . Wal, reckon we might as well turn in."

I spoke up and asked Tom where Lowden was.

"Aw, last I seen of him he was lookin' on red likker with that black-eyed dame."

"I think Lowden will be all right," I put in. "I didn't tell you fellows before, but I believe Flo is all for us."

"Wal, thet's Jack all over," replied Shaw. "We won't go back after him an' we won't wait up for him, but he'll catch hell if he gets drunk. This new job of ours won't stand for much drinkin', especially now we've got Ruby to take care of."

I took a few turns around the camp fire, hating to forsake the dying red embers, and the sough of the wind in the trees near by, and the blinking of the great white stars. When I returned to the wagon, all was quiet. Shaw lay on the floor between the two bunks. He was covered with the blankets, all except his boots which he had not removed.

I softly sat on my bunk and this night, as a beginning, I did not remove anything but my shoes and my coat. The air was nipping cold and I felt that was a good excuse. I stretched out and covered myself with a blanket. A low steady hum came from the town street, and out on the prairie I heard what sounded like a pack of wild dogs barking. They had the sharpest, wildest, strangest bark or yelp that I had ever heard in nature. They emphasized the wildness of the prairie. All at once I recognized the barking from what I had read about coyotes, and I lay there thrilling until I fell asleep.

Something awakened me. It must have been near dawn. Some kind of noise around the wagon had broken my slumber. Before I heard it again I felt a pressure on my feet, and raising myself on my elbow I saw that Shaw was sitting up, his gun gleaming darkly in the starlight. The pressure of his hand seemed to prompt me to silence. I saw him put the same cautious pressure upon Darnell. Then I heard shuffling footsteps outside. It was not an animal. There was a man out there who had on boots. Whoever it was, he was muttering in a half-maudlin way to himself. Pulling me down, Shaw whispered in my ear:

"It's thet damn geezer, Jack. I reckon he's half drunk. He's gonna try to sneak in the front of the wagon to keep from wakin' us."

"But he'll scare Ruby," I whispered back.

"Wal, she won't be so easy to scare. Let's wait. This is goin' to be funny."

Darnell also propped himself on his elbow, tense and alert of posture, which relaxed as he looked at us. No doubt he figured the situation just as Shaw had. I realized then, from the gray light that shone in the back of the wagon and made Darnell distinct, that the dawn was at hand.

Then I heard Jack trying to climb up on the wagon seat. It was rather difficult for him without making a noise, but he was evidently sober enough to try it. It was plain to hear him panting and he muttered once or twice. Presently he got to the driver's seat and was nonplused to find the curtain that we had stretched behind it.

"By damn, wassa 'ells zis? Bet million—wrong wagon."

Just then Ruby awakened and let out a scream. It was neither loud nor piercing nor indicative of actual terror, but she was scared.

"Vance, Vance, wake up," she called. "There's a drunken bum trying to get in the wagon."

A gasping intake of breath, a sound of scraping boots, and a sodden thud as Lowden fell off acquainted us with the catastrophe that had befallen him.

"Shore, honey, we're all awake," spoke up Shaw. "We heard the drunken bum all right. It's Jack."

Whereupon Shaw arose and leaped out of the wagon to the ground.

"Come here," he bawled, and as he disappeared from my sight I heard Lowden utter an amazed snort. I decided to get out myself. I was in time to see Shaw collar the cowboy and give him a tremendous boot in the rear which landed Jack on all fours.

"My Gawd, pard, is it you? Or hev I got the willies?" called out Jack.

"There ain't nothin' the matter with you except yo're drunk," declared Shaw.

"Wot the hell? Wot kinda deal—up agin? If I ain't drunk or crazy, you got a woman in thet wagon."

"Shut up. Not so loud," ordered the cowboy, peremptorily. "Shore we've got a woman here. It's Ruby an' she belongs to our outfit."

"Wal, I'll be damned! Gee, I reckoned I hed the jim-jams. Sorry, pard, but how in hell was I to know?"

Shaw led him back to the wagon where Lowden presented a rather ludicrous and shamed figure. "Climb in, you no-good pard, an' get a little sleep. Boys, the day is about to bust but I reckon we can get another snooze. As soon as we wake up again we'll build a fire, get some grub from the store, an' have a bite to eat here, an' a cup of coffee."

I was the one, of course, who did not sleep any more. I marveled at the way those cowboys apparently could turn on slumber at will. I saw the gray brighten, and day break in the east, and the ruddy sky grow suddenly resplendent with the rising sun. When ever, in my life, had I seen the sun rise like that?

I slipped out of the wagon, carrying my boots and coat; and after putting them on, I proceeded to search for wood to make a fire. It was no slight task. Bits of firewood were few and far between. I packed back as heavy a load as I could carry. I found Darnell and Shaw up and about to leave the wagon on some errand.

"Ruby," called the cowboy, through the canvas, "are you awake?"

The answer came in a soft affirmative.

"You lay low in there until I come back," went on Shaw. "I'm goin' to get some stuff to make a Mexican out of you, an' we'll fetch back some grub too."

Then Shaw turned to me. "Mawnin', pard, I see yo're some gazabo of a wood-packer. Heat some water when you have the fire goin'."

He and Darnell strode away then. I thought I had better awaken Lowden and get him up before the boys came back. After so little sleep it was amazing to see the cowboy awaken about the same as usual.

"Boss, what the hell come off last night?" he queried.

While he splashed and sputtered over a pan of water and brushed his tousled hair, I gave him a brief résumé of what had happened up to the present time. "I don't mind pard Vance bootin' me so hard," he replied, ruefully, as he rubbed his rear, "but I shore ain't gonna stand fer bein' called a drunken bum. I ain't no sech thing. I wasn't drunk atall. Last night I got the lowdown on Pierce an' his gang an' I couldn't hev been smart enough to do thet if I was drunk, could I?"

"I'm awfully sorry, Jack," spoke up Ruby, from within the wagon, but her voice sounded as if she were having difficulty repressing a titter. "I apologize, but what in the world could I think? You plumped your feet right down on my bunk."

"Okay, Ruby, it's all right," replied Jack, at once his old self again. "Jest you put in a good word fer me with thet dawg-gone pard of mine."

Presently Shaw and Darnell appeared laden with bundles which they deposited on a piece of canvas. "Mawnin', pard," Shaw said cheerfully to Lowden. "You fellers get breakfast while I fix up Ruby. Betcha two-bits none of you will recognize her."

We all accepted that wager.

The fragrance of the ham and coffee was so appetizing

that I quite forgot about the little drama within the wagon. But when Shaw called I was keen to look. He had gotten down out of the wagon and Ruby was in the act of following. I knew, of course, that the figure was Ruby but she was far removed in appearance from the girl I remembered.

She was a slim boy in well-worn jeans and a dark jacket and an old gray slouched hat pulled down to hide her hair. That was contrast enough but her face was simply unrecognizable. It had been stained or dyed quite dark and it was my opinion that if she was supposed to be the counterpart of a Mexican youth, she was an attractive one.

She approached the camp fire where several savory dishes had already been laid upon the tarpaulin. Lowden halted in the act of pouring the coffee and stared incredulously. Darnell stood motionless.

"Pards, meet our Mexican handy boy about camp," drawled Shaw. "He answers to the name Pedro. You can all boss him around when there's any of these other men within hearin', but when we're alone don't forget yo're talkin' to the little lady who is goin' to be Mrs. Shaw."

It was quite impossible to discern Ruby's expression, but she exhibited shyness, disguised as she was. Shaw sent her back to the wagon, saying that he would fetch her breakfast, whereupon we all fell to and ate heartily.

While we were finishing the meal more laborers attached to the wagons nearby approached from town, and from their actions it was evident that there was work to do. The last man to appear was Liligh and he called to us:

"Good morning, cowboys. Rustle with yer grub, hitch up yer oxen teams, an' git ready to follow me. Who's boss of yer wagon?"

"Wal, Liligh, we've got four bosses," called back Shaw, "but Cameron is the boss who'll say what goes."

Some hours later we drove eastward out of Gothenburg in our prairie schooner, which I called an improvised lodging house on wheels, and which Lowden nicknamed the "B'Gosh." I sat in the high driver's seat beside Darnell with Ruby on her knees behind us peeping out. I

73

must say that Ruby could have been no more thrilled over her new adventure than I was over mine. I was at last on the actual working of building the line of communication across the wilderness.

There were three wagons in front of us, the last of which was Liligh's. We were following in his wheel tracks just far enough back to escape the dust. The telegraph pole holes had been dug all the way from the town back along the Trail to wherever Creighton had halted with his outfit. The wire had already been stretched along the ground and beside every hole was the insulator, the little green glass cup which was to hold the wire. When the poles arrived the line would go up for these last few miles as if by magic.

I saw that we were approaching nearer to the river, and after several miles, when we topped a slow gradual rise of ground, we saw stretches of water and sand running along a line of green willows which led my eager gaze to concentrate on a clump of white canvas wagons and grazing oxen, smoke and dust that marked the construction camp. On each side stretched away the prairie, somehow beautiful in spite of the monotony of the rolling barren reaches. At a distance all merged into a gray haze along the horizon. There was not a hill in sight.

At last, as we approached the camp, Shaw came forward to lean over my shoulder and survey the ground ahead. "About ten wagons," observed the cowboy. "Thet means Creighton's outfit, an' none of his other wagon-trains are in."

"Look a little farther south, Vance," suggested Darnell; "you'll see a real big bunch of prairie schooners an' a lot of oxen an' horses. Thet's a big wagon-train."

"Shore, I see it now. Thet's a regular trail wagon-train in camp here."

Instantly I gazed in the direction indicated by Darnell. Could the girl I had, no doubt foolishly, allowed myself to dream about, the one I meant to meet—could she be with this outfit?

"Wonder where Slade's wagon-train is, that we heard about?" I commented, bringing myself back to earth.

"He had his wagons in town. Tom, drive a little off

the road toward thet nice clump of willows, an' we'll make a stop there. Just a little outside of Creighton's camp but not too far."

"Oh, Vance, what shall I do while we're here?" murmured Ruby, with a catch in her breath. "Shall I hide under my bunk?"

"I should smile not. All the same when there's men around you better make yoreself a little scarce. Don't worry none, Pedro. We'll figure out things for you."

"Pard, I reckon one of us ought to hang around the wagon to keep Pedro company," suggested Lowden, slyly.

"You bet, Jack," returned Shaw, who did not see the humor. "One of us must always be near her when it's possible."

We halted on the bank of the river near the green clump of willows, on the edge of a low bank beneath which the water ran clearly over white sand. Shaw suggested that I report to Creighton and find out what we had to do and that if I did not return promptly he would hunt me up.

I threw off my coat and after a moment's hesitation, unbuckled my gun belt and laid it on the ground too. The hawk-eyed Lowden saw me do this and he said, "Hey, boss, don't ever lay off yore hardware," but I laughed and walked away thinking his advice at the moment was more of his dry humor. I directed my footsteps toward the concentration wagons and when I reached them, I saw men at work on repairs, greasing wheels and doing odd jobs I did not understand at the time.

I noticed a wagon full of coils and telegraph wire and then over to one side a big vehicle different from the others which I at once recognized to be what Darnell called a chuck wagon. There were two fires still smoldering, around which a short, thick-set, jolly-faced man and a Negro helper were washing cooking utensils. There were pots and pans and packs on the ground and sacks which had been used for seats. Still farther over was a fine, big, white-canvas covered wagon along the banks of the river where several men were seated around a table in the shade cast by the tall canvas dome.

I had hurriedly walked right through camp but all the

time I was tensely aware of the color and movement, of the sound of hammers and rough voices of men, the smell of wood smoke, and outside on the prairie, the grazing groups of oxen. The man with the jolly face directed me where to find Mr. Creighton. As I approached I saw that one of the men seated by the table was Creighton and the others, except Liligh, were strangers. When I got up to them I bowed and spoke.

"Mr. Creighton, I am reporting for work. We have just arrived behind Liligh's wagon, and the cowboys are ready."

"Good day, Cameron," returned Creighton, genially. "Liligh here tells me you're all raring to go. Well, that's fine. I anticipate a good deal of rarin'. . . . Sunderlund, this is Wayne Cameron, a young Easterner and Harvard man who has come West to help me build the telegraph line. . . . Cameron, this is Jeff Sunderlund from Texas. He has a big wagon-train bound for the Sweetwater Valley in Wyoming. He has a brother out there in the cattle business."

I greeted a fine-looking man who extended his hand and spoke with the identical accent I had learned to know and like in my intimacy with Shaw. He was light haired and light complexioned though somewhat tanned, and he had penetrating kindly blue eyes and a lined, strong, serious face to which a long, drooping, tawny mustache gave a dolorous touch. I was introduced to two other Texans, Bligh and Stevens, who were cattlemen associated with Sunderlund, in the big wagon-train, and the herd of four thousand cattle they were driving to Wyoming. The fourth man was Liligh, who spoke to me in his dry way.

"Cameron, pull up that box and have a drink with us."

"Thanks, don't mind if I do," I replied.

"Mr. Creighton has just told me about these cowboy men of yores," said Sunderlund, "an' I will be glad, especially, to meet the one who has just come from Wyomin'."

"You mean Darnell," I replied. "He is certainly an interesting chap. I'm sure he can tell you all you want to know about the Sweetwater Valley."

"Thet'll shore be good," rejoined the Texan. "Lately we've heahed conflictin' reports about the Indians an' buffalo, an' we need to get at the truth. It's a job to drive even a small herd of Texas longhorns this far north, but when it comes to four thousand haid, wal, then it becomes somethin' to keep you awake nights."

"That I can well imagine. Mr. Sunderlund, my friends will be coming over presently, but in case you are in a hurry I'll go after them."

"Thanks, Cameron, we'll wait, by all means. It's pleasant heah in the shade."

"Mr. Creighton, are we stuck here?" I inquired, earnestly.

"Stuck! Not by a damn sight," returned our leader, grimly. "One of my scouts reported this morning that my brother James was on the way in with six wagonloads of telegraph poles. I'm looking for him to show up out there on the prairie any moment. Then there's a wagon-train of supplies due from Omaha. That load of supplies will have to do us until we get to Ft. Laramie. I expect my brother John with his wagon-train in from the north in a few days. And the other wagon-trains that have been hunting for poles will follow and catch up with us sooner or later. We'll have the line up as far as Gothenburg sometime early to-night."

"That's just splendid news!" I ejaculated, happily. "I want to get out of that town. I've already had one fight and if I don't watch out I'm likely to have another."

"Cameron, you'll have fights everywhere and the big one will be out in the open," said Creighton, with a smile that minimized his assertion. "We've struck a bad delay here but I don't think it will detain us much longer, and in any event, we will go ahead with my outfit and my brother's load of poles, and leave some men behind to repair the damage done to the Western Union line by the cattle herd belonging to our southern guest here."

"Damage! How was that?" I exclaimed, in surprise.

"Cameron, it's the silliest thing to happen," said Sunderlund, in great annoyance. "You could have knocked me over with a feather. I wouldn't have been surprised if my herd had stampeded, but they knocked over miles

77

of the telegraph poles just by rubbin' their backs against them!"

"Can you beat that?" queried Creighton, in stern amusement. "It shows that everything in the world that can possibly happen, is going to happen to retard and obstruct the development of my telegraph line. But it can't be stopped."

I glanced across the space between the wagons and saw Shaw approaching with his erect stride and forceful presence. Without a jacket he appeared a splendid figure, built like a wedge, graceful and handsome with his fine alert face and tawny features. As usual he wore his gun and he gave me an impression that he would be a dangerous man to try to escape from.

Sunderlund's back was turned to the cowboy and he did not look over his shoulder until Shaw had approached within a few paces. Then he stared and, uttering an exclamation, he arose to his feet in haste. Shaw, swift to see that motion and eternally vigilant, halted in his tracks, his clear eyes registering the fact that he was never to be surprised. The meeting frightened me a little. Then the Southerner spoke out in a hearty voice, just a little too deep to be casual.

"*Vance!* If it isn't you, I reckon I have gone loco."

"Wal, you old son-of-a-gun!" ejaculated Shaw, without his drawl. His expression underwent a lightning change. Suddenly his face glowed. And it worked with a smile that I had never seen there before. The eyes lost their piercing hard light. "Colonel, I'm most damn glad to meet you here an' not a little surprised."

"Same here, cowboy. I wondered if I'd have the luck to run into you somewhere. An' shore, I hoped for it. This is a big country, but I guess it's shore still a small world."

They strode the few intervening steps and met with a strong clasp of hands. The older man lifted his left arm and put it around the cowboy to show further evidence of his delight in this chance meeting. The sight of them standing there looking intently into each other's eyes heightened my regard for Shaw. He was the most surprising fellow. Excitement, events, romance seemed to trail him. They broke apart then.

"How come I meet *you* way up here, old timer?" queried Shaw.

"I've got a wagon-train out here, an' a big herd of longhorns. Two partners who shore know you if you don't know them. Tom Bligh and Jim Stevens from the lower Brazos. We're on our way to Wyomin'."

"Wyomin'," echoed Shaw, tensely. "Got yore family with you?"

"Yes. We pulled up stakes an' left Texas. It shore was hard, but Texas is in bad shape now an' will be wrecked when this Civil War ends."

"Too bad! I'm damn sorry. Mebbe I oughta have stayed home but it got a little too hot for me."

"Vance, I've got good news for you. You rode away too soon. After you left, it all came out about Stanley. Yore killin' him, instead of bein' a crime, turned out to be a good thing for the community. He lived a double life an' you were one of the few who knew that he was the haid of one of the toughest gangs of thieves the border ever knew. You have been absolutely cleared. You would be welcomed back in Texas, but I'm goin' to try to take you with me to Wyomin'."

"Wal, thet's good news, Colonel. I'm shore glad. How come? What happened? Who found out the truth about Stanley?"

"Vance, it was due to the loyalty of yore ranger friends. Siddell an' Hardin'. They got a hunch somehow— or mebbe they found out the truth—thet Stanley was not what he posed to be. An' with Stanley dead his gang under Duke Wells went on the rampage. Siddell and Hardin' got wind of their raid, an' takin' some rangers with them, they ambushed the gang. There was a bloody fight in which the rangers came out on top, all shot up bad, but no one killed. They wiped out the gang, Duke Wells lived long enough to confess Stanley's treachery an' to-day, Vance, you are a hero on the Rio Grande border, if you weren't one before."

"Dawg-gone! Things do come about. I'm glad. My

pard Jack will be happy to hear this. . . . Colonel did *all* yore family come north?"

"Yes, cowboy. Even Kit came along. She didn't marry Bert Knowles after all. I reckon their split was because Knowles had persistently harped on yore bein' a bad hombre an' when the truth came out, Kit shore told him where to get off. She'll be mighty glad to see you. Kit's spunky, you know, but I imagine she's game enough to tell you an' take her medicine."

"Ah-huh. Wal, wal—I don't know. Things can happen to me, too, Colonel. . . . Now, about yore goin' to Wyomin'. Where to?"

"Sweetwater Valley, Vance. Do you know anythin' about thet country?"

"I've heard plenty," returned the cowboy, darkly. "There's a Jim Sunderlund out there, an' I'll gamble he's yore brother."

"Indeed he is, Vance. I've heard from him twice the last year, but not these last few months. He says the Sweetwater is the finest range in the West an' if I can drive a good herd in there, we'll get rich in no time. I've a half interest in his range. If you know anythin' about the Sweetwater, spill it pronto."

"Wal, Colonel, I'm sorry to say I've heard there's hell to pay out there," returned Shaw, soberly. "It must be a magnificent range. Lots of settlers movin' in. A dozen or more big cattle outfits at the haidwaters of the river, but a bad war is comin' pronto between the cattlemen an' the cowboys."

"War!" ejaculated Sunderlund. "Between cattlemen an' cowboys! Vance, I'd discredit news like thet from anyone else but you! Man, what's it all about?"

No doubt I was as intensely interested as the other four men around the table. Sunderlund and Shaw apparently had forgotten there were others present. Creighton coughed once and spoke up, but as his question was not heard, he subsided.

"Wal, it's the damnedest cattle deal I ever heard."

"Shore it must be. What kind of a deal?"

"Wal, it's one thet'll be new even for Texas." Vance hesitated, appeared about to go on. Then he evidently thought better of what he must have intended to say. "Colonel, you ain't goin' to turn back, an' what I've heard is still only hearsay. We'll all be there together. An' after we get this telegraph line built I'll be goin' back to cattle. Thet war may blow over an' never come. Let's talk about somethin' cheerful."

"Shore, you're right, Vance. I'll not cross bridges until I get to them. . . . Say, what'll you take to go with me? I'll pay you anythin'. Give you a half interest in my Texas longhorns. Four thousand haid in the herd! An' Kit would sure be glad."

"Sorry, old timer, I cain't take you up. I've made a deal to work for Mr. Creighton, an' me an' my pard Lowden have throwed in with Cameron here an' a Wyomin' cowboy named Darnell. It was from him thet I learned about the Sweetwater deal."

"Vance, I want to talk to thet young man. Will you fetch him to see me?"

"I will, Colonel, an' I may say I'm damn glad luck threw Darnell in our way, because he'll give you the low-down on the trouble out in Wyomin'."

Shaw bowed to Creighton and me and the others present as if to make excuses for the situation and hurried away along the river bank.

"Sunderlund, who is this young cowboy, Shaw?" queried Creighton, keenly interested.

"Vance Shaw? Wal, I couldn't tell you in a week all about him. He belongs to an old Texas family. His father was robbed an' murdered yeahs ago by rustlers. Vance was the hardest ridin', hardest shootin' cowboy in Texas. He belonged to the Texas Rangers for a while. He is like Bowie and Travis, who lost their lives in the Alamo. He looks a young man to you but he's all of thirty an' thet's a lifetime in Texas. He rode for me for three years. He killed my bitterest enemy. He fought the Comanches on my range, an' his outfit saved all our lives. I couldn't begin to tell you about Vance Shaw."

"Well, indeed Shaw *is* an acquisition to my construction work," said Creighton, with feeling.

Presently he suggested to me that I walk to the rise

of ground about opposite his camp and see if I could get a glimpse of his brother James' wagon-train.

As I strode along through the coarse grass, I milled over all that I had heard. Prominent in my mind was the fact that Vance Shaw had turned out to be one wholly worthy of my hero worship. I could not even have dreamed of a more remarkable fellow with whom to become friends. It had hardly been news to hear of his being what the Texans called a gun-man, but Sunderlund's eulogy simply made Shaw great. And I was to work beside him, to fight beside him, to know him in all the unpredictable happenings that were to come! And this girl, Kit Sunderlund. She must be the girl I was hoping to meet. I felt it in my bones that it was inevitable. If there were ten girls with that wagon-train, the one who had waved to me would be the one who had been sentimentally involved with my cowboy friend. And, which was plain to see, an affair upon which Sunderlund had looked favorably. But what would happen when Shaw met this Kit Sunderlund again?

He had fallen in love with Ruby and if I was any judge of character, it was genuine love, prompted by the young girl's beauty, her loneliness and her passionate yearning to escape from the life into which a rotten prank of fate had forced her. The questions that my skeptical mind asked were all answered in the negative. No matter what the relation had been between Vance and Kit Sunderlund, I was positive that he would not desert Ruby.

Meanwhile my rapid stride had carried me almost to the rise of ground to the right of Sunderlund's wagon-train and from its summit I had unobstructed gaze down the valley. I saw a large group of prairie schooners, drawn in a great circle, and all around it the prairie was spotted by grazing oxen and horses.

Down along the river road, far beyond the camp, I made out a line of telegraph poles standing stiff and erect, connected by a thread of wire that shone in the sun. Then came the point where the poles were down, some flat on the ground and others in various stages of leaning, until still farther on I could dimly make out that all the telegraph poles were down. And at the limit of my sight

I saw what I concluded was a gang of men at work prob-ably repairing the line. Then swinging my gaze around to the south I was tremendously thrilled to find a wagon-train of eight wagons, only one of them covered with can-vas, winding along like a huge snake. They were loaded to capacity with telegraph poles, the ends of which stuck out from the wagons. I hurried back to camp to break the good news to Creighton.

His face lighted up into a beaming smile. He thanked me and said he would put the gang to work raising poles the moment they arrived. Whereupon I made my way through camp toward our wagon out by the river. I found Ruby and Lowden sitting in the shade peeling potatoes in preparation for our supper.

"Say, Jack, you look pretty happy, and I thought you positively hated any such menial work as that," I re-marked, "and Rub—I mean Pedro—you don't look so down-in-the-mouth yourself."

"I'm happier than I ever expected to be again," whis-pered Ruby.

"Where in the hell you been, boss?" queried Lowden. "I been a-wonderin' about you. I seen you an' Shaw with them men over there, an' when Vance come back after Darnell an' dragged him off without as much as a word to me, I thought it was funny. Who the hell was thet tall geezer Shaw was talkin' to? Looked like a Texan from hyar."

"A Colonel Sunderlund, Jack. Vance has a good deal to tell you."

Jack swore in astonishment. "Sunderlund, eh? You bet Vance'll have a lot to say, Wayne. Did he say he was goin' anywhere in particklar—I mean anywhere far from here?"

"Jack, Colonel Sunderlund's news was good, from what I could make of it."

"You mean thet fiasco in Brownsville? The truth come out?" Jack asked earnestly.

"It certainly did, and all to Vance's credit."

"Wal, the old son-of-a-gun. He might have taken a couple minutes to tell me after I've ridden a thousand miles with him half starved, half drowned, shot at a dozen times."

I could see beneath Lowden's agitation the deep joy of learning that his friend had been cleared of anything approaching crime.

"Did . . . did Sunderlund bring his family—his women folk?" Lowden asked, his piercing eyes intent upon me.

"Why, yes, I believe he did," I replied, trying to keep calm, the significance of his query suddenly dawning upon me.

"An' Vance knew this?"

"He and Sunderlund mentioned a girl named Kit. . . ."

"Aw, I knowed it," Jack exclaimed. "That feller just cain't keep away from trouble. I thought the Indians we'll hev to fight an' mebbe the buffalo stampedin' an' prairie fires, an' storms would be enough. But thet ain't nothin' to this Kit Sunderlund. Supposin' she should find out about Ruby, which is shore inevitable sooner or later? Wow!"

Chapter Six

"JACK, IN less than a half hour we'll be on the job." I wanted to ask Jack a million questions, but I decided to let well enough alone.

"What! Me an' Vance diggin' holes an' puttin' up poles? Ump-umm! Not on yore life. I'd rather fight Indians."

"Jack, I've heard you cowboys hate fences, especially digging post holes. But this is different. I'll bet you dig and like it before this job is over. I expect Liligh will get pleasure out of making us all work hard. Let's hurry and cook a meal so we won't have to go to work on an empty stomach. If we don't make Gothenburg by dark I'll miss my guess."

In less than an hour Creighton with his own wagon and several others were headed back for town. Presently our vehicle was the first to follow the wagon-train of James Creighton as the wagons rolled out along the telegraph line westward toward town. Men on the last wagon, whenever they came to a post hole in the ground, threw off a telegraph pole.

Soon, under Liligh's dominating direction, we were engaged in strenuous labor. There were four groups of laborers carefully raising the poles and easing them down into the holes in the ground. We filled in the earth and tamped them down tight. Darnell drove our wagon. Ruby stayed out of sight. We had a stalwart companion from Liligh's outfit to make up our quartet. His name was Sullivan and he was a jolly Irishman.

To my surprise, Shaw put on a pair of heavy gloves and helped us with right good will. It was Lowden who complained. I began to suspect that Lowden's grumbling was more of a pose than a real habit of character. I noticed that he worked as hard as any of us. And it was hard, slow work.

I got tired of counting the poles, but they seemed innumerable. I could hardly believe there were only about twenty-five to the mile. The sun beat down hot and the dust was thick. The strength I proudly boasted of during my school days was being put to the test. In an hour my clothes were wringing wet with perspiration and I was burning up and parched with thirst. But my spirit was willing if my flesh was weak. I was simply heart and soul in that work.

Despite the strenuous toil, the afternoon passed by quickly and before dark we erected the last pole just outside of town. We decided to make camp right there.

When I sat on the earth cross-legged after the fashion of my comrades, I thought I had never been so hungry and had never smelled anything so fragrant as the steaming food. Ruby waited on us, and her quick movements and bright eyes attested to her happiness. Vance was silent as usual, but I saw him look often at the girl.

While we were eating supper a messenger called on us to notify us that the construction camp would be held

85

up on the following day to permit Sunderlund's wagon-train and herd of cattle to get ahead of us. This was disappointing news to me, yet, on account of my physical pangs, it was very welcome.

"Aw, hell," growled Lowden, "we jest cain't get away from this burg without trouble."

Darnell said that the telegraph line would probably keep up with the wagon-train, that Sunderlund, with all those wagons and cattle, couldn't average more than five or six miles a day.

After dark I paced to and fro a bit to try to ease my aching muscles and succeeded to some extent. Vance and Ruby wandered off toward the river which was close by, and I was left to myself. Soon I sought my bunk and it seemed that for the first time in my life I fully appreciated a bed on which to rest.

The sun was high and shining in my face when Darnell gently shook me and told me to get up for breakfast.

"That's easy to ask, Tom, but how on earth am I going to do it?" I replied, with a groan. Still, after washing and limping around a bit, I began to feel better.

At breakfast Shaw asked his comrades: "What the hell makes you gazobos so glum this mawnin'?"

"Dawg-gone-it, pard, I hate to tell you," admitted Lowden, remorsefully.

"An' I reckon there ain't no way of gettin' out of it," added Darnell.

"All right, shoot," said the cowboy, curtly.

After hesitating and halting, Lowden replied, "Cain't you send Rub—Pedro off somewhere to look at the scenery?"

"Wal, I could, but I won't. Ruby is in this deal with us now. She's game, an' you might just as well speak out before her."

"Okay. There's sense in what you say. It's about Slade. We shore hed him figgered correct. He's all right sober, but he's one of these bloody hombres who, when he gits to drinkin', sees red an' has to spill red all over the landscape. He killed one of his drivers yestiddy, an' from what I heared he killed the man without any reason atall, 'cept his ornery disposition. Shore, mebbe the man was

ornery too, but one killin' like thet don't make any difference to us one way or the other. I reckon we'll see a
plenty of them. But what made me an' Tom sore was thet
Slade hed been heared to make a dirty crack about Ruby
—an' pard, for us Southerners, thet kind of vile talk don't
go about *any* woman, let alone a girl we hev taken to
like all our outfit hev. Thet's all there was to it, pards. . . .
An', Pedro, yo're not to get fussed up atall about this."

"Oh! How in the world can I help but get what you
call fussed up?" asked Ruby. "It means fight, doesn't it?
And maybe—maybe——"

"Naw, it don't mean no fight," returned Lowden.

"I told you-all what a funny feeling I had when I seen
thet hombre Slade makin' up to Ruby," observed Shaw,
in his slow, pondering way. "I figured wrong, when I
reckoned in this construction work we might escape them
ordinary incidents of range life, but I see thet it just
cain't be done."

"Wal, pard, thet's all right an' proper talk," went on
Lowden. "We got the day on our hands an' let's go up
town soon an' get it over. I forgot to tell you thet I went
in Pierce's dive last night an' asked fer Ruby. Somebody
said she had disappeared, but I got ahold of Flo an' she
said Ruby was sick, an' she winked at me when she said
it. She's wise an' she's not agonna give us away."

"Shaw, if it's jest the same to you, I'll stay in camp,'
said Darnell, moodily.

"I don't know about thet, pard," returned Shaw,
thoughtfully. "I reckon you better come along. Ruby can
keep out of sight in the wagon, an' we won't be gone
long."

The cowboys' calmness gave me further clear insight
into their fiery and deadly spirit. They spoke in commonplace manner of meeting a desperado and killer as if it
were one of the simple events of any day. Ruby, too, surprised me. She had this frontier spirit. She showed no
particular stress or fear when Shaw said good-by to her
and said he would be back soon.

"We'll split up an' Jack will trail with me," said Shaw,
once we reached Gothenburg's dusty thoroughfare. "I
don't want to go into any of them stores an' saloons

lookin' for Slade onless I have to. If I meet him on the street, okay. But it's dollars to doughnuts thet I won't run into him. Tom, you an' Wayne go into the saloons an' stores—every place—an' if you see Slade tell him thet there's a man out here who thinks he's too yeller to come out an' face him."

We separated then, and entered town on opposite sides of the street. I was too stirred to remember my physical pangs, and Darnell evidently was not in the mood to talk. We sauntered, although I must have walked rather stiffly, into the tavern, into the lobby and then the saloon and out again into the stage-coach post without seeing anything of Slade. Whereupon we started down the dusty street and we looked into the several restaurants and stores.

Finally we came to Pierce's place. Through the wide open door we could see that the hall was full of smoke and noise and men, just as it was at night. Suddenly Darnell's eyes flashed.

"There's the damn hombre," he whispered, "gamblin' at that table next to the roulette wheel. Why, you wouldn't recognize the feller, hardly. Funny what likker will do to a man. Mebbe he ain't drunk now, but he has been."

Slowly we entered and I was aware of a constriction of my throat and the pounding of my heart. I resented this agitation. Was I never going to take things in stride and meet them coolly?

"Tom, suppose you let me tell Slade," I suggested.

"The idea ain't so good in one way. If Slade is as mean as he looks, he might bore you for jest speakin' to him."

"Nonsense. I'm not a Westerner. I'm a Yankee tenderfoot and the man would have to be crazy to do me harm for just delivering a message."

"Wal, mebbe, but I'll trail alongside of you, and I'll be between you an' Slade, you bet. Let's walk up to the table slow-like, look at the game, an' when I give you a little kick you tell Slade an' talk loud so every damn man in this saloon will hear you."

We approached the gambling table. There were four men playing and Slade sat facing us with his face bent over his cards. At that distance he was easily recognizable, but he was vastly different from what I remembered. His unkempt hair hung down over his forehead and his face was dark and unshaven. We stopped behind the players and watched the game for a moment, then Darnell edged around to the right close to Slade and I kept my position.

Presently Darnell gave me an almost imperceptible signal, at which I drew a deep breath.

"Gentlemen," I began in a loud voice, "excuse me for interrupting your game."

I waited for a moment. All four of the men looked up quickly, but I saw only Slade's face. His eyes were the gloomy furnace windows of an evil soul.

"What d'ye mean buttin' in here?" he queried, irascibly.

"Slade," I shouted, rising to the moment, "there's a man waiting for you outside who says you're too yellow to come out and face him!"

Slade heaved inwardly like the rumblings of a volcano about to erupt. His face grew malignant—black in his fury. His violence, as he jerked with his right arm, scattered cards and chips on the table and made his chair scrape loudly on the floor. There was absolute silence in the place. It could not have been possible that anyone there did not hear.

Slade whipped out his big gun with foul and menacing speech in which I distinguished the names tenderfoot and Yankee. But before he could level the gun Darnell seized his wrist and with powerful sweep extended his arm high over his head and held it there.

"What would you do, you bloody murderer?" demanded Darnell, harshly. "Kill a man in cold blood jest for bringin' you a message? That'd prove you're a yeller dog."

All three of the other gamblers got to their feet and one of them wrenched the gun out of Slade's hand.

"He's right, Joe," said this man, stridently. "You can't do this sort of thing in here. They'd lynch you. Cool down. Don't give in to your temper like that. I'm your friend, Joe, and I'm talking sense."

With that Darnell let go of Slade's arm and wheeling to me, dragged me from the spot where I seemed to be rooted. I was completely in the throes of a hot and terrible passion. In another instant I would have leaped upon Slade and have beaten him to the floor and kicked him half to death. Darnell pulled me out of the saloon, and it was there that I was again able to breathe deeply.

"Good Lord, Tom," I gasped. "The man would have —shot me. Why, he's not human! He's a blood-lusting beast."

"Pard, we got out of it fine!" ejaculated Darnell. "You shore told him. Everybody in town will know pronto that Slade has been called out. An' if he comes we'll see Shaw bore him."

"Gosh, Tom, look there!" I exclaimed, aghast. "There's Shaw in the middle of the road. What's he doing there?"

"Wal, 'cordin' to the rules of the gun game, he'll walk up an' down until Slade comes out. Come, let's get away from the front of this place."

We hurried up the sidewalk fifty paces or more and then stopped to watch. The crowd was spilling out of Pierce's. Part of them went one way and part another. Their actions as well as their excited speech told the passing pedestrians that there was something amiss.

Shaw walked down the middle of the street until within fifty steps of Pierce's door and there he halted. It was wonderful to behold him standing there motionless, tall and slim, his right side turned toward the direction from which he expected his enemy. His right arm hung by his side.

"There, look, you'll see Jack on the other side of the street," whispered Darnell. "He'll motion to Shaw if he sees Slade comin' to the door."

After a few tense moments Shaw resumed his pacing the street, this time walking down past the saloon. Presently he turned to come back. The drivers of vehicles, and others who had not been in Pierce's saloon, were quick to realize what was about to happen. Those that were close to Shaw moved back out of range and those on our side of the saloon halted on the sidewalk close to the buildings, and the one teamster turned in close to the rail.

All seemed set, then, for one of the famous frontier duels—what the West called an "even break." The noise of shuffling boots and excited voices died down and there was silence. It seemed to last for an interminable time. But Slade did not appear.

I heard a scream and a clatter of hoofs to our left. As I wheeled, Darnell ejaculated, "Gosh, look at them horses comin'. Runaway!"

I saw a team of furiously plunging horses dragging a high-wheeled buckboard down the middle of the street. The driver was a girl, and she was desperately hanging on to the reins trying to stop the horses. It was plain her attempt was futile. The shouts of onlookers attested to that. Instinctively, I strode forward and leaped the hitching rail into the street. Darnell called for me to look out, but he jumped to my side.

Suddenly, as the runaway drew rapidly close, I recognized the driver as the prairie-schooner girl who had waved at me. My instinct had been to do something, but when I saw that girl, all caution vanished in flaming impulse. I bounded forward, and as the horses came on, I broke into a run that would enable me to keep pace with them as they came abreast.

I timed the instant correctly and leaped for the bridle of the near horse, and seizing it with both hands, I hung on and sagged with all my weight upon it. I was dragged along. I brought that horse to his knees and would have stopped the team if the other horse had not kept on in his mad action. But I checked their speed.

Darnell flashed by me in front of the horses and he leaped to get hold of the bridle or head strap of the free horse. Lying back with all his weight, he yelled, "We can't stop them. Make the girl jump!"

I let go, floundered to my feet, and started to run again even with the driver's seat. "Jump!" I yelled. "I'll catch you. *Jump!*"

She stood up and propelled herself into the air, striking me squarely in the chest. I caught her, and I went down, but I broke the force of her fall as we landed in the dust.

She had fallen half across me. I extricated myself with difficulty and dragged her to her feet. I turned to see men had run to Darnell's assistance and had stopped the team halfway down the block. Then I turned to the girl.

"Well, for Heaven's sake, if it isn't you," she exclaimed, seeming to ignore the fact that she had just recently avoided a possible broken neck.

"Are—you—hurt?" was all I could stammer.

"No, thanks to you. I should really ask you if you're almost broken in two," she replied, appraising me with level blue eyes. "Some fresh hombre threw a pebble at my horses. Ace is a bit fractious an' he bolted. I'd have held him, but one of the reins broke."

It was indeed the girl of the wagon-trail. We stood gazing at each other and it was certain I forgot where we were or what had just happened. I saw the same bright chestnut hair which was now flying over her face, eyes which were of a darker blue but which I had remembered, the same striking face that had so affected me. She was quite tall and, as she instinctively brushed the dust from her blouse, never removing her glance from my face, I saw that she was of graceful, superb build.

"I'm a lucky man—" I found myself saying. "You see, I've never forgotten you. I thought of you constantly, Miss—"

"Sunderlund. Kit Sunderlund. And I'm the one who is lucky," she smiled.

"I didn't mean about the near accident," I went on.

"You're not any slower on talk than Texas cowboys, I can hear. But—I remembered you, too. You're not a cowboy—or a Westerner."

"I'm a Yankee tenderfoot from Boston. I hope the Yankee part won't prevent our being friends, Miss Sunderlund."

"You didn't act much like a tenderfoot," she replied, with a warm smile and a light in her eyes that added further to my subjection. "I should know an Easterner when I see one. I was born in Texas, but I went to school in Philadelphia. Aren't you the young Harvard man on this Western Union work?"

"Yes, I am Wayne Cameron."

"Here comes my father now. He will want to thank you, and I shall want to too, later. We are staying at the hotel to-night, and will catch up with the train to-morrow. Will you come to see me?"

"Will I? Thanks, I surely will. I don't know just what to say—or how—but this meeting has been the most wonderful of my life."

"And mine too," she averred. Then she turned to meet her father who stepped from the board walk to meet her. Evidently Sunderlund had witnessed the whole proceeding for he certainly looked alarmed.

"Kit, you're not hurt, are you?"

"Not at all, Father, thanks to this young man."

"Cameron, I thank you too, but thanks are not enough. I saw the whole thing. I was waitin' in the crowd—you know, for what we all expected to come off—it was a nervy thing for you to do. Thet's a heavy, fast team of horses. Yore partner Darnell must also come in for his share of thanks."

"I'm sure he deserves more than I, for I would never have thought of calling for your daughter to jump."

"Wal, it was shore fortunate for the Sunderlunds," he returned, with courtliness. "I'll see you later. We are remainin' in town all day. . . . Come, Kit, let's get out of this crowd."

The girl's dazzling, promising smile as she turned away with her father left me quite overwhelmed. Was this meeting really a consummation of my dreams? Something tremendous had happened to me.

No doubt if I had met that girl back in Boston, though unquestionably I would have been struck with her, I believe I should have maintained my composure even if it is doubtful that I should have kept possession of my heart. But after that romantic sight of her in the wagon-train, after my gradual subjugation to the West, to meet her out in this wild frontier town and to be able to help her at a moment when I was keyed up to extreme height—that was too much for me, and I knew I had fallen head over heels in love with her.

I leaned against the hitching rail in a daze, a confusion of thoughts making me oblivious to my surroundings.

Suddenly my memory took me back to the object of this visit to town. The crowds were dispersing and lining back upon the board walks; two laborers were leading the runaway team away, and on the moment Darnell came to my side to say:

"Wal, our pard bluffed the great killer an' made a yeller dog of him in the eyes of every man here. There ain't anythin' to come off. Shaw an' Lowden have gone up the street, I reckon on the way to our camp. Let's go."

"Tom, did you see that young lady jump into my arms and knock me over?" I inquired, in somewhat awed tones.

"Shore I seen it. You caught her even if you did take a tumble, an' figgerin' from the way you looked jest a couple of minutes ago, she must have given you another kind of a tumble."

"I guess she did. Tom, that girl's name is Kit Sunderlund and she's the daughter of the Texas cattleman whom you talked with."

"Hell! Is that so? So Jim Sunderlund of the Sweetwater is her uncle, an' she's goin' with her father to live in that valley. My Gawd, that's tough."

"Tough? Why so?" I asked, quickly.

"Wal, I reckon it's hard to say jest what I mean. She's too beautiful to be stacked up against all those woman-hungry cowboys an' cattlemen."

"It doesn't seem reassuring from your point of view," I reflected, soberly. "I wonder if our pards saw us save the young lady? . . . Shaw knows that girl. They were friends down in Texas. Her father intimated as much, and Lowden implied that Shaw was once in love with her."

"Shore, how could he help but be? But I reckon he's gotta deeper case on Ruby. There's somethin' about a gurl like Ruby that appeals to a man's sense of protection."

By the time we reached the end of the street we had caught up with Shaw and Lowden and soon turned out into the prairie toward our camp. I did not note any difference in Shaw, but Lowden seemed to be letting off steam in his relief. He called Slade a number of range epithets that were raw indeed.

"Vance," I spoke up, "you called the turn on this fellow Slade."

"Wal, I reckon so," he drawled, "but, of course, it wouldn't do to be too damn shore. What come off in thet saloon? When I seen you come out your face was as white as a sheet."

"Did you notice that, Vance?" I asked, wonderingly.

"I did, you bet. I seen every face on thet street. I might say I didn't miss nothin'."

While Darnell interposed to tell in forceful words what we had done, I wondered if Vance had also seen the runaway team and who was driving it.

"What the hell!" burst out Lowden. "If Slade ain't about the orneriest cuss I ever heared of."

"I tell you, boys," Darnell said, "if I hadn't had a hold on Slade, Wayne would have slugged him sure. I never seen anybody act so mad as Wayne."

Talking thus in this heightened state of mind, we arrived at our wagon and Shaw called out cheerily, "Wal, Pedro-Ruby, we're back without mussin' a hair. Nothin' happened, at least to me, but if I'm any judge of things, somethin' turrible happened to our Yankee pard."

Ruby came out to sit down on the end of the wagon bed and let her little feet hang over. To a casual glance she was merely a good-looking Mexican youth, but the eyes she fixed upon Shaw were darkly strained and dilated and there was an expression in them that actually hurt me. The fading out of agony to let in a beautiful light of utter worship betrayed what that ordeal had been to her. Her breast heaved under her blue blouse and her little brown hands shook. She managed to whisper huskily that she was glad he had gotten back safely.

"Pards," spoke up Vance, "it might be a good idee for us to pull out of town along the river an' make camp somewhere in the willows."

"That'll—be fine," I said, haltingly. "I suppose I can walk back to town to-night."

"What for, you darn fool?" queried Shaw, quickly.

"You'll get hurt in this burg, shore, if you keep on runnin' chances."

"But I've got to come, Vance. I made an engagement with that—that girl. Didn't you see the runaway? Didn't you see Tom and me stop the team—and the girl jump out in my arms to pile me on the ground?"

"Shore, me an' Jack seen thet, but we were pretty far away. . . . Holy Moses, pard, you seem doomed to have bad luck. It just couldn't be bad enough, but thet the girl you saved was Kit Sunderlund."

I gazed steadily at my Texas comrade and strove to control the disturbance in my breast, for his look, his tone caused me to sense something dire and calamitous. "Yes, Vance, the girl *was* Kit Sunderlund."

Lowden had the queerest expression that I had yet observed. "Oh, Lord, Vance, it's shore turrible the way things kin happen around you."

"Come here," snapped Shaw, and he laid hold of me. "Come over here where I can cuss you by yoreself."

He dragged me out of earshot of the others and, as he whirled me around to face him, I spoke somewhat stiffly.

"Vance, with all due respect to your state of mind, I see no reason for any force or mystery over the simple fact that I have a date with Kit Sunderlund, unless you're still in love, yourself."

"What in blazes has thet to do with what I'm tryin' to tell you? But if yo're still in possession of yore senses, you'll listen to me," rejoined Shaw, a little caustically. "Don't get yore Yankee back up, now. I'm yore friend. Pard, you look an' talk like a man who's lost his haid an' his heart. I know the sign."

"Shaw, you're hitting me below the belt. Your cowboy eyes are too keen. Some days ago, back along the trail, you remember I told you I saw that girl in a prairie schooner? Well, even with that short glimpse I was pretty hard hit. And to-day—well, damn the luck, there's no guessing about it—I never in my life fell so deeply in love."

"Thet's tellin' me, pard, I feared it," returned Shaw, earnestly, and he kept strong hold of my arm. "It's kinda hard to say an' I couldn't mean no disrespect to Kit Sunderlund, but yo're my friend an' I gotta give you a hunch. Kit Sunderlund has been the belle of Santone for years, ever since she was fifteen, an' she's twenty now. She was the purtiest girl in Southern Texas, rich, blueblooded. Kit is a natural born flirt. She's had more suitors, more pore devils in love with her, than anyone I ever heard of. I was one of them. I rode for her Dad for three years.

"Kit just cain't help makin' the boys love her. She never done anythin' but smile and be gay. It's just the way she is. There's somethin' intense an' alive in her. Why, with all the chances I had, I never held her hand but a couple of times, an' I kissed her once. Thet was when I got mad an' yanked her off her saddle, an' just had to kiss her or die. Thunder an' blazes! I'll never forget thet. She was mad as a hornet."

"Vance, I don't see anything in what you've said to—to make me regret falling in love with her. You've paid her nothing but compliments even if you do say she is a flirt."

"No, pard, it ain't atall," replied Vance, positively. "Thet's the whole trouble. I just cain't see Kit fallin' for any man. An' thet's what I'm afraid of—you fallin' so hard for her an' her not returnin' it. I do know, consciously or unconsciously, she leads men on. Us southern fellers are all alike. But I reckon an Easterner like you might be so hard hit thet it'd ruin yore life. An' this job we're on is shore no job for a broken-hearted man."

"Vance, I can very well see that, but I protest. Even if my heart is involved, that isn't saying that Kit Sunderlund will break it."

"The hell it ain't! I've seen too many fine young fellers go plumb to hell on account of bein' in love with Kit Sunderlund."

"You put me in a difficult position, Vance. You see—during the few moments I talked with Kit she gave me the impression that she had entertained precisely the same feeling for me."

"Oh, Lord, pard! You must have been loco. Even Kit couldn't have done it thet quick."

"Vance, I could discount her looks and actions, though

97

heaven knows they were sweet enough. But it was what she *said* that convinced me."

"Wal, an' what did Kit say to you?" queried Shaw.

"I don't care to betray her confidence. . . . I'm taken aback at your argument, Vance. You know the girl and you're kind enough to think of sparing me possible pain. You've also made me most intensely curious about her. It seems to me the sensible thing to do here will be to wait. If I have actually fallen head over heels in love with Kit Sunderlund—all right. I'll give in to it and I'll take my chances with her out along the Trail. Our telegraph line and that wagon-train are to travel west, probably keeping close together."

"Hell, pard, you make me feel bad," returned Shaw, remorsefully. "I ain't no prophet. I tell you I'm mebbe wrong. I was only playin' the cairds as they come to me in this deal. Let's go back to the wagon an' get ready to pull out. I reckon you can do some more tall thinkin' but yo're purty damn clear-haided at thet."

Without more ado we returned to the wagon and busied ourselves in preparation to leave. I was aware that Lowden cast skeptical glances at me. And evidently he or Darnell had acquainted Ruby with the facts for her eyes dwelt very softly and understandingly upon me. In due time we were ready to start and Lowden appeared with the three horses belonging to the cowboys.

It was an indication how deeply I was stunned that I hardly looked twice at the three most magnificent horses I had ever seen. We turned westward, taking the percaution to travel outside of the town following the wheel tracks of some of our wagons. Darnell drove the oxen as usual, and Ruby sat on the driver's seat beside him. Shaw and Lowden rode ahead on their horses, while Darnell's animal was haltered to the back of the wagon.

I lay down on one of the bunks and contended with the commotion within me, nor could I quite make Vance out. Was he giving me friendly advice or, as I prayed not, was he telling me in his cowboy way that he was still in love with Kit?

When we passed the long line of shacks and high board-fronted buildings, I found myself sentimentally looking for that high buckboard and spirited team of black horses that had come running headlong into my life and had left me, I was sure, somehow transformed. Soon we entered the wide trail, and in a little while only the dust and smoke of Gothenburg remained in my sight above the horizon.

In my melancholy reflection regarding Kit Sunderlund, there seemed to be contention between what little sanity I had left and the facts which Shaw had told me. I had sense enough to realize that all my emotions had been tremendously sharpened and augmented by this first contact with the West. My reactions to circumstances were bound not to be normal, at least until by hard knocks and privation and catastrophe I had been hauled down out of the clouds to actual reality. It was hard to overcome— my romantic obsession.

I let the fact speak for itself—that I had decided to give up seeing Kit Sunderlund and was already on my way out of sight of that town. But I found how useless it was to try to imagine I was not hurt. I had never been so in love with a girl. Often the sensations would creep into my mind that I had felt when she leaped solidly from the wagon into my arms, propelling me headlong to the ground. I remembered the feel of her as we lay there an instant, and then when I scrambled to my feet lifting her with me, how she leaned against me holding to me and gazing into my eyes with wonder and joyful recognition. It was something that I could not contend with. That was an unforgettable moment and had only grown to be bitter since Shaw had undermined my exalted estimate of her.

Yet deep in my heart there was some instinct, some rebellious significance which clamored that Shaw was only a repudiated lover and that his opinion was biased. Perhaps I had acted with wisdom but I was full of regret and I had a conviction that the romance was not ended by a long way. I must have lain there a considerable time slowly working out of my misery and reconciling myself to fate. And presently the stern call of this building of Western Union returned again with zest and thrill.

The halting of the wagon attested to our arrival at our new camp. Shaw and Lowden were unsaddling their horses and I walked over to admire these wonderful steeds at close range. I was at once struck with the spirit of these animals. They looked at me as intelligently and as skeptically as a human being might have. Shaw's horse was a sorrel, racy and thoroughbred and quite a contrast to Lowden's mottled chestnut mustang, a really small animal, but so sturdy and muscular that he looked large.

"Pard, don't lay a hand on him. He'll try to kill you," advised Lowden.

"Gee, aren't these beasts friendly?" I asked. "I don't want to try to ride a horse that's wild."

"Wal, I wouldn't advise yore learnin' on my hawse or Jack's, but Tom says his hawse is gentle."

"If Tom's hoss is gentle I'll eat him," remarked Lowden, sarcastically.

"Anyway, yo're due to find out," drawled Shaw. "When we passed Liligh an' his gang back heah a few miles, he said for us to ride back an' go to work."

"Then we passed the end of the construction work?" I asked.

"Shore did," replied Shaw. "They're stuck there over somethin' or other. Wayne, have you looked around atall?"

"Yes, I have, but I couldn't see anything."

"Look at thet smoke off down the river. See thet? . . . "Thet's Sunderlund's wagon-train. He's halted for camp. I reckon not over five miles away."

"Well, Vance, five miles is as much as a thousand as far as I am concerned," I replied, shortly.

"Tom is goin' to stay heah in camp," said Vance. "He's got some work to do on the wagon an' we'll grab a snack of grub an' rustle back to work. From now on it'll be work an' hell, which is sayin' there won't be any tellin' which is one an' which is the other."

I gazed off at that smoke which marked Sunderlund's wagon-train, and I thought that for me there could not be too much of the work to assuage the pain and longing that flooded my heart.

That evening as we were sitting around the camp fire, Creighton sent for me to take down in my rather amateurish way an emergency message which he was expecting from the East. It had to do with wire and poles and men. And it also had to do with men of the same country who were fighting a war with each other.

"Fellows," I said soberly, when later I returned, "the Civil War is on in a big way. Big battles are being fought, and a lot of us fellows from the North are shooting a lot of you fellows from the South, and vice versa."

There was a silence for a moment, broken only by the quiet crackling of the fire and a slow wind moving through the grass.

Darnell finally broke the silence. "I suppose we fellers here ought to line up against each other across the fire and shoot it out."

"Thet's a right good idea," said Lowden. "Pedro, what side are you goin' to be on—because I want to be on the same side."

Ruby replied, "Lowden, I know I'm s'posed to be Pedro to all of you but for the moment I'm going to be Ruby."

"Meanin?" Shaw asked her.

"The side of women . . . not wanting war at all."

Looking backward across an interval of days and weeks of back-breaking toil and pain, it seemed an endless time to our camp near Ogallala from that one back along the river at our first stop out of Gothenburg. It remained in my memory only because at the Ogallala camp Sunderlund had driven by in his buckboard with his daughter, and they had stopped to inquire for me. I had spied them coming and had left camp, determined to stick to my resolution not to see her, for the present at least. Even from a distance, I was further distracted by her lovely face.

That memory was fresh beside the intervening ordeal. I had labored until there was no thrill left of pleasant sensation any more. Perhaps I had plunged into the thing too eagerly to conserve any energy and strength. The men of Creighton's outfit hated above all else the digging of post holes. Marvelous to recall, I had dug most of the telegraph pole holes along that weary endless stretch of miles.

When the day's work was done there were always other tasks that seemed to keep on and on till I went down exhausted. If there had only been the stretching of the wire, digging holes and raising poles, the work would not have been such a nightmare. But there were jobs too numerous to remember that mounted in all to one weary grind. The telegraph line had to go almost straight. This prairie that looked level and unobstructed to a casual glance was a deceit and a snare. There were deep dry washes to cross, marshes that would have been bottomless in wet weather, live streams to ford, and always firewood to gather and telegraph poles to find where there were none.

As if the manual labor were not enough, never a day passed in which I was not called upon to minister to some injured laborer. At first I was proud of Creighton's reliance upon me and his outspoken gladness that I was with him; but as time went on the medical tasks grew to be a great burden. Superficial cuts and bruises, burns and abrasions, all the minor injuries that happened along were easy to contend with. But I had broken arms and broken legs to take care of, gunshot wounds, one of which was fatal, fever and dysentery, and all kinds of serious ailments that put a tremendous responsibility upon my limited medical knowledge. Sometimes, weary as I was, I could not sleep for worry.

Always I had Creighton as an example. He was indefatigable, indomitable, a leader of men. If we had to stop for a day, he redoubled the work on the next. Yet he was cheerful, kind, patient, untiring, forever the unquenchable leader. I tried to emulate him, but my failure often dispirited me greatly. Upon this day at sunset I found a few minutes to sit and rest, and look backwards to that camp where I had got my last look at Kit Sunderlund. Though the weeks seemed endless by reason of the ordeal, it was really a short time. I gazed at my ragged garb, at my worn-out boots, at the calloused blisters on my palms, and the backs of my hands sunburned to blackness; I felt the stubble on my chin and could not remember when I had cared last to shave. I felt my spare limbs that had grown thin and hard as iron, and I marveled at the changes labor and pain and endurance could make in a man.

I did not want the West, with all its beauty, its wildness, its increasing grandeur, with its catastrophes, with all that could come along in duty to an extraordinary enterprise, to kill that in me which had made me so eager and happy to throw in my lot with it.

I bent my gaze upon my comrades at their camp tasks, and I was ashamed of my past indifference, the discouragement and exhaustion that had let me fall away from the enthusiasm and loyalty of our first meeting. Despite my lethargy they had grown increasingly dear to me. All of which convinced me, as I sat there in the sunset, that I had really a magnificent opportunity to be worthy of Creighton's trust and to attain the simple western nobility of my comrades.

We were camped on a rise above the river about half way between Ogallala and Julesburg. It was late August. The weather had been hot and dry, and a red haze obscured the sinking sun.

The fragrance of savory bacon and coffee and hot biscuits awakened me eagerly to thoughts of supper. Evidently it was not ready yet for they did not call me. It was pleasant and sweet to watch Ruby. She looked like a boy and might have deceived uninterested spectators, but to me her womanliness and charm stood out all over her. She could not pass Shaw without some outward manifestation of her regard. Certain it was that the new life that had come to her centered in him.

As I watched her I could not help but yearn hungrily for some woman to care for me that way. And as that thought bitterly reminded me of Kit Sunderlund, I dismissed it.

Several times during the last half hour I had seen Shaw halt in his tracks, lift his head with that hawk-like action so characteristic of him, and face the north. He did not seem to be looking, as much as feeling. Something attracted him out there across the plains, and it developed that Lowden had not missed it either.

"Pard, what the hell is eatin' you?" he queried.

"Nothin' is eatin' me, Jack, only I'm gol-durned hungry. Why do you ask?"

"Wal, I seen you stop an' look acrost the river there, like you used to look when you sensed trouble fer the herd, or hed a hunch Comanches were around, or some sech little trick as thet."

"Jack, old pard, up here in the north yore sense of fear seems to have been lulled. If you was as keen as you used to be, you would have seen thet it had to do with my nose."

Lowden, who was kneeling beside the fire, lifting the lid off the Dutch oven to see if the biscuits were brown enough, slowly arose to his feet. "Nose? Hell! What d'ye smell?"

"Turn around an' take a sniff or two."

Lowden was quick to answer to that suggestion, while Darnell looked up with keen interest and Ruby stopped anxiously beside Shaw. I, too, curiously faced the north and smelled the cool breeze in my face, but I thought I could not catch anything but the dry tang of the open that I had become used to.

"Dawg-gone!" ejaculated Lowden. "Smoke! Smoke, by gosh. Tom, do you ketch it?"

"No, I don't, pards, but that ain't sayin' anythin'. My smeller is not much good. It hasn't worked very well since I got kicked by a hoss."

"Jack, I was hopin' you'd tell me thet was camp-fire smoke," said Vance.

"Wal, I cain't," responded Jack, shortly, and he walked away from the camp fire toward the river bank.

My curiosity grew into intense interest. There was something wrong. These open-range men smelled smoke and evidently smoke meant peril. By straining my faculties I made sure that the cool wind was almost imperceptibly increasing, and if I did not catch a hint of smoke, I certainly imagined it. I strode toward the bank to join Lowden and presently Shaw followed me. We stood there silently for a few moments. Then Ruby came and stuck her arm through Shaw's. "What is it, Vance?" she whispered, in troubled tone.

"I was hopin' I wouldn't have to say," responded Shaw, "but it's been growin' on me the last half hour. All afternoon I didn't like the look of the clouds an' the feel of the air. It was heavy an' felt like it was bein' pushed south. But only in the last half hour did I catch the smell of smoke."

"Thet smoke ain't so good," returned Jack. "We're in the wussest place we've been in since we left Ogallala. Kinda a low swale hyar along the river for fifteen miles back an' Lord knows how far up the river. Grass an' brush awful thick an' dry as tinder. It ain't so good!"

"Boys, out with it. Tell me what's wrong," I demanded, anxiously.

"Prairie fire!" exclaimed Shaw. "An' if it runs before a norther it will be hell for us. I'm afraid it's comin' but I cain't be shore for a half an hour mebbe. Let's eat an' wait a bit."

We returned to the camp fire which Jack replenished with bits of brush. They burned up brightly and we sat down around the tarpaulin and fell to in hungry silence, but I emulated the cowboys in that while I was eating I faced the north and strained my perceptions. The coyotes had begun their hue and cry. The sharp concatenation of yelps seemed more piercing than usual. Then, from across the river and not so far away, there sounded a deep bay, somewhat similar to that of a hound, only wilder, a long, mournful, bloodcurdling howl.

"What's that?" I asked, my cup of coffee poised in hand.

"Thet's a wolf, my Yankee friend, an' he ain't very cheerful," returned Shaw, grimly.

I noticed that the cowboy got along with his supper somewhat more quickly than usual. About that time the breeze suddenly increased to a wind that blew hard and cold and steadily. It moaned through the willows; it rattled the canvas flaps on the wagon; it quickened the fire, and made the embers glow and scattered sparks along the ground. With it came a perceptible dry pungent odor of burning brush. Shaw finished his cup of coffee and rising to his height once more, gave his attention to the north.

"Pards, no use hopin' against hope," he said, with decision. "Jack, you an' Tom clear away heah, then get the hosses in an' the oxen an' hitch up. Wayne, you come with me. We'll go tell Creighton. It's a prairie fire an' a norther an' we're right in the track of both!"

Chapter Seven

WE HURRIED out into the darkness, buttoning our coats and turning up our collars. The north wind was cold. We followed the road a little way and then threaded our zig-zag way through the bare spots in the grass and brush until we reached the construction camp. That evening Creighton's force was much larger in camp than usual, at least a hundred wagons and probably three hundred men. The men around the camp fires apparently had no inkling that possible danger was blowing down upon them.

Creighton was at the table in his wagon writing before a bright light.

"Hello, boys. Come on up," he greeted us in answer to our call. "Well, Cameron, you look kind of pale behind the gills, and Shaw, you look as if you were about to pull a gun."

"Boss, I shore wish it wasn't anythin' wuss than throwin' a gun," replied the cowboy. "There's a norther blowin' down on us."

"Yes, I thought I had begun to feel a little chilly. But that in itself can't be bad news."

"Boss, it's blowin' a prairie fire ahead of it."

"Indeed! That's different. How serious is it, Shaw?"

"I cain't say, Mr. Creighton, but even at the best it'll be bad enough. This stretch along the river here is very thick with grass an' brush an' it will burn. With thet wind behind it, it'll run along like powder. It'll be wild fire."

"That'll be something new. With Liligh away I wouldn't know how to meet it."

106

"You cain't take time to send for Liligh. We've got to do somethin' pronto."

"I appreciate that, Shaw, but *what?* Spill it."

"By all means I'd advise packin' all yore supplies, hitchin' up all the wagons an' drivin' them into the river bed. It's pretty wide along here. The water runs mostly on the north side an' there's sand bars thet have dried out an' will hold up the wagons. I've had to do this before down in Texas when I was drivin' cattle. It's good we haven't any cattle except yore little bunch of beefs because we couldn't keep them from stampedin'. With the oxen an' mules hitched to the wagons, we gotta chance to hold them. Lucky for us, sir, thet thet space between the river banks is pretty wide, else we'd have to leave everythin' an' run for our lives."

"Indeed it is serious," returned Creighton, rising and picking up his coat. "I'm lucky to have a plainsman like you in the outfit. Is there any way to tell how quickly this fire will be down upon us?"

"Not yet. The sky has begun to get red up toward the north. I'm advisin' we rustle, sir."

"That's enough, Shaw. Go back to your wagon and get that in shipshape. Cameron, you come with me and we'll give the men orders. Liligh ought to be here."

I followed Shaw down out of the wagon to see him stride swiftly toward the river. Creighton came after me putting on his coat and we both stood motionless for a moment watching the strange ruddy glow in the north. It now reached almost to the zenith. The wind was harder and colder and it bore a pungent odor that closed my nostrils like pitch.

"No time to be lost, boy," said Creighton. "You can repeat my orders to the men below and I will take care of these at hand."

I stayed long enough with Creighton to hear him shout at the first group of men around the camp fire. An army officer about to meet unexpected attack could not have called out more forcefully and sternly. Standing in the glow of the fire light, Creighton looked a man to command obedience and respect. He stood with bare head, his hair blowing in the wind, and his eyes reflecting the fire. I left him then, and running down the line I burst upon the next group of men around the camp fire and yelled: "Creighton's orders! Prairie fire. Teamsters are to bring in the oxen and mules—hitch up—and the rest of you pack everything with all possible haste!"

As I ran past them I had the satisfaction of seeing that my trenchant words had the effect desired. In short order I had acquainted all the men on that side of the camp with our leader's orders and the need for haste. Then I slowed down to catch my breath and made for our camp on the river.

Tom and Jack were hitching up the oxen, the horses were tethered near at hand, saddled and bridled, and Shaw stood on the bank peering ahead.

I joined Shaw and told him how I had followed out the orders of our leader and asked him if the situation had changed anything for the worse.

"I'm darned if I can be shore, Wayne," replied Shaw. "But I'm scared. If there was any high ground near I'd get on my hoss an' ride out to make shore. But it's all low an' flat hereabouts. . . . But look, don't you think it's brighter than it was?"

"Perceptibly. It's a lighter red and it reaches up higher."

"I reckon it's shore bad. I can see yore face plainer than I could a while ago. An' it shines pretty red. Now look out in the river. We can see the bare spots of sand an' the puddles an' the big patch of water out yonder. We'll have to cut down this bank a little because it's too steep to take off. Go get some shovels an' tell the boys to come help us when they've hitched up."

Presently we were all laboring strenuously to cut the river bank into a slant over which it would be safe to drive the wagon. Darnell got the ax and cut out saplings and overhanging branches. I purposely did not turn toward the north until my share of the tasks was finished. Then, with Ruby standing beside me holding my arm, I looked, and for the first time felt awe and fear. The sky was a strange red and all the stars had been blotted out.

"Wayne, I've been in a couple of prairie fires," said Ruby. "But not in a place like this. It's bad."

"But, Ruby, where's the danger?" I asked. "Those sand bars are a hundred feet from this side and three hundred feet from the other side. The fire can't touch us there."

"Oh, you don't realize!" she exclaimed. "The wind will carry fire—flames will leap on high and reach ahead— oh, hundreds of feet! That is, if there's a hard enough wind. But isn't it beautiful? See the ruddy sky reflected in the water, the sand bars are red. Look at the dark line of willows across there. They shine as if they were on fire already. And then that dark, wild horizon line with the fiery color beyond! Wayne—the wind burns my cheeks —I'm beginning to be frightened."

"Well, you may be frightened but you still can be poetical," I replied. "Here come the boys with the wagon and the horses. We'll have to get out of the way. Come, Ruby. If we run into any patches of water or mud, I'll carry you."

But by proceeding carefully and picking out the way we arrived at the sand bar without incident. It was hard-packed sand and gravel, an area of perhaps half an acre in extent, and at its edge there was running water. I felt that we had a very fortunate position and wondered how it would be for the other wagons. Then I turned to see how my comrades were faring.

Shaw led the way riding his horse and leading the other two. I heard him call out directions to Darnell who was driving the oxen. Lowden was on foot. When the oxen reached the foot of the slant they sank to their knees, but that was nothing to the powerful brutes. They waded right through the deep sand. When the heavy wagon struck the soft place the wheels sank hub deep and finally ceased to turn.

"Come, Jack, fork yore hoss an' get yore rope out. We gotta help pull the wagon out of thet hole."

I was the interested spectator then of seeing the cowboys fasten rope to the tongue of the wagon and help the oxen haul the wagon out of that bad place. It required strenuous pulling but they accomplished it and soon our vehicle and supplies and animals were safely with us on the patch of solid sand.

Shaw dismounted and he and Jack tethered the three horses to the wagon wheels. Shaw remarked the while that we were all right in that location unless there should be a regular cyclone blowing. He and Jack were not so sanguine about the other wagons. We could still see the fires burning in the construction camp and a great deal of bustle going on there, but so far as we observed, none of those wagons had got started yet.

"If they don't get goin' soon some of them will be in for disaster," Shaw remarked.

"We've got the best place all along here," Jack said. "I reckon there's room fer two or three more wagons on this island. What you say, pard?"

"Okay, I'd say you better run over and tell Mr. Creighton to drive his wagon over here, an' a couple of other wagons thet he wants. One of them shore ought to be the grub wagon."

Lowden trudged away and soon disappeared shoreward. And then Shaw said that they might be going to burn up but it was darn cold right then and he was going to build a fire. He told me to take a shovel and make a bank of sand behind the only clump of willows on the island. While I was engaged at this task, he and Tom went ashore for firewood.

Ruby got off the wagon seat where she had climbed and came close to me, evidently lonesome and probably frightened. Her pretty face, stained dark by whatever Shaw had used upon it, shone ruddily in reflection from the sky. It was growing brighter every moment. That prairie fire could not be so very far away.

"Wayne," spoke up Ruby, timidly, "I remember back on the Trail days and days ago, that I saw you leave camp when that Sunderlund girl with her father drove by our camp. Vance saw you, too. I'm wondering what in the world made you do that?"

"Well, Ruby, it's not a very long story," I replied.

"It doesn't strike me that you'd be afraid of any girl," she said, as if to herself.

Then I frankly told her about the first time I had seen Kit Sunderlund, that it was probably love at first sight, that I was sure of it the day I rescued her from the runaway, and that I really was in a seventh heaven until Vance dragged me down by the things he had said.

"But, Wayne, he's a cowboy," she expostulated. "He's a prince—the finest fellow in the world, but he's a cowboy. And cowboys don't know anything about girls. He told me right out he used to be in love with Kit, and that he knew that he had no show at all with her."

"Ruby, you surely are a fine kind to talk that way," I replied, feelingly, "knowing Vance was crazy over that girl. You're not jealous, but I suspect that Shaw was jealous of me."

"I don't believe it, Wayne. Even if Shaw loved Kit more than he did me, he's too big for that. He'd die before he showed it," Ruby said earnestly.

"It'd be good to find one flaw in that cowboy's character. . . . Well, I'd like to know what would have happened if I had gone to see Kit Sunderlund that night. And I just wonder what I'd do if I ever met her again."

"You probably will, Wayne. That wagon-train can't be far ahead of us."

The cowboys returned, each carrying an armful of wood with which Shaw soon built a fire. In spite of the wind-break the flames roared and blew out almost on a level while the sparks went flying. In my excitement I had not realized my hands were almost numb with cold and that I was extremely uncomfortable. The fire felt very good. I was learning that back in the effete East people did not know what it was to be hungry and exhausted and cold, not to say frightened.

"Tom," spoke up Shaw, "grab a bucket an' let's get some fresh water before it is all full of dirt. Wayne, you bring some water-bags."

While we were filling these receptacles I realized from the reflection of the bright sky in the water that it was now almost as light as day, but the color was red. Shaw stood up with his bucket and scrutinized the north. Then he turned his ear to the wind.

"It looks lots brighter," he said, "an' my nose is all clogged up. I can't hear anythin' yet but it's blowin' right smart now an' if it gets harder, we can look for thet fire to blow down on us pronto. I wish Creighton an' those other fellers would get a move on. Mark what I tell you, Tom. They're gonna lose somethin' if they don't rustle."

We went back to the wagon and carefully covered the buckets, and I stowed away the water-bags inside the wagon. It was blowing so hard now that we had to speak loud to make each other hear. Presently a crashing in the brush on the bank and a driver yelling at his oxen acquainted us with the fact that one wagon was approaching. It finally reached the bank and, directed by Lowden, labored across to our island and took up a position at the lower end. This man drove his oxen until they were all knee deep in water.

From that moment the shouting of men and crashing of brush on the shore attested to the fact that other wagons were approaching the river. We saw one come out below us fifty feet or more and get in trouble in the sand. Above us wagon after wagon worked out into the river bed, some of them in the water and some of them more fortunately located on sand bars.

It was light enough now for us to see distinctly, only everything was strange and unreal in that red glow. Another wagon came lumbering out to our position and took the upper end of our island.

When I attended once more to the spectacle in the North I found that I could not take my eyes away from it again.

The scene was changing. The sky was the color of flame. That augmenting red meant the approach of storm-driven fire. Above the sound of the wind, the loud crashes in the brush, the piling of oxen off the bank, the groan of wheels and rattle of wagons, and hoarse, excited voices of men attested to the fact that they were having trouble getting out into the river far enough to be safe.

"Wind about forty miles," I heard Shaw call out. "Not bad yet, but too bad for us. And the worst is thet wind is growin' harder. An' Lordy, ain't it cold!"

Ruby seemed fascinated by the approaching holocaust. She clung to my arm and gazed and gazed and kept crying out. Presently all across the line where the black of the horizon met the crimson of the sky, clouds of smoke

112

rolled upward. The cowboys yelled at sight of this. The rapidity with which the clouds rolled upward amazed me and gave evidence of the power of the wind behind.

In a few moments a quarter of the red sky was blotted out by these rolling, mushrooming, bellowing clouds transforming, marvelously beautiful in their colors of yellow and black and white, all streaming upward and forward vividly reflecting the fire underneath. Every second I expected to see flame.

Low down at the bottom of these clouds a bright line intensified. Then a loud yell from Jack, who had climbed on top of our wagon, heralded something terrific that was still hidden from me.

"I see it, Vance," he yelled. "Comin' hell bent for election, an' I reckon if we don't take to the water we're gone goslin's."

"Hell, no," shouted Shaw, as he faced the north, his lean grim face red in the firelight. "We'll get blistered shore, an' have hell with the stock, but our lives will be safe here."

Tom climbed up by the big wheel beside the driver's seat and, holding to the hoop of the canvas top he gave vent to exclamations of awe if not of fear. I supposed that nothing could scare these cowboys. My skin was tight and that queer internal commotion which I had learned to become familiar with here on the frontier beset my body again.

"Whoopee!" yelled Lowden, from the top of the wagon. An instant later, as if by magic, I saw the curved tips of fiery forked flames leap into sight all along the horizon. There was something supernatural in that sight. The leaping, upflinging motion showed the powerful energy of the wind and fire. If they leaped into sight in one instant, in another they had lifted high above the ground, and then I knew what was meant by wild fire on the prairie.

It was a monstrous wall of flame, in furious swift action, motivated by a gale of wind. Marvelous and unbelievable the way the streaks and streams of smoke shot upward to roll and spread into clouds that formed the immense curtain, a color of infinite varied hues, a canopy that now swept upward and toward us with frightful celerity.

Shaw joined us and called out, his voice now ringing, "She's a humdinger an' she'll be on us pronto. Hear thet roar!"

I became aware of a low strange sound increasing in volume while I listened. It was not like any sound that I had ever heard. The wall of fire topped by the waving, flinging tongues of flame could not have been more than half a mile away now, and it was approaching us with awful rapidity. It stayed level at this period although its leaping points varied along the line. The heavier, thicker brush and grass bordering the river bottom would, of course, add to the height of the flames.

Now in the intense light, the opposite shore did not seem so far from us and our danger lay in the possibility of these flames reaching out toward us, possibly spreading over us, in which case we were doomed. Even if we submerged ourselves in the river the heat would be fatal. But I still hoped and felt sure that the flames could not leap far enough across the river to make our position untenable.

I now saw flaming bits of wood and brush and millions of sparks racing low and ahead of the wind and these certainly would cross the river and fire the brush on the opposite side. The wall of fire, the forked tongues of flame, the mounting roar rushed down upon us and held us spellbound and mute.

I felt Ruby's little hands like bands of steel on my arm. The spectacle was at its grandest and most appalling when the fire struck the thick grass and brush on the edge of the river. There came a tremendous explosion all along back of the river and immense puffs of smoke and sparks and flames, and a hissing, crackling, destroying roar, the like of which I had never dreamed. I observed birds in flight, and hundreds of jackrabbits and other animals, some of them coyotes and antelope, fleeing like phantoms in the eerie light and leaping over the bank to disappear. I saw antelope swimming across the red flaring patch of river.

It was a magnificent, hellish, appalling storm of fire

that blotted out the shore and leaped out half across the river. The smoke was over us; and underneath a streaking flood of burning bits of wood, flying on the wings of the wind. Fiery sparks as large as my hand fell all around us. The oxen surged in their yokes. The cowboys leaped down to hold the plunging horses that had been covered with blankets and tarpaulins.

Then the wave of heat struck us. I seemed to shrivel up. Ruby fell on her knees in the front of the wagon, and I, with seared eyeballs, watched for a moment longer to see that awful spectacle of fire reach its limit on the shore and then become obscured in dust and smoke. I covered my burning face with my scarf and bent to my knees, terror stricken, yet never losing that horrible roar of gale and fire.

Measured by my agony and terror the culminating moments of that catastrophe seemed endlessly long and torturing. Gradually, however, the roar lessened and passed from the opposite shore across the void and became louder behind us. The crackling, bursting force receded and I realized the wind was carrying the fire onward, away from us.

Once more I heard the men shouting. The cowboys were yelling, and, as I opened my eyes and uncovered my face I once more attended to what was going on about me. The terrific roar had passed away. All about me was dim, gray, smoky. I found breathing extremely difficult. On the bank near us were denuded willow trees with their stems still blazing. Here and there on the ground small fires burned. The holocaust had passed, leaving hardly anything to burn.

Up and down the river there was commotion among the men and hoarse shouts everywhere. Wagons were in flames. Everywhere the men were throwing water, hanging on to the plunging oxen, tossing burning articles from the wagons, or rolling telegraph poles into the water.

Shaw, who was working madly, screeched at me to come out of it and put out the fire in our canvas top. I leaped down and seizing a bucket, I ran into the water. Then I saw Lowden trying to hold the surging oxen.

"Throw some water on them, pard," he yelled. I complied with all the haste I could muster. They stopped their plunging as I put out the fiery embers on their backs. Then, refilling the bucket, I ran to the wagon. Darnell was on top beating out burning places.

"Here," he yelled. "Throw some here. Never mind *me*. That water shore feels good. I'm burned to a cinder. Throw some here, and here. Rustle another bucket."

Shaw had succeeded in quieting his horse and he joined me with a pail. Lowden remained with the oxen.

Vance and I promptly put out all the fires in and around our wagon and then had a chance to catch our breath and see what was going on around us. The teamster on the wagon below us bawled lustily for help. We ran to his assistance.

The succeeding couple of hours were a nightmare. Up the river for two hundred yards we found the wagons in bad shape. The canvas covers of many wagons had been completely burned off and contents badly damaged. Many loads of telegraph poles had been left standing on the bank. Wagons and poles had both caught on fire. Creighton was raging over his burning telegraph poles and he was trying to work everywhere at once to put out the fires. He did not seem to mind the ruined wagons at all, but he was grateful whenever we saved some of his precious telegraph poles.

By midnight we had all the fires out and both oxen and wagons safe on the shore. We left our wagon on our little island but we unhitched the oxen and freed them of the heavy yokes. Ruby had replenished our little fire back of the bank and after the blast furnace we had just faced, it surprised me how welcome it was. I sat down to warm my numb hands and was further amazed to see Ruby laugh at me.

"You're a ragamuffin," she said. "Holes in your clothes, and hands and face black—oh, you're a sight. But, Wayne, can't you do something for my back where it was burned?"

"Of course I can, Ruby. Let me catch my breath and wash my hands. I'll bet two-bits you're not the only one who is burnt."

The smoke had blown away on the strong wind. Only

in a few places could I see the red of charred embers glowing. It had grown night again. The stars were bright and the norther was still blowing, though not with the velocity which had accompanied the fire. That beautiful and hideous spectacle seemed to have been a nightmare dream. But my own burns and bruises assured me of its actuality.

By the light of the camp fire I ministered as well as possible to Ruby. She had sustained a bad burn in the middle of her back and I thought that it would leave a scar. I used oil and salve on her wound and bound it up with soft linen.

"Ruby, you have a lovely back. Just as white and soft as satin," I said. "But I'm afraid that it will have a scar."

"What do I care!" exclaimed Ruby. "I'll never show my naked back again. I'm through with that dance-hall job. . . . And say, Doc Wayne, thanks all the same for your kind services, but I'd hate to have you set my leg if it got broke."

"You ungrateful little imp! Why, I'd like to know?"

"Why? You're rougher'n hell, that's why," she retorted.

"I guess I was at that," I replied, contritely, "but my own hands are scorched. They're sore and clumsy and I'm so gosh darned tired that I couldn't be gentle."

It developed that there was no rest for the weary. Almost all had burns and abrasions that needed attention. It went the rounds that I was ministering to these needs, and one by one, other men of the wagon-trains called upon me for services. Ruby went to bed but the boys remained awake and helped me all they could. They kept the fire burning so I had a light and so we would not freeze.

Creighton's wagon had not escaped unscathed and would need a lot of canvas patched and he himself had sustained a bad leg burn. In his haste to save the precious telegraph poles he had fallen over a red hot coal and burned his leg severely below the knee. While I worked over him, man after man called to report. When I finished with Creighton and commented upon the catastrophe, he smiled and replied:

"Only an incident of construction work on the Western Union, my boy, but you certainly fit in handily."

Shaw accompanied me from wagon to wagon and so many were the hurts of the men that gray dawn was breaking in the East when Shaw and I returned to our camp.

"Pard, we better snatch a little sleep, 'cause Creighton will have us on the job at sunup just as if nothin' happened."

Despite my pangs, my extreme weariness caused me to drop to sleep at once and indeed the sun had been long up when I awoke. The boys were cooking breakfast and when I painfully clambered out of the wagon, I was astounded at the seared and blackened spectacle of the prairie on all sides. To look about me was to dispel any doubt that the prairie fire had been a nightmare. Still, we were a cheerful lot.

"I'll tell you, honey," drawled Shaw to Ruby, with his cool humor, "gettin' acquainted with fire ain't such a bad idee because where yore goin' some day it'll be like thet last night all the time."

"Meaning hell, you heartless cowboy," retorted Ruby. "Well, I'll have a lot of company, and you and your pards, all except maybe Wayne, will be sitting around with me trying to keep cool."

"Ump-umm on thet escape for Wayne," returned Shaw, with a grin. "Accordin' to all signs he's haided for hell just the same as we are."

"If you ask me," chimed in Lowden, "we'll all hev our hell hyar an' our reward will be heaven."

I hurried over to the new camp to find Creighton and get the orders for the day, but he was extremely busy and I saw from the havoc that had been done to the wagons and oxen, it would hardly be possible for the construction work to get under way that day. Liligh had not shown up and we did not know what had happened to him and his men. It appeared certain that all telegraph poles and line in the path of the fire would have been destroyed.

On the way back I talked with Herb Lane and it was his opinion that Creighton would form one outfit of all the wagons and men in good shape and set them to repairing the line.

I bethought myself of changing my tattered clothing when a messenger arrived from Creighton telling me to report at his wagon at once with my medicine kit. As I gathered up my things Shaw dryly observed:

"Ten to one you'll have to look up Liligh an' his men. An' I've a hunch thet Sunderlund outfit may need you. They were traveling without a doctor. If their wagon-train was in the track of thet fire, I'll bet they're in a hell of a mess."

"Vance, that seems far-fetched to me," I returned, thoughtfully. "Of course, I'll go if Creighton orders it, but there's no end of work for me here."

Ruby slyly called after me: "Wayne, look sharp and dodge that violet-eyed girl."

I hurriedly made my way across the blackened ground to the new camp. Before I reached Creighton's wagon I saw a buckboard with high wheels and a team of black horses that I most certainly recognized. Shaw was correct. Upon arriving at Creighton's wagon, I found him talking to the driver who was sitting in the seat of the buckboard.

"Cameron, there's a hurry call from the Sunderlund wagon-train. Some of Sunderlund's men have been badly burned and his daughter especially needs your services. Go and do what you can for them. This messenger ran across Liligh on the way over and found that he and his outfit had not suffered materially from the fire. You might look him up on the way back and report to me."

I acquiesced in few words, and climbing into the buckboard, put my kit under the seat. I seemed divided between chagrin and irresistible thrill. "So Miss Kit Sunderlund is injured and I'm called upon to minister to her," I soliloquized. At once we were off and that fast stepping team of blacks looked as if they would make short work of the miles.

"We had a bad night here, as you can well see," I remarked to the driver, by way of opening conversation. "How did the Sunderlunds' wagon-train make out?"

"Wal, we had the wust time since we started from Texas," he returned. He was a stalwart young man and had the earmarks of a teamster more than of a cowboy. "Our camp was about ten miles up the river from heah. And some of the wagons were in a bad place, but most of them were safe on bare ground. It blew like hell and the fire was fierce but the grass and brush wasn't thick or we couldn't have come out of it without loss of life."

"Did you take to the river with the wagons as we did?" I asked.

"Some of the men did and they come out all right barrin' some burned canvas. It was the wagons thet got stuck in the brush and stalled in the sand thet suffered the most."

"What about Sunderlund's horses and that big herd of cattle?"

"The cattle stampeded to hell an' gone, an' it took one man to every hawse to hold him. About fifty riders went out this mawnin' to round up the cattle. Looks like a forlorn hope to me. Just before the fire reached the river one of our scouts reported a band of Injuns—Cheyennes, he thought—ridin' by not so far from our camp. We've about struck the range of the Cheyennes an' they're hostile to the whites these days."

"Cheyennes!" I ejaculated. "That's pouring it on thick and hard. Just as if we didn't have enough trouble!"

"Wal, thet's it. I heahed Sunderlund say thet he was glad the cattle stampeded, 'cause if they hadn't they'd all been burnt to death. We've got a lot of good cattlemen in our wagon-train an' if our herd didn't run off the range they'll round them up."

"How badly is Miss Sunderlund injured?" I at last came out with the question that I had wanted to ask first of all.

"I didn't heah, Doc," replied the driver. "She was in her wagon—she has a wagon all her own, shore fitted up in style an' she was in bed tended by her maid. But Sunderlund certainly sent me off in a hurry."

With that I settled down to thoughtful silence and concern. I certainly hoped the girl had sustained only superficial burns. As we sped along about five miles from our camp, I discovered Liligh's wagons ahead and soon saw his men at work. I remembered that his job had been to work along ahead of our camp, stretch the wire and dig the post holes. The men saw us drive by and Liligh waved to me. Beyond this point the ravages of the fire began to diminish.

After speeding on a few more miles I saw a long line of white-topped wagons. I noticed a good many oxen out on the plain apparently grazing, but I did not see that there was much left to graze upon. The driver drove off the trail along the first line of wagons and very shortly I was in the presence of Mr. Sunderlund with several of his associates whom I had met.

There was not any doubt about my welcome. Sunderlund shook hands with me and anxiously inquired how Creighton's wagon-train had fared. When I acquainted him with the details of our troubles and injuries he expressed sympathy and replied that he had escaped any serious injuries but had lost some wagons and supplies and all the cattle.

"And Miss Sunderlund?" I inquired. "How is she?"

"Come with me to her wagon," he replied. "Kitty's foot was badly burned. It happened after the fire had passed us. She was running around in the dark tryin' to help an' she caught her foot between a couple of logs or branches thet were still red hot. She couldn't get it out an' it was some moments before her cries brought assistance. If you will take care of her I will be greatly obliged to you, Cameron."

The wagon he led me to near at hand was not so large as his own, but it was more pretentious and better cared for. I saw at a glance that the driver had been right in his reference to Miss Sunderlund's home on wheels. There was a step leading up to the curtained opening in the back of the wagon, and at Mr. Sunderlund's call, a buxom Negro maid appeared and spread the curtain. Sunderlund directed me to go up into the wagon, and then thanking me, he departed.

There evidently were several compartments in the wagon and in the middle one, which was very comfortably, not to say luxuriously, furnished, lay Kit Sunderlund on a bed, her head propped up on pillows. A light coverlet was spread over her, from under which protruded a little bare foot clumsily bandaged. I remembered her face as tanned but now it was white and her large eyes, darkly violet, held an expression of pain. She wore something white with short sleeves to her elbows and altogether she made a picture that sent the blood back to my heart.

"Good day, Miss Sunderlund," I said, cheerfully, as I deposited my kit on a chest. "I hope you're not badly burned."

"I'm in considerable pain, but I want you to understand that I did not send for you." Her tone was distinctly spirited and the aloofness of it surprised me and took me aback somewhat.

"Your father, as you must have heard, has asked me to attend you. I—I'm not a regular doctor but I'll try to relieve you."

"Thank you. Of course, it was good of you to come. I just wanted you to know I didn't send for you. . . . Martha, you open the curtains to let in more light and wait near in case the—the doctor might need you."

"I won't require anything but a pan of hot water." Then without glancing at the girl I opened my medicine kit and laid out the bandages and medicines necessary. Drawing up a cushioned stool, I said in as professional a way as I could assume: "I'll look at your foot now."

She pulled up the coverlet slightly further exposing her right foot and a shapely ankle. I now could not help looking at her and I could not fail to see the doubt and disdain in her beautiful eyes. I would hardly have been normal if I had not felt some resentment, but I went calmly to work.

I removed the bandage from her foot, not without several emphatic protests from the girl, and I found the burn to be on the instep, a superficial one, not serious at all, but one that necessarily would cause considerable pain. Lint from the bandages had stuck on the raw spot and that had to be carefully washed off which I simply could not do without hurting her. Once she asked me very sweetly:

"At Harvard did you study regular medicine or to be a horse doctor?"

I passed by that comment, but for a moment I relaxed somewhat in my gentleness; moreover, with my sore hands it was difficult to work lightly, with the result that she cried out:

"Oh, you hurt me! You're a brute! And you're takin' so much time. Are you going to be all day at this task?"

"Miss Sunderlund, I told you I was not a regular physician," I replied, with what dignity I could summon. "I am doing it as gently and rapidly as possible. I do not want to *prolong* the job. You have a lovely foot and ankle and you make a very bewitching picture here in your wagon-train boudoir—but really that is nothing to me. I didn't *want* to come any more than evidently you wanted me."

"Cain't you get through quickly and get out?" she flashed, the red coming to her cheeks.

"I'll get through quickly if you'll stop wiggling—and making unnecessary comment about my work."

"But you're hurting me."

"Of course I'm hurting you. You've got a bad burn. You won't be able to wear a shoe or a boot for a month," I replied, exaggerating somewhat. "Are you a baby that you can't stand a little pain?"

"Mr. Cameron, you are as rude and ungentlemanly as you are uncouth in appearance and action."

"What would you expect, girl?" I demanded hotly. "I was up till midnight last night fighting fire and then dressed wounds until daylight."

"Very noble of you, Mr. Cameron, but I can't see that you're helping me much," she returned, sarcastically.

"Oh, shut up," I said, thoroughly nettled. "I'm beginning to believe some of the things I have heard about you."

That apparently subdued her for the moment. I anointed the injured member and then made a neat job of bandaging it; whereupon I turned away to the chest and began to pack my things, remarking casually:

"There. That will relieve you presently. I would not have the bandage removed for a day or two and I advise staying off your foot."

"My father will reimburse you, Mr. Cameron, for your time and trouble."

At this sally I laughed outright. There was no longer any doubt that this young lady was distinctly angry with me. I thought her most unreasonable. Fortunately the heat that she had roused in my veins kept me from looking at her, which I most decidedly longed to do, and saved me from betraying myself. I purposely took several moments to pack my kit. I handed the pan of water down to the maid.

"Why didn't you keep the engagement with me the day we met?" she asked, in a tone that made a challenge of her question.

"Why do you suppose, Miss Sunderlund?" I returned, and I certainly looked at her then. The red spots had left her cheeks and if there was not battle in her bright eyes I mistook the expression. I grew curious at what I thought was an exaggeration of feeling in the situation. It was possible, of course, that she had wanted to see me as badly as I had wanted to see her.

"I had never wanted to keep a date with a girl so much in my life," I continued.

"Well, how do you think I felt?" she retorted, scornfully.

"I don't know how *you* felt. I only imagined it. I daresay such a romantic meeting is merely an incident in your young life, but it was tremendous for me. That day I saw you first on the seat of that prairie schooner I—I was deeply struck with you, and I couldn't forget you. I kept hoping and dreaming that we would meet out here. Just as we did, worse luck! When you leaped into my arms from that runaway wagon in Gothenburg and knocked me sprawling into the dust, I realized that I had fallen in love with you at first sight!"

"Yes, and you played up to it very well," she retorted, derisively. "But you ignored the opportunity I offered you. And now you talk just like a cowboy."

"Yeah. Well, if I've learned to think and talk like a cowboy, I'm certainly proud of it."

"What did Vance Shaw tell you about me?" she flung at me, and she sat up in her bed, letting the coverlet fall somewhat and further distracting me with the revelation of her beauty.

"He told me a lot of things," I retorted.

"I can divine what, so you need not demean yourself by telling. If you knew what cowboys were, you would understand how a girl has to protect herself."

"Because cowboys are flirts and no doubt worse, that is no reason for you to trifle with their affections. He said you made them love you without a notion in your head of returning even a little."

"That's true, Mr. Cameron. I liked all cowboys. But I always hoped to meet one or some young men who might make me serious. . . . And when I did meet him, what happened? He turned out to be even worse than the cowboys."

"What do you mean, Kit Sunderlund?" I demanded, curiosity overcoming my anger.

"You're not as intelligent or subtle as first impression would indicate. You may be from Boston, you may have an eastern background, and you are a self-confessed Harvard man. For that reason you're more despicable than any of those cowboys, even Shaw."

"And may I ask why?" I queried, quietly, burning inwardly.

"You may ask, and I'll tell you," she cried. And now a crimson wave spread upward from her neck to her temples and her eyes resembled hard blue diamonds. "When I rode up to your camp with my father and asked for you and found you were not there, I made a discovery. You had a girl with you in that wagon. Disguised as a boy! I *saw* her. She was back in the wagon partly undressed and she hastily tried to screen herself from my sight. But I saw her. She was a girl, and young and pretty. She was living with you all in that wagon. You were sharing her with your cowboy friends or they were sharing her with you."

"So you saw Ruby! Well, and *that* is what you think." I spoke with a caustic scorn that matched hers, only there must have been genuine astonishment in my expression.

"Yes, that is what I thought. Do you deny it?"

"Why should I? You seem to use your feminine prerogative. I fail to grasp any of the southern chivalry that you Texans are noted for."

"I am indeed a sentimental Southerner and I've suffered more than once from that weakness. But I'm not an utter fool. If seeing that dance-hall girl in your wagon was not enough, you will be interested to know that my father was told in Gothenburg that you paid marked attention to this girl, Ruby, and it was you who took her out of the dance-hall."

"That is true, Miss Sunderlund. I did and I am most heartily proud of it. And I would like to inform you that that little dance-hall girl is bigger and finer than you and far more worthy. Good day."

Chapter Eight

I ALMOST leaped out of the wagon in my bitter disappointment and fury and I made my way at once to where the buckboard and driver were waiting for me. Mr. Sunderlund was not in sight. Climbing into the buckboard, I told the driver to take me back to the construction camp at once. And at a word we were off.

What a devil that girl was! It was unthinkable that there was any justice in her accusation of me, from my point of view. But yet, even in my bitter anger and resentment, there came the memory of her dark, proud eyes and her beauty which had been so enhanced by her agitation and the intimacy of the moment.

The drive back to Creighton's camp seemed short, undoubtedly owing to my state of mind. I saw that Creighton was moving wagons and evidently the catastrophe of the night before was merely another obstacle surmounted. I saw Shaw pacing up and down beside our wagon and it was certain that he spied me long before I had seen him. As I alighted from the buckboard his piercing eyes took me in at one glance and I felt as if a searchlight had been turned on my emotions. Right then and there I gave him hurried but minute information of what had happened to me in Sunderlund's camp. The cowboy made no comment but, as he faced across the river, there was a convulsive working of his throat. Outside that all the sign of agitation he betrayed was the steel-like clutch of his fingers on my arm.

We were set to work at once, our wagon and crew along with half a dozen others, at repairing the eastern portion of the telegraph line that had been burned. Creighton's short order was imperative and yet it showed that he left our particular party without the services of a foreman. He said he would leave it to us, that he could not spare a man for that overseer duty.

Naturally we worked all the harder because of his faith. For three days we toiled with twisted wires and charred poles, camping along the line where darkness found us. On the fourth day, we had the line again in running order, and traveled westward out of the blackened belt made by the fire. In the evening we came up with Creighton.

We pushed westward with all possible speed, sometimes erecting as much as seven miles of telegraph line in one day. A regiment of thirty dragoons met us out on the prairie, having come from Ft. Laramie. They reported an uprising of the Cheyennes and Sioux over in Wyoming. Sergeant Kinney said that Sunderlund's wagon-train was about a score of miles ahead on the trail and that they had been able to round up only a few hundred of the Texas longhorns. This, I imagined, had proved a bitter blow to Colonel Sunderlund and I felt sorry for him.

We settled down to hard work from daylight till dark. But the work was far from monotonous, especially after we saw our first small herd of buffalo and lean wild Indian riders. They gave us a wide berth, but they sat their ponies on high ridges and watched us. Sometimes they sent aloft smoke signals communicating with other Indians. I wondered what was in these red men's minds. They certainly appeared the opposite of friendly. These nights the wagons were drawn in a circle and we made our fires and did our cooking on the inside. All night long soldier guards patrolled the line of wagons.

The days multiplied into weeks, the telegraph line was approaching the border of Colorado. Julesburg, with its unsavory fame, was not many days away. So many things had happened that I no longer could recount them. Still many stood out unforgettably.

I had killed my first buffalo, and I was tremendously proud of that beautiful, glossy, black and tawny robe. One of the most pleasant incidents of the whole trip so far was my sensation at my first taste of buffalo rump steak. It was the sweetest, finest meat I had ever tasted and the game flavor was not too strong.

I had seen my first Indian in the act of pulling down the telegraph wire, and I had taken a shot at him, deliberately missing him, but scaring him away. I knew that my apprenticeship on the frontier would be ended as soon as I had actually shot a man, either red or white. I still did not want to graduate into a killing frontiersman, but it was inevitable and I was resigned to it.

It had begun to grow very hot along the trail during the middle of the day, and the continuous labor grew at times almost unendurable. But we kept on.

Creighton eventually put me on the job of nailing sharpened spikes around the telegraph poles about four feet from the ground in order to keep the cattle from rubbing against them and knocking them down. Darnell accompanied me and he packed the cumbersome sack of spikes and our tools while I carried the heavy rifles. We never went any place any more without a rifle.

We saw mounted Indians every day. They gave us a wide berth. But they would make a detour around us and always approach the telegraph line in our rear. I watched them through my field glasses. Evidently they regarded this wire stretched along on poles as something about which there was mystery and danger. Sometimes a couple of Indians would dismount and sit down beside the telegraph poles and remain there a long time. At length Darnell solved this problem by saying he was "gol derned if he didn't believe the crazy redskins were listening to the hum of the wires." I told Creighton about it that night and I suggested that it might be possible to work on the Indians' credulity and primitiveness by somehow connecting the telegraph wire with the Great Spirit.

When the Indians decided to do violence to the line, which happened rather frequently, they would pile some buffalo chips against a pole and set fire to it. This rarely did any damage. Then they would hack at a pole with their tomahawks. It took a long time for them to cut through one of the green poles with their little hatchets. But in this way they would bring the line to the ground. The telegraph message would still go through unless they broke the wire. This happened often enough to cause Creighton to tear his hair. He had a repair wagon escorted by soldiers always working in our rear. Then again the Indians would show their resentment and destructive spirit by roping the wire with their long lariats and pulling it down. Liligh claimed these straggling couples and bands of savages were out scouting for buffalo and that no real danger menaced us until we ran into a large body of Indians. Some of these roving Indians were marauding thieves. At night they would sneak up to a wagon and steal anything they could lay their hands on, in spite of guards. They were thin, slippery, red devils, and like snakes they could glide along in the short grass absolutely without sound or disturbance of grass or brush.

Toward the end of our drive on to the Colorado line, two wagon-trains passed us, one of about ordinary length of approximately sixty wagons and the other fully three times that number. This caravan, viewed from a distance winding over the plain like a colossal serpent, made an imposing and an inspiring spectacle.

Its meaning was tremendous. Thousands of men and women from the South and East had become imbued with the hope of finding a better life in the West, and fired with this pioneer spirit they had pulled up their roots and started across the plains. It was the beginning of a great empire in the West.

Sunderlund was the only pioneer we had met who envisioned the plains of the West sloping up to the Rocky Mountains as the future cattle range that would dwarf all the cattle ranges he had left behind. But of course Sunderlund had a brother in Wyoming who had got cattle there somehow and had found that they had prospered exceedingly well.

When I approached Shaw about this, he said, "Shore. All the time I knowed it. I figured it before I got out here an' once having had a look at this buffalo grass I said it would support millions of cattle. Why not? There are millions of buffalo, an' in time the cattle will take their place. There's goin' to be an all-fired battle between the redskins an' the whites before the West ever can be settled. But it's goin' to happen. The pioneers an' the hunters who'll come after them, an' then the hide hunters will kill off the buffalo. An' Uncle Sam with his army will have to fight the Indians from the Comanches in my country to the Blackfeet of Montana. An' I tell you what, pards, somethin' I've said before. If I ever come out of this Western Union job, I'm goin' in strong for cattle raising."

The telegraph construction camp, again short of poles and with men and mules and oxen sorely in need of rest, rolled into camp on the banks of the South Platte River at Julesburg, Colorado, one sultry summer day at dusk.

It was too dark for me to make out what kind of place this Julesburg was. The camp along the river was not an attractive spot even under cover of darkness. All I could see of the town was some blinking yellow lights. I sat until the camp fire died down to smoldering red coals. The night air was chill, and used as I had become to the cold at these increasingly high altitudes, I needed my coat and I missed the heat of the fire. The coyotes had long been howling quite near at hand, and I never tired of their racket. They were curious, sneaky, thieving animals that would approach quite close to the camp fire at night. I heard their soft rustling footsteps and I had grown thoroughly familiar with their thin, high-pitched, concatenated, piercing yelps. But the cry of the prairie wolves—that was another thing. It was a wild hungry mourn. It rang of blood and tragedy, yet it had a singular rhythm and beauty—a full-throated, piercing cry, a deep bay faintly similar to that of a bloodhound, and it was prolonged and sustained in its terrific melancholy.

As always when I yielded to an hour like this I remembered Kit Sunderlund. She seemed far away now. I had forgiven her unjust suspicions and remembered only the beauty of her as I saw her last. I could have loved that girl, I thought, far more than I had ever loved anybody.

At sunrise the next morning I rolled out in answer to Darnell's gentle boot to find myself rested and feeling fit except for sundry bruises and sore places on my anatomy. Mentally I was again alert and somewhat approaching my earlier happy moods.

The boys were getting breakfast. Ruby, who greeted me with a bright smile, was pattering with light feet between the camp fire and the wagon. The morning was cold and clear, and the air had a nip to it. When I washed in the river, I knew what Darnell meant when he called it mountain water. I decided I would celebrate our arrival at Julesburg by shaving off my bristly beard. By dint of great patience I succeeded. Ruby rewarded this ordeal with one of her nice compliments.

"Gee, Wayne, but you look different with a smooth face. All the blisters gone, face thin, and your skin clear and dark—you shore will play hell with the girls, if we meet any out here."

"Thanks, lady. I noticed that some of your disguise is worn off and you look uncommonly pretty this morning."

While we were at breakfast Liligh made the rounds of the wagons to give us our instructions for the day.

"Wal, boys, hyar we air in Julesburg. No telegraph poles, an' a hellish lot of wagon repairin' to do, an' Julesburg threatened by redskins. Shaw, yu an' Lowden ride out on a scoutin' trip, an' Cameron, yu an' Darnell look after yer wagon. It's good to git hyar, but then it ain't so good."

I was completely disillusioned by my surroundings. Entirely without reason I had built up Julesburg into something that would be great to see. But the prairie was unfriendly and barren; the river was a turgid muddy stream bordered by stunted cottonwoods, denuded and stripped all along its banks by the wagon-trains; and the great Julesburg itself turned out to be a row of five unsightly buildings, crude, drab, rugged with their high board fronts facing the west apprehensively.

I was bitterly disappointed. But I went with Tom into the town, looked over the improvised telegraph station, stopped at the Overland Trail and Pony Express Station, went into the trading store which was as uncouth inside as it was outside, made purchases of tobacco and some supplies of what they had on hand, and bought a lonesome box of candy for Ruby.

We looked for Slade and then inquired for him to learn that he was off on business on the Overland route toward Denver. This was a relief. I knew he and Shaw would clash if they ever met again and I did not see any sense in my friend's courting trouble. There was a considerable crowd of men and soldiers in town, mostly from our wagon-trains and a few from the wagon-train camp across the river. They stood around in groups conversing and drinking over the counter. Most of the talk was of Indians.

Having exhausted the few sights of Julesburg and feeling that the less we heard about the possibilities of being scalped, the better, Tom and I returned to Creighton's camp and our own wagon where, after ceremoniously presenting Ruby with the box of stale candy, we took off our coats and addressed ourselves to much-needed tasks. We were busy all the rest of the day.

Shaw and Lowden returned at sundown, having traversed a fifty-mile circle around our camp. We got their reports after Shaw had talked to Creighton. They had seen a considerable number of buffalo passing north, to the west of Julesburg. No Indians had been sighted, which news was unexpected and not so reassuring. However, from every distant ridge on the horizon the cowboys had seen Indian smoke signals, some of which they had studied with the field glass.

Shaw said he had interpreted these signals to Creighton and Liligh, but he did not vouchsafe as much to us. He was far too serious to suit me. Except when he looked at Ruby, he had a hard steely glint in his amber eyes. Shaw's eyes appeared to me to vary in the color of their clear intensity. I had never forgotten them after the march he had made back in Gothenburg waiting for Slade to come out and fight.

"Pards, I'm worried," Shaw said suddenly. "We're in for a fight here, shore as God made little apples. South of here about twenty miles Jack an' I run across a deep swale with water in the bottom. It shore was a grand place to hunt, full of game, deer, antelope, bear, elk, and we saw two big grizzlies. Jack had to pink one with the rifle an' you bet we made tracks out of there. But on the steep side of thet gully grew a lot of little fir trees. An' when I was makin' my report, one of them wagon-train bosses, Beal by name, heared me. He follered me an' asked for specific directions an' then without askin' Liligh or anyone else, he went after these fir trees. It's dollar to doughnuts that wagon-train never gits back."

That was that. I tried to take the unfavorable news in the same light which characterized my companions. We were rather more than usually quiet at supper. The sunset broke gold and purple and white out of clouds in the West and at least changed the dreary landscape to something colorful and beautiful.

Liligh visited us before dark and asked Shaw to repeat the report that he had made to Creighton and to add to it any observations or opinions that he had omitted to the leader. The cowboy's much enlarged recital obviously made Liligh more serious than ever.

"Wal, thanks, cowboy," he said. "Thet dovetails in with my own figgerin'. I reckon we hev been purty lucky all the way along an' we'll git it rubbed in from now on."

"That's shore. What I'd like to know is how our boss is goin' to take bein' held up in the work."

"Shaw, he ain't goin' to be held up. Yu remember the line must be up and in operation before the snow flies. An' yu know, of course, it's purty cold early up in western Wyomin'. We ain't goin' to tell the boss what we think."

"But man alive, there is such a thing as sense. If we don't advise Creighton to go slow, why, the line might not go up atall, much farther."

"Mebbe a good brush with the redskins might be fun

for a change. We're well armed an' we'll play safe. There's no sense alarmin' Creighton. But I reckon yu better haul yore wagon over in line with ours an' take yore turn standin' guard."

"Yo're daid right, Liligh. We can't be too watchful. I was goin' to do thet on my own accord."

Liligh left us then and it was evident that his visit had impressed Shaw rather unfavorably.

Soon after that Shaw told us to turn in and he would take the first guard. I went to sleep at once and barring one period during the night in which I lay awake a while listening to the lonesome howl of the coyotes, I did not know any more until sunrise. The three cowboys had divided the guard duty among themselves. I objected strenuously when I found out that they had not awakened me to take my turn, to which Shaw dryly remarked: "Pard, yo're a pretty good-lookin' gazabo shaved, but you wouldn't look so good without all your hair."

"Yeah. I guess I must be a tenderfoot still," I retorted. "All right. After this I'll stand guard duty with one of you every night until I learn how."

"Thet's a fine idee," agreed the cowboy.

We spent most of that day working on our wagon and after the necessary tasks had been accomplished we did further work to make it as impregnable to attack as possible. Above the sides of the wagon, as well as the end, we raised a defense a foot or more higher and in lieu of wood or metal, we used pieces of dried buffalo hide which Lowden got in town at the store. They were as stiff and hard almost as iron. A man could kneel behind this barricade and be pretty well screened from bullets and safe from arrows.

We were told by some of the other men that there were a lot of Indians in town lounging around, surly and hostile, with eyes like hawks. Some of them were Utes, who were supposed to be friendly at that time, and there were several Arapahoes. Shaw did not like this news a bit and said he was going into town to look them over. I went with him only to find out that the Indians had departed. The next day, however, they were back again and in greater number.

After our tasks were ended next morning, we went into Julesburg and I had my first sight of real plains Indians at close hand. I could not tell the difference between Utes and Arapahoes. They were not by any means a reassuring spectacle. It was a hot day, as usual, and the Indians had on practically no clothing at all. They wore breech clouts and leggings and moccasins of buckskin, and carried their blankets and weapons. Their bodies were lean, muscular, darkly red in hue. They had wolfish visages, some of them lined like parchment, and their black eyes were sullen and smoldering. In most cases they wore their hair long. No one of them exhibited any elaborate head dress but several had bands around their hair and a single feather stuck in them. While we were in town they spent the time in the neighborhood of the shack where the telegraph operator worked at his instrument. That strange metallic clicking evidently had a fascination for them. They gathered that it meant some kind of message coming in or being sent out, the evidence of which they doubted. The sound of the telegraph wire equally concerned them. It was easy to see that the wire had for them some relation to life.

"Wal, it's this way," spoke up Shaw, reflectively. "Every damn one of them redskins is hostile an' treacherous as any Comanche or Apache I ever seen. They are no more than spies. I'd bet my gun an' my hoss to boot thet there is a big bunch of Indians out here somewhere waitin' to hatch some kind of deviltry."

"I guess that Sergeant Kinney didn't like their looks any better than you did," I replied.

"Neither did Liligh," said Shaw. "Come on, we'll hunt up both of them."

By midday all the Indians had departed. They had mounted their wild mustangs in small groups and had ridden away in different directions. Concern was being felt about the wagon-train that had, without specific orders, gone out for poles.

We finally found Sergeant Kinney with Liligh and several of the wagon-train bosses. "Liligh," spoke up Shaw "what do you think about these Injuns leavin' town?"

"Dunno," answered Liligh tersely. "There's nothin'

fer us to do but stick an' hope it won't be as bad as it looks. Now, I've jest been talkin' to Sergeant Kinney about what to prepare fer. Would you be good enough to give yer Texas angle on it?"

"Short an' sweet, boss. Haul all the wagons into town, run them as close together as you can between the houses, an' drive the oxen down in the brush along the river. I'd suggest Sergeant Kinney puttin' half his soldiers in each end house an' let the rest of the men take their posts among the wagons an' the other houses. It'd take an all-fired lot of Injuns to get the best of us. But we must expect the worst about thet wagon-train thet went out after poles, an' some of us who are doin' these odd jobs near to town will get a run for their scalps, if I can still figure redskins."

"Right, cowboy," agreed Liligh. "I was jest tellin' Sergeant Kinney my idee which wasn't so far from yours. Now, Shaw, go out on the detail yu was ordered on with Herb Lane an' yu cowboys keep yer eyes peeled. Don't go too far away on thet job. Yu'll hev mule teams an' as the Injuns can't surprise yu on thet level prairie yu'd git a good start back if they did show up."

By mid-afternoon our two wagons under Herb Lane got about five miles from town. Four men working in relays dug a post hole in short order. Shaw rode on one side and Lowden on the other and they ranged a mile and sometimes two miles ahead of us or to either side, scouting for the possible approach of Indians.

The afternoon was very hot and sultry. I labored without even a shirt and the sweat ran off my brown body. Storm clouds hung low in the west and we saw faint streaks of lightning but it was so far away that we could not hear the thunder. But the terrible storms that we had been told about were slowly forming. Darnell, except when he was driving from one post hole to another, stood up on his driver's seat, searching the horizon with his field glass. For that reason, none of us workers bothered to scan the prairie, but there were none of us who did not expect something to happen before the sun set.

So we were all prepared for Darnell's ringing shout.

"Injuns! Off there to the west! Pile in, for we're gonna have a race!"

With a violent start I looked in the direction Darnell pointed but I could not make out any moving objects. While he and Lane were turning the mule teams back toward camp we threw our tools into the wagons and leaping aboard, took up our rifles and cartridge belts. By that time the drivers had the big wagons rolling along at a lively clip. The precaution of taking mule teams instead of oxen now served us in good stead.

There were four men in each wagon and the extra men in our vehicle were Edney and Cliff Nelson, both hardy Missourians and men calculated to inspire confidence. Neither of these wagons was canvas covered and that enabled us to stand anywhere in them and see all about us. It was with tremendous excitement that I scanned the prairie to our rear. I saw clouds of dust puffing up but still no horsemen.

"Tom, are you sure you saw something?" I queried.

"Shore as hell," responded Tom, grimly, as he hauled back on the reins. "These pesky mules wanta run an' mebbe that's gonna be good. . . . You're not lookin' right, Wayne. More to the south. They're in plain sight now—an' look! Here comes Jack hell-bent for election along the river bottom."

Then I saw Shaw on his red horse flashing across the gray prairie and behind him, I could not tell how far, a group of wild riders. Even at that distance of several miles they looked wild in every sense of the word. They were silhouetted black against the horizon line. Tails and manes streaked out in the wind. It was a breathtaking sight. I had no fear for Shaw mounted on his grand horse but I knew, of course, that those Indians would overtake us. Then I switched my gaze around toward the river and soon espied Lowden tearing down toward us. He was less than a mile distant. How he could ride!

I searched the river bottom and the plain behind him for signs of possible foes, but there were none. Then I shifted my gaze back toward Shaw. I was astounded to see that the Indians had changed their course and were making directly for the two wagons. And it did not take a moment to see how rapidly they were gaining. Shaw, too, had turned toward us.

We three men in the second wagon gripped our rifles and watched with strained eyes and waited for the attack that would soon close in around us. I did not fail to observe then what a superb driver Darnell was. The trail road was fairly good and except for ruts here and there we rolled on with the mules at a gallop. Lane must have been letting his mules go for his wagon drew a little ahead of ours. When we came to a bad place in the road Darnell would yell for us to hang on, and even so we were hard put to it to stay in the wagon.

The next few moments for me were singularly fraught with queer sensations up and down my spine. Lowden had crossed the trail and was heading to join Shaw, who had cut across to come between the Indians and the wagons.

"Look! Smoke!" shouted Edney, pointing. "The ball's opened. Some of them damn redskins have got guns. Some more we've got to blame the traders for."

Puffs of white smoke arose above the group of Indians and my keen sight picked up smaller puffs of dust where the bullets struck far behind the cowboys.

"If we don't bust somethin', we'll beat that bunch of Indians into camp," shouted Nelson, in elation.

"If the Indians are firing, why don't the boys shoot back?" I yelled.

"Too far, I reckon," replied Edney. "This is an old game for Shaw. I'll bet when he shoots you'll see somethin'."

How long that rear-end chase kept up without any material change, except nearer approach of all the horsemen to the wagons, I could not accurately judge. It seemed to be very long but probably was short. When the cowboys were some few hundred yards in our rear and the Indians perhaps a quarter of a mile farther out, all riders again changed their course. The Indians swerved off to our right in single file. Shaw and Lowden likewise swerved and took a course parallel with ours.

I counted fourteen Indian riders in that long line, and now they drew close enough for us to see their color and all the physical aspects of mustang and rider in their wild detail. Some of them had bows and arrows but most of them were armed with rifles. They kept shooting. I marveled at the way they were able to reload riding along at that pace. Still the cowboys withheld their fire and it was not until the savages drew parallel with us and began to come closer that they shot. The distance was pretty far and, for all I could see, they missed, but their shots brought a remarkable transformation in that spectacle.

All at once the mustangs appeared to be riderless. Had the redskins fallen off? I rubbed my eyes to get rid of the dimness which affected them. Then I saw that each Indian rider had slipped down on the offside of his mustang and was riding at that swift pace with only one leg in sight and that was over the back of his mustang. They presented no target at all. And as they forged ahead of us they also drew closer. The cowboys rode between them and the wagons and it was evident that they intended to keep on doing so. The running of those Indian mustangs had the splendid pace of the cowboys' horses would have been something beautiful to watch if it had not been for their deadly significance.

Then the Indians were shooting from under the necks of their ponies and I saw the bullets whip up the dust in front of the cowboys, showing that the Indians had gotten within range. The perilous time for the cowboys had arrived, if not quite for us. Darnell had let the mules have their heads and they had almost caught up with the wagon in front. We now could plainly see Julesburg and the big group of wagons filling the spaces between the houses. We were hardly two miles distant. But I noted that the cowboys had to swerve closer to us to lessen their danger of being hit. Again they held their fire.

The Indians came close enough for me to see dark heads and arms under the horses' necks. In that position they were firing. It was incredible what good marksmanship they showed. Sooner or later they were bound to hit one of the horses or cowboys. At that juncture the men on the wagon ahead of us opened with a volley. It was futile so far as we could see. The Indians were plainly bent on circling around us and as they kept on, the cowboys maintained their place between them and the wagons, at the same time always drawing somewhat closer to us. The savages crossed the trail and circled around on the river side, passed beyond and behind us, then crossed the trail again to take up their former position on our right except that they were closer. Hardly four hundred yards distant now! And the cowboys were less than half that far away.

Presently my sensibilities were tightened at sight of Shaw leveling his rifle. Frightened as I was, I could not help reveling in the picture he and his horse made. He did not shoot quickly. But when he let go, I saw an Indian pony pitch headlong, flinging a dark savage form to roll ahead of him. Possibly the bullet went clear through the horse to wound the savage. I heard the ringing crack of Lowden's rifle sounding above the reports of the Indians' guns but I could not unrivet my gaze from Shaw at that moment. He shot again and again. One more mustang went down and in the next three shots another. Then as I counted the Indian riders I saw that four of the original fourteen were missing and I knew that Lowden had accounted for one. The savages swerved again then, to draw out of range of the cowboys' fire and to cease shooting, though continuing to run parallel with us.

"Wal, they'd shore have cooked our goose if it hadn't been for the cowboys," shouted Edney. "We'll make it on in now. . . . Hello! What's goin' on there in town?"

"Injun attack," yelled Darnell. "There's a whole mob of them. If they see us drivin' in it'll be Katy-bar-the-door with us."

But as we drew closer it was evident that the engagement, luckily for us, centered on the far side of the town. Through the dust and smoke I could discern Indian mustangs dashing to and fro, but I did not see a soldier or any of our men.

With the mules at a furious gallop we made the remaining distance into town before our Indian pursuers could join the main body and have us cut off. As we entered the bare circle before the town Shaw and Lowden raced up to us. Shaw yelled: "Rustle! Drive up behind the nearest house."

We held on for dear life, and what with the jerking and jolting of the wagons and the infernal screech and rattle all around us, I heard and saw nothing of the combat in the town until Darnell halted with a tremendous jerk and I half leaped and was half thrown to the ground. Then a hideous uproar assailed my ears. It seemed to be an infernal chorus of piercing Indian yells punctured by volleys of rifle shots.

Out of the dust and the smoke Liligh appeared with fire in his eyes, his face begrimed with powder and with a bloody streak on the side of his head. "Somebody unhitch while the rest of yu stand guard," he roared, above the din. "Turn the mules loose. Look after yer hawses. Fight from behind yer wagon or inside. Look sharp fer there's a million Indians on the other side."

"Rustle this job, boys," shouted Shaw, standing with rifle in one hand and the bridle to his horse in the other. "I'll look for Ruby."

With seven men in a hurry and one at least actuated by fright, the tasks indicated were done in a twinkling. Our own wagon was not in a position for us to reach at the present. The seven of us hid behind the two wagons and peered out on each side with cocked rifles ready. I became aware of an intermittent rifle fire, sometimes in heavy volleys and then again in scattered reports. The din came mostly from the demoniacal war cry of the Indians.

With our backs to the last house and the wagons in front of us, we peered out looking for a redskin to shoot at. There did not appear to be any on that side. I noted shiny streaks coming out of the smoke to strike the earth, and then the quivering objects turn into Indian arrows half imbedded in the ground.

In a few moments Shaw rejoined us looking terribly concerned.

"Ruby's not in our wagon," he said, hoarsely, close to my ear. "I reckon, of course, she must be in one of the houses. Didn't see any soldiers and only a few of our men. But I seen a bunch of wagons rushin' toward the river an' them wagons shore wasn't here when we left. I don't like the looks of it. But, hell, we gotta be smart or

141

all our scalps will be lifted. There's a big outfit of Indians an' they're shore mad as hornets."

"What'll we do?" shouted Lowden, as he and Darnell joined us.

"Do! Keep hid here and blaze way at any redskin thet shows himself."

Shaw's speech was calculated to put us all on edge. Agitated as I was, I still could see that my comrades were cool and grim. I had to force myself to be the same. But inside me there was a terrific conflict going on. This was going to be my test and it had come with such amazing suddenness that I had no time to prepare myself. All of a sudden a screeching mob of redskins appeared to rise up out of the dust and smoke and dart here and there, some with rifles at their shoulders, others with drawn bows, and some with tomahawks. They were hideous, painted, phantom-like images that never stood still for a second.

I heard my comrades firing and I began trying to get a bead on this redskin and that one. I knew I missed several before I hit one. As he crumpled into the dirt and jerked spasmodically I let out an involuntary screech that emanated from a side of my nature that I had never known. I stared at the fallen Indian until he lay still. I had killed him! I gasped but I did not shrink. I did not know how I felt, but on the instant there came a ring against the wagon wheel and then, with a shock of agony, I saw an arrow with its head buried in my thigh. Instinctively I grasped it and pulled it out. It came easily and the arrow head was covered with blood. It had hit me after glancing off the tire. The pain and its meaning seemed to transform my nature. All of a sudden I wanted to rush out among those Indians and with a clubbed rifle beat them down. An iron arm dragged me back behind the wagon.

"Here ends yore tenderfoot days, pard," shouted Shaw, in my ear. "Now fight an' be careful not to expose yore-self."

The fury of the yelling and shooting and the whirling of dust and smoke that had seemed a hideous pandemonium to me may have swelled in volume but my reception of it was different. I knelt low and peering from behind the wagon-bed I shot at every Indian I could get a bead on. There was a steady, continuous rifle fire from behind our two wagons. There were fallen Indians all over the ground behind that part of the barricade. I saw the rest of them dart and glide out of sight in the smoke round toward the other side of the town from which most of the yelling and firing came.

There came a period then in which all these sounds of battle augmented and swelled to one tremendous point and then suddenly diminished so that only the hoarse shouts of white men and the bang of their rifles continued. We waited there strung behind our barricade, peering out, ready for anything.

"Pards, they've been drove off," shouted Shaw. "You cain't hear the sound of shootin' any more an' the whiz an' thud of arrows has stopped. By gosh, there's some of us left alive anyhow. It was shore damn hot for a spell."

"Men, they've taken to their horses, packin' their cripples," yelled Edney, from the other wagon. "Look! There's a whole hell slue of them. I'll bet they got a sweet reception, an' if we haven't got some men hurt or mebbe killed, it'll be funny."

"Hurt!" ejaculated Lowden. "What you call thet arrow stickin' in my laig? An' I stopped a bullet, but it must have glanced an' hit me, 'cause I can feel it under the skin."

"Never touched me," returned Shaw. And then I looked to see his rifle on the ground and that he was reloading his two guns. He had emptied them all. I considered what execution he must have done because I knew that he seldom missed anything he shot at.

We ventured forth and warily looked about. I saw Edney knock an Indian on the head as he lay trying to rise from the ground. Here and there lay other savages. With the cessation of the firing the dust and smoke clouds began to blow away and soon we could distinguish the houses and the barricades of wagons between them. Hoarse voices of men were augmented and then soldiers held guns and appeared to be looking for Indians still alive. We joined them and when the smoke entirely lifted

I was relieved of a fear that had assailed me, and that was of the Indians having set fire to either houses or wagons. We met Liligh.

"How about yu, men? You don't look hurt much."

"I reckon we missed the worst of it," said Shaw.

"It was short but bad all the time. The redskins charged the store fust of all an' I'll bet we'll find bloody work done there."

"Liligh, did you see anythin' of our boy Pedro?" queried Shaw, sharply.

"Yup. Shore I did. But jest at the minnit I forgit where."

"Whose were those wagons I saw makin' for the river as we came up?"

"They belong to a wagon-train thet jest come in before the attack. I asked them to form their wagons in line an' fight it out with us an' thet's the last I saw of them."

"Wal, they rustled for the river. I seen them just as we reached the town."

From all accounts the engagement had been short and bloody. Liligh said the Indians had counted on superior numbers and after circling the town two or three times they had charged the southern end of the line of wagons and houses. Fifteen soldiers had been killed, most of them in or around the trading store, and five of Creighton's men, one of them belonging to our crew. The retreating Indians had carried away all of their cripples and most of their dead men. A messenger came from Creighton asking us to come to him in the Pony Express station. He had been shot in the shoulder, a painful but not necessarily serious wound. He greeted us with grim mien.

"Boys, I'm sorry we ran into this," he said. "Cameron, I see you've been hurt because you're all bloody. If you're able to navigate it'll be a busy time for you. There's not many men, according to Liligh, who haven't sustained an injury of some kind."

"Boss, mine is only a scratch," I assured him. "Soon as I get my things and tie it up, I'll tend to you."

"I'll wait," replied our leader. "There are men hurt far worse than I am. Take care of them first."

I ran around to our wagon and called for Ruby but

received no response. I had the same sinking of my heart that I had felt before my own injury. I climbed aboard to find the wagon empty. But I realized this was no time for qualms. I smeared some antiseptic on my wound, and tying it up tightly and buckling my belt, I reached for my kit. There on the floor of the wagon was a note. I picked it up. It was addressed to Shaw. Hurrying over to where he was standing with Tom and Jack, I dared not think whether or not I was the bearer of good or bad news. I only knew this note was for Vance, and that he should have it without delay.

"Here," I exclaimed, "this is for you."

He read it quickly and turned ashen white. "Here . . . Pard Wayne, you read it—to the boys." His voice broke and he walked away.

Slowly with grieving voice, I began. " 'Vance: I couldn't marry you to-day like you asked. I should have told you before. I was already married. So I have left with a wagon-train. Good-by. Ruby.' "

Chapter Nine

NOT IMPROBABLY I would have suffered severely from the wound in my hip, and from a sickening revulsion in reaction to the shedding of human blood, had it not been for the cardinal necessity of my taking care of the injured. Even my great distress over the disappearance of Ruby and my sorrow for Shaw yielded to that.

It had been an unusually bloody fight according to Liligh, and there were not many men of Creighton's force that had not been hurt in one way or another. Vance Shaw had seemed to bear a charmed life. No doubt he knew how to think about saving himself while he was fighting. But how much worse for him had been the loss of Ruby than any wound he might have sustained!

I had two seriously wounded men. It did not seem possible to save Jenkins, one of the teamsters, as he had been shot through the middle. The other man, who was suffering from a severed artery, I managed to help. I did not rest a minute that long night nor did the faithful Darnell, who kept at my heels with the lantern and helped me all he could. It did not make things easier to find out that Sergeant Kinney and the remaining soldiers of his command anticipated a return of the savages. But they did not visit us that night.

I stopped in the telegraph shack to see if the operator was wounded and he gave me some bad news that he had received over the military telegraph of a west-bound wagon-train that had been attacked by the Indians twenty-five miles out of Julesburg. This wagon-train, having been warned of a possible attack, had secured a military escort.

Knowing this, the Indians had assembled there a band several times larger in number than the whites, and before the Indians were finally beaten off, many soldiers and citizens were killed. The survivors had retreated to the military post, which was only about two miles distant, where they established communication with Julesburg and the outer world.

At midnight, they strung an emergency wire from the main line to a temporary pole which they had erected. Adorning its top were a tattered flag and an Indian arrow, grimly and determinedly pointing west. Then the survivors buried at the foot of the pole a paper signed by all which, the operator said, had been sent East over the wire to the outside world. He showed me a copy of this sad message which he had scrawled:

"The lives of fifteen soldiers and five citizens were lost during this terrible raid, and their remains are interred near by. While this pole stands the wires will whisper a mournful requiem over the graves of the gallant dead. . . ."

When daylight came it was not possible for me to overlook the dead savages that were lying all over the place. Naked, gory, malignantly fierce in death, they presented a ghastly sight. During the morning Kinney had the corpses carried out on the prairie for burial. The remainder of that day, I went my rounds without food and with scarcely any drink until I felt assured that I had done all that was possible for my patients. Creighton was up and around scanning the horizon to the south with his glass in the hope that he would see his wagon-train returning.

When about dusk I staggered back to our wagon, I was almost ready to collapse. It turned out to be more than exhaustion. Tom and Jack took off my boots and put me to bed, redressed my wound which had become inflamed, and they gave me a hot drink. During the following period while I was half out of my head, one or both of them stayed beside me all the while.

I fell asleep at last and did not awaken until late the next morning. Then, outside of a stiff and very sore hip, I seemed to be all right. Against the wishes of my comrades, I got up. But weakness forced me down again. Sitting on my bed, I asked for news.

"Wal, there ain't a hell of a lot," offered Lowden. "The opinion of the agent an' everybody about town here is thet the redskin attack was against Creighton an' his construction work. The telegraph line is down east of heah but thet will be repaired by to-day or to-night an' then Creighton can telegraph. Gee, we're goin' to see yet what a great thing thet telegraph line will be! Th best news was the return of the wagon-train thet was sent out three days ago," went on Lowden, ponderingly. "All except Beal an' two wagons with three or four men. It'd be too much to hope for thet Beal an' his men also got off free. Anyway, Wainwright is in with four wagons full of posts of slim, fine, strong telegraph poles, an' you'd think Creighton never had any back-set atall."

"But shouldn't someone ride out there and look for Beal?" I asked.

"Shore as shootin'," returned the cowboy. "Me an' Tom an' Vance are about to saddle up an' rustle, that is, if you don't want one of us to stay with you."

I assured them that I was quite all right. Indeed, despite my weakness, it was an ordeal for me to try to rest, but I did manage to doze off for a couple of hours. Upon awakening and getting up, I found to my satisfaction that

I was much stronger and was not to have any fever or other serious results from my mental and physical ordeal. I made the rounds of my patients once more to find that after all I had not been such a bad doctor. They were all grateful and even Creighton showed his appreciation.

Toward the end of the afternoon the cowboys returned, their horses dusty and caked with froth. They dismounted at Creighton's wagon and remained there for a little while. Tom was the first one to come over to our wagon and I did not need to ask him about the fate of Beal's men. Under the dust and grime on Darnell's face was a shade that was gloom. He unsaddled and unbridled his horse and rubbed him down while I went for a bucket of water. When I returned from the river Shaw and Lowden had come back with their horses. Shaw's narrow slits of eyes still showed the lightning of his fiery spirit, but he was not silent. However, something about his talk seemed forced, unnatural. He asked me about myself and my paients and said:

"Reckon you've won yore spurs, boy. . . . Wal, you shore ought to see thet we've had a brush an' run with the Injuns. An' if you had been ridin' you would have seen how a fast hawse is the difference between life an' death. We found Beal's wagons burned to black skeletons, but we only found three men, all naked, scalped, and mutilated. The other man must have got away, at least from the wagons, but he shore must have been followed an' killed. We couldn't find out. A bunch of Indians camped down the creek got wind of us an' came ridin' down like a pack of wolves. We waited until they got within rifle range an' then we rode off shootin' back. We made it pretty bad for them redskins. They couldn't hit us or our hawses an' finally some of them tried to ride around an' head us off. Then we cut loose an' rode away from them."

Next morning we rode out under Creighton's strict orders, four wagon-trains, strong, minus the men we had lost, and several brace of oxen. We had not lost a mule. The wagon-trains of John and James Creighton that had gone off in different directions to bring back telegraph poles were left to catch up with us as we continued the construction work. There was some grumbling on the part of the men but the few who were badly hurt were put in the bunk wagon and the others, crippled or not, went at the work as if nothing had happened. By noon we had poles up five miles out of Julesburg beyond the point where we had been surprised by the Indians. I was still nailing spikes in telegraph poles to ward off the friendly contact of plains animals. It seemed so absurd to me, and I always felt silly when the cowboys grinned mysteriously at me.

It so happened that Darnell and I reached the end of the line to meet Shaw and Lowden riding in and we were all struck with the same thing at the same time. This was the spectacle of our leader in his shirt sleeves with a bloody splotch on his shoulder, red-faced and sweating under the hot sun, digging a post hole with one arm. That was the way with Creighton. He would never ask a man to do anything or to attempt anything that he was not willing and glad to do himself. We were short of men now but the work had to go on.

We camped that night for the last time on the banks of the South Platte River. From there the trail was to head northwest back into Nebraska following Lodge Pole Creek.

Shortly after supper we had the disquieting news that one of the two wagons destroyed by the Indians had been full of supplies, and we had to go on rations.

Thus far, particularly when we had buffalo meat, we had fared very well indeed. We had had flour to bake biscuits or bread, bacon, plenty of coffee and sugar. There was even butter kept in tin cans. Now we were to be deprived of a sufficient amount of these foods. We would soon have recourse to *pemmican,* made of buffalo meat thoroughly dried and ground into a powder and kept in bags of skin. When served mixed with flour and boiled, it made a wholesome dish and one that I liked. There was also *penole* which was parched corn ground up and mixed with sugar and cinnamon. It needed no preparation except mixing with water and it was amazingly satisfying and strength-giving. For vegetables we used various herbs from which the juice had been extracted and the remainder dried in an oven. This residue when cooked in a dish swelled up to four times its ordinary size and was really tasty and nutritious. But we were not concerned at being put upon rather slim rations for we knew that very soon the buffalo would catch up with us.

It developed, however, that if the rains did not come we would suffer for lack of water on this long trek through the corner of Nebraska and over the barren lands of Wyoming as far as the Laramie River. Liligh had heard rumors that Lodge Pole Creek which we were to follow to the next divide sometimes ran dry in the summer.

On the following morning before we left the big river Liligh had us fill all the barrels and water-bags and other receptacles that would hold water, and asked us to make sparing use of it until we had crossed the bad lands.

Some miles from the river, on rising ground above the creek bed, we got into the most barren country we had yet seen. At a distance it looked like rolling prairie but near at hand it seemed flat enough. There was a scant growth of sage and the most meager buffalo grass we had encountered. The bleached bones of cattle and buffalo and other animals lined the trail, grim reminders of what starvation and thirst could do. We did not find any water until the third day out from the South Platte, and we were not able to make more than three or four miles a day.

It cheered us materially to receive a message that John and James Creighton had reached Julesburg with two wagon-trains of poles and were on their way to join us. There was also another detachment of dragoons on the way from Ft. Kearney to join us. Creighton sent orders for these soldiers to repair any damage done to the telegraph line as they traveled along.

One day we were visited by a group of Indians. They were serious but not unfriendly. Liligh said they were Sioux which tribe had not openly gone on the war path at that time. They had a fine type of chieftain named Black Hawk. He was intelligent and somber and knew a few words of English. He, like his band, became absorbed in the sounds of the telegraph. At this camp it chanced that a message wired to Julesburg brought back the information that there were Indians there at the time, also several Ogallala, one of whom was a distinctive chief. Creighton wired back to get his name. His name, translated from the Julesburg end, was War Cloud. Black Hawk was asked if he knew the Ogallala Sioux chief, War Cloud. His reply was a gutteral, "Ughh!" and a change of expression that denoted interest and wonder. Thereupon Creighton and Liligh and another one of the plainsmen who knew Indians extracted a message from Black Hawk to telegraph back to War Cloud in the endeavor to get an answer that the Sioux chieftain would know was honest. The message sent was something like this:

"No rain! All dry. Sun burn up grass. Where buffalo?"

Back came the answer from Julesburg:

"Rains come. Plenty buffalo. War Cloud greets his brother Sioux."

Wonderful as that seemed to the chieftain he was not wholly convinced. He was crafty as well as intelligent. He sent back another message which had to do with the whereabouts of his braves and what they were doing, which obviously was something white men would not know. And the answer, though far from reassuring to the white men present, was "Iron horse plenty braves. War dance at White Rock That Stands High."

That reply convinced the Sioux of the magic of the wire and it also convinced us that we could look for more Indian trouble ahead. But Black Hawk was apparently certain that Creighton could invoke the power of the Great Spirit to send words through the air and he was strong in his assurance that the Sioux tribe would protect the telegraph line. He would send word to all the tribes that the White Chief meant no harm with his line of poles and wires across the plains and that they should protect it. This delighted Creighton more than anything that had happened. It was also good for us to know.

Liligh said, "These Sioux are sincere people. If they believe yu, thet yu mean them no harm—an' thet yer not goin' to kill off the buffalo—they actually will protect the telegraph line. Fer them, it means the voice of the Great Spirit, but"—his pause was pregnant—"wal, I wanta hev the line finished an' patrolled by dragoons."

From that day as we progressed along the trail we always had Indians with us. They guided us to water or tcld us where we could find it, and that meant much where sources were few and separated by weary miles and hot blistering days. Sometimes we had to give the oxen a drink out of a bucket, to save them from parching and falling in their tracks. The days grew hotter, the prairie more barren, and we grew thin from hard work, insufficient food, and the hot sun. A Pony Express rider reached us from the West with most disquieting news. Sunderlund with his wagon-train had stopped to fight off Indians. Also he sent word back by the rider that half of his herd of cattle, instead of having been stampeded by Indians, had been run off by rustlers who had followed him all the way from Texas. Shaw evinced most unusual interest at the rider's story. And he wanted to know what the name of the Texas rustler chief was. I wondered if Shaw suspected Red Pierce.

One evening after we had made camp, we were sitting around trying to keep cool when Lowden told us that Sunderlund's wagon-train was only about eight miles off.

"Well, Wayne," said Darnell, "I reckon you'll be ridin' out that way to-night, no doubt, to talk to Mr. Sunderlund."

"If you do speak to Sunderlund," Jack broke in, "be sure to give my regards to his daughter."

"I know you're all kidding me," I replied, "but as a matter of fact, if Mr. Sunderlund's wagon-train is only about eight miles off, then I'm definitely going there to-night."

Up to this point Shaw had been quiet, but suddenly he motioned me to one side.

"Wayne," he said, "I know yo're supposed to be boss of this wagon-train and all, but I'm boss of this evening. And you just ain't goin' to see Kit Sunderlund."

"Can it possibly be that you're intending to call upon her yourself?" I asked, suddenly stung by this apparent determination of Vance's to keep me away from Kit.

"No!"

Without another word, Shaw walked over to saddle up his horse. I strolled over to him, my anger somewhat subsiding.

"Vance, you're probably the best friend I have in the world. How about going for a ride with me to-night?"

"No, Wayne, I've got to do a little scoutin'. So long." He leaped astride and wheeled away. I watched him go, wondering why he had again brought up this subject.

It was a most beautiful night and very calm. But to me it was a night of utter distress. On the one hand I was drawn toward riding over to see Kit. But on the other hand, I could not quite make Shaw out. Did he have some specific reason for not wanting me to go there? Was he heading that way himself? I could not bring myself to think that Shaw would actually go to see Kit after refusing to go with me. My brain welled around, but through the confusion one single thought came out. And that was that I was heading that moment straight for Kit Sunderlund and that her bitter accusation was as if it had never been.

As I threw a saddle over Darnell's horse, he called out, "Pard Wayne, you do thet like you bin doin' it all yore life. Funny how wimmen affect a man."

Lowden told me how to find the Sunderlund camp, and soon I was riding along a slight swell between two draws. A moon that seemed red had just risen in the east. The breeze that swept over the Plains was hot and dry. I seemed to be following an Indian or game trail, so I gave Wingfoot his head. My thoughts strayed from one thing to another, but always back to Kit Sunderlund.

I intended to declare myself once and for all. Kit had evinced an interest in me. If not, why had she bothered to accuse me of having an affair with Ruby? If there was no hope for me with this high-spirited Texas girl, I wanted to hear it myself.

The point where I reached the Sunderlund wagon-train was at the end of the small ridge I had been following. I gazed on the number of wagons, the ten or more camp fires glazing brightly. Wingfoot champed his bit as if eager to descend. I picked out Kit's wagon home and gave the horse his head.

Kit's wagon had been unhitched under a spreading cottonwood, somewhat apart from the others, yet not on the outskirts of the camp. As I neared it I heard voices. Then to my utter amazement and chagrin I saw Vance Shaw's horse standing, reins dragging, at the rear of the wagon. And silhouetted against the fire stood the tall cowboy, with Kit against his breast.

They seemed entranced with the moment. Ordinarily Vance would have heard Wingfoot within a quarter of a mile. Sitting there on my horse I knew that what I should do was ride away as quickly as possible. But a feeling I could not control made me burst upon them. Speaking furiously and without allowing either of them to interrupt me, I pointblank accused Shaw of lying to me.

Before he could reply I turned to Kit. "Vance and I were friends, Miss Sunderlund. And I entertained hopes that—hopes that you would not understand."

With my world crashing about me I leaped for the horse. Somehow I swung into the saddle, blindly grasping for the reins.

As Wingfoot plunged away, I heard Vance's startled entreaty, "Pard Wayne . . . wait!" But I kept on.

Chapter Ten

WE STOPPED one day, at an hour when the heat was most intense, within sight of the famous Chimney Rock which was one of the most eagerly sought landmarks along the Oregon Trail. It was situated not far from the Wyoming line. It was a dim, spectral, chimney-shaped shaft of rock rising above the haze of the horizon to pierce the sky. It had no color unless it was a ghostly dim gray. After the endless days of monotonous sweeping prairie it seemed a thing of beauty, unreliable, a mirage from the highlands. It was between fifty and sixty miles away, but it might as well have been a thousand miles distant. Creighton's wagon-trains were stalled. For the first time they could not go on. The men were exhausted from hard work in the broiling heat and starved from a meager diet which lacked meat, and so thirsty that they spat cotton. Their lips were blistered, their cheeks peeling, their eyes seared from peering through hot air. The oxen amd mules had been two days without a drink and there was only a little water left to slake the thirst of the men. Every day in the afternoon, clouds would appear on the horizon and there would be a low rumble of distant thunder, but the storm never broke.

Creighton sent for Liligh and the cowboys and several of the Westerners. Our leader showed as much as any of us the ravages of this long ordeal across the barren lands from Julesburg. He was thin, the sun had bleached his hair tawny, and except where his face was protected by beard it was burned to a crisp. But the eagle look of him, the unquenchable, seemed enhanced.

"Men," he addressed us, "I have made the decisions on this trek across the plains. I have taken the responsibility. I realize that we are stuck here momentarily, hourly, perhaps for longer, but my mind simply cannot accept that we *can't* go on! I say, *carry on,* and, of course, that is what we will do. But for the time being, what?"

"Boss, we can't go back an' we can't go forward," returned Liligh. "We hev reached our limit. To push the oxen an' mules any further without water would make them strangle in their tracks. If it doesn't rain——"

"Don't say *if,*" thundered our chief. "How many times have I told you to say *when?* . . . Shaw, with all due respect to the older Westerners, I'm leaving it up to you. You are younger and your vision has not been impaired by failure and defeat. What shall we do?"

"Wal, sir, as I see it, I reckon we should stay put, as Liligh thinks. I disagree with him that we could not move on if we drove the animals, an' see what's beyond thet rise of ground. But, boss, you may not believe me, but I can smell rain."

"Smell rain?" queried Creighton, incredulously.

"Yes, sir, I can," returned the cowboy, his voice strong and vibrant. "I always could smell rain an' I can now. Thet sense of mine has never failed me. I don't attempt to explain it, boss, an' thet's not important. I've lived all my life in the open. I've learned thet some men can see things at a distance thet are invisible to the crowd. I have known Indians thet could see farther than any white man. My senses are keen. I can hear stampedin' buffalo farther than any plainsman thet I ever knew. An' I can smell rain now."

"You encourage me, cowboy. Men, here we stop until something happens. Unhitch and make the animals and yourselves as comfortable as possible."

"All right, boss. Thet's fine," returned Liligh, and spitting a gob of tobacco juice to the dry sand, he eyed Shaw with an unfathomable glance. "Wal, you wolf-nosed Texas *vaquero*, yer shore takin' a lot on yer shoulders. But I'll be damned if I'm not glad to lean on yu. We're almost shot to pieces. Come on, fellers, let's get at it."

Liligh's words rang in my ears. How we all depended on that cowboy! And despite the bitterness that had assailed my heart, I could not help but pay tribute to him.

While Darnell and I unhitched the drooping oxen and turned them loose, Shaw and Lowden relieved the three horses of their saddles and led them into the shade of the wagon. Then we all sought some point where the burning sun could not get to us. It was relief to rest, yet as the hottest hour came and passed, it was difficult to breathe or move. A scant drink of water made our dry skin break out with moisture.

While watching the south for some sign, however small, of a change in the weather, my thoughts drifted to that night when my world had crashed about me. Or had I any reason to think this? I had not been on a basis with Kit Sunderlund to object to anything she might do or any choice she might make. It had been finding Shaw there, his seeming betrayal of the close friendship I imagined existed between us, that had rocked my equilibrium. What had he meant when he called for me to wait? Could he have justified his presence in the Sunderlund camp that night after having told me he would not go there?

We had never spoken of it since. I had seen Shaw looking at me peculiarly many times during the days that ensued. But he said nothing and it was impossible for me to broach the subject. As far as an outward relationship was concerned, we had conducted ourselves as if nothing had happened. Our very lives were dedicated to the task of stretching the telegraph line across this barren country, and now we were confronted with the problem of survival.

This afternoon was different from any I remembered. It did not seem hotter, but it was more sultry. There was an oppression in the air. The stillness of that vast prairie was something appalling. There was not a bird or an animal in sight. What had appeared to be blue heat haze in the south gradually took on the form of clouds. They could not be seen to move, yet they spread up over the sky, and the afternoon gradually darkened, not because of the lateness of the hour, but because of some peculiar thickening of the atmosphere. It became a thick, rich amber. Gradually the cloud forms spread to the zenith and beyond and the darker center, almost purple in hue, intensified, and then for the first time that afternoon we heard muttering thunder. It began faintly and far away, and rumbled along the sky until it almost reached us.

"Pard, as shore as God made little apples, we're in for one of those turrible electric storms," said Shaw to Lowden. " 'Course I never seen one way up here, but you know we've been told they're awful bad."

"Wal, if they're as bad as them on the Panhandle we're in fer brimstone, hell, an' blazes," added Lowden.

"I don't care what it does," said Darnell. "Storms are bad in Wyomin', yes, but I'd rather be struck by lightnin' than strangled from thirst."

"Boys," I chimed in, hopefully, "I don't know anything about it, but I tell you it's going to rain."

"Ha!" exclaimed Shaw, rising in one motion to his tall height. "You all see what I see?"

Lowden had been his shadow in action and he burst

out, "Injuns, by damn! An' a whole bunch of 'em. Now what the hell air they up to?"

"Up to? Cain't you see?" snorted Shaw. "They're ridin' along under the wire, tryin' to make up their minds just where they're goin' to do some dirty work."

Finding the field glass, I went forward to stand on the driver's seat. Liligh came running along the line of wagons.

"Hey, men, listen to boss' orders," he yelled. "A gang of redskins out hyar up to some mischief. Creighton says to let them do what they damn please. We can't take on a fight now. What the hell air a few telegraph poles now leveled to the ground in our young lives? No shootin' unless they should happen to charge us. Stretch tarpaulins an' any extra canvas from wagon to wagon to ketch the rain."

Shaw yelled out to Liligh, "Hey, old timer, you reckon it's agonna rain?"

"Yas, yu gimlet-nosed rooster, it's gonna rain!"

"Boys, have you noticed the sun has gone behind thet cloud? An' thet the fire is out of the air?" asked Shaw.

"Shore hev," replied Lowden, "but I reckon I'll stay in the shade a bit longer."

"Wal, my Yankee pard, cain't you tell us what you see?" went on Shaw.

"Must be about forty or fifty Indians, maybe more," I rejoined. "You can see now. They've stopped about a half a mile away just at the curve of the telegraph line before it turns up this way. They don't look like any Indians I've seen before, but surely not Sioux or Arapahoes."

"They have the lean, hungry look of Crows," called out Shaw.

"If they're Crows we can look for dirty business," said Darnell. "But I reckon we're not in for a fight."

"I think I see a chief haranguing that bunch," I went on. "They've gathered around him in a circle. . . . There. A lot of them have dismounted from their mustangs. They are shaking the telegraph pole. Others are rubbing the wire . . . Whoopee! They're dragging the poles and wire down. I can see them chopping at the wire with tomahawks. There! They've got the wire down at that point. Indians riding back like the wind along the line. They're followed by another bunch, perhaps a dozen, and they're pushing over the telegraph poles as they go along. Looks to me as if they were knocking the insulators off. . . . Say, boys, way down beyond there's another bunch of Indians. I hadn't seen them. They are a mile away and working away from the telegraph line. . . . By George, boys, they're dragging the telegraph line with them. Some of them are on foot leading their mustangs and hanging on to the wire."

"Dawg-gone me, thet's a new one fer Injuns!" exclaimed Shaw.

"I reckon the pore damn ninnies hev got it into their heads thet if they cut out a mile chunk of wire an' march off with it, it'll keep us from gettin' the Great Spirit to send more messages." That was Lowden's sally.

Presently there was a long line of Indians, some mounted and others on foot, stretched along fully a mile of wire and dragging it over the prairie somewhat to the north. At this close end of the line I made sure that there was not a single savage, either mounted or on foot, who did not have hold of that telegraph wire either by his lasso or by hand. In the still, peculiarly noiseless moment, their weird cries came to our ears. It was a strange thing for Indians to do. They were all children. They might have been doing it for fun but it did not appear that way to me. I wondered what Creighton was thinking about a mile of his telegraph line having been cut out and dragged away.

A loud clap of thunder disrupted my attention and lowering the field glass I saw that in the interval of time when we had been distracted from the storm, the atmospheric conditions had remarkably changed. The clouds now were moving on us and they were very low. The center was inky black and the rolling prairie land this side of it was obscured by a gray moving wall. That was rain and I rejoiced at sight of it and yelled aloud the glad tidings. But others among the men had observed this before I did. They were rushing to stretch tarpaulins between the wagons.

As far as my comrades and I were concerned, the catching of rain could wait a little because we were still interested in watching the savages. I was interested, too, in the darkening thickness of the air, the unnatural amber light that seemed to envelop everything, and the approach of the inky black cloud with its bright zigzag darts. It was no longer silent. The men were shouting at their tasks and huzzaing at the welcome coming of the storm.

Suddenly there came a dazzling, blinding stroke of lightning followed immediately by an ear-splitting crash of thunder. For a moment my eyesight was impaired, yet I knew the stroke had fallen closer to the Indians than to us. But hardly had I realized this when that blinding, dazzling, white and blue bolt of lightning ran along the ground with incredible swiftness, leaving a wake of electric sparks. The lightning had struck the telegraph wire that the Indians were dragging and the sound of it, the seething, hissing ring of metal as if it were being melted, ran the whole length of it, seeming to explode all the way.

For an instant the lurid white light obscured the line of savages. When it cleared I saw that they had been knocked flat. The riderless mustangs were wildly running across the plain. For a moment I wondered if the Indians had all been killed, but then I saw them, one after another, rising up out of the grass, to grope here and there, to come to their senses and flee across the prairie like frightened quail.

Shaw's rolling laughter rang out. "Pards, what you make of thet? The Great Spirit pitched a lightnin' bolt into thet telegraph wire the redskins were stealin'. It's dollars to doughnuts they'll never come near thet telegraph line again. *Whoopee! Ki-Yi!*"

"The Lord is shore with Creighton," yelled Lowden.

But I was still too awe-struck and stunned by that tremendous phenomenon to see any humor in the situation. I felt more like thanking God for a miraculous escape.

"Here comes the storm, boys," shrieked Shaw, "an' she'll shore be a humdinger."

Then on the instant the sky appeared to rain streaks of lightning, and balls of fire seemed to rise from the ground where the lightning had struck and bounce over the prairie for all the world like huge blazing white cotton-balls. The splitting crack of ropes of lightning, the crash and boom of thunder, the terrific glittering brightness that illumined the scene, the pungent odor of brimstone, and envelopment of all in weird unreality, and a cataclysm of sound that became deafening—these caused me to fall upon the driver's seat and cling there half stricken, all my senses strained beyond their limit.

It was almost dark as night but the flashes of lightning were so thick that it seemed dazzling bright and duskily dark almost at the same time. From where I stood I could see part of the roped-off corral where the men had put the mules. Shaw had told me that in one of these electric storms mules were likely to become almost insane with terror. Incredible as it seemed, I actually saw balls of electric fire run up and down the backs of those mules, play up and down their short manes, and drop off their ears. For the most part the mules stood legs apart, quivering as if they were about to collapse.

The black cloud had almost reached us. It was like an inky curtain swinging along close to the ground. It must have been higher but it did not seem more than a hundred feet up. Darnell came running to me and shouted something in my ear which I did not hear. But as he leaped into the wagon, I had sense enough to follow suit. In another moment the electric storm had passed on and the rain clouds, reaching us on the wings of the wind, burst over us, obscuring everything in a gray pall and almost swallowing up the rumble of thunder in the thudding impact of water over and all around us.

Shaw and Lowden were lying on their bunks calmly smoking cigarettes; Darnell sat on his bed and I knelt at the end of the wagon peering out. If anybody spoke I didn't notice. I had the feeling that I could not hear myself think. My heart swelled with thankfulness. We had prayed for rain and now it looked as if we were going to be washed off the plain. This storm had broken the drought, filled the waterholes, flooded the streams, and had been Creighton's salvation. It must have been a vindication of his faith.

The solid downpour lasted less than half an hour; the gray pall passed on, and it grew light again. I could see patches of blue sky in the clouds to the south. The lighter rain diminished and passed away and by the time the cracks and bolts of the electric storm and the peals of thunder had passed out of our hearing, the storm was over and, incredible to see, the sun burst out again, gloriously bright but tempered of its blasting heat.

We emerged from the wagon to find all the men and the soldiers in action. Our camp was on high ground but there were inches of water everywhere. In the wash below us that had been dry there roared a muddy current. Lakes and ponds shone everywhere, mirroring the sun and sky. I could hardly believe my eyes when I say that the sage and the grass had been washed of their dead gray and already showed a tinge of purple and green. Every tarpaulin that had been stretched between the wagons was sagging full of water. Some distance off to the left of camp the oxen were drinking at the little pools and runnels, and even beginning to graze off the sparse vegetation.

"Wal, who's the plumb best prophet about this wagon-train?" drawled Shaw.

"Pard, yo're purty good but yo're lucky," observed Lowden. "You know damn well you told all thet stuff to Creighton to keep up his nerve. . . . But, at thet, I knowed it was gonna rain."

"Boys," interposed Darnell, "won't the buffalo be comin' along after this rain?"

"They shore ought to, sooner or later, an' do I want a hunk of rump steak!"

"Here come Creighton and Liligh," I said. "Wonder what's working on them now? Lord, I'll bet two-bits he'll put us to work digging post holes."

"Take you up, pard. It's past mid-afternoon now, an' look down the desert to the southward about ten miles."

"What! By gum, if it ain't a wagon-train," ejaculated Lowden, joyfully.

"Jack, yore eyes are pore, except maybe for girls. Thet's two wagon-trains."

They were indeed a welcome sight to me. And I rejoiced at the realization that Creighton's fortunes had again risen. It may have been in my mind, but the prairie had taken on color, a waving rolling beauty clear to the purple horizon. And close at hand that colorful expanse was split by the broad Oregon Trail now shining white in the sunlight and winding down to meet the long serpentine wagon-train.

Camp was a busy place late that afternoon. Creighton gave orders to slaughter two of the oxen that had been crippled and which threatened to be a drag on our progress. There was promise of fresh meat for several days but the problem of fire wood still confronted us. None was in sight. And there were very few buffalo chips left in the wagons that had roamed to and fro across the trail in search of this peculiar but satisfactory fuel.

Next morning bright and early the telegraph construction was in full swing again. It developed that we had been too sanguine about our troubles being over. They were not.

Every day Chimney Rock stood up in the distance seemingly no closer. The work along this stretch was probably the most strenuous that we had encountered. But it lacked the distress and suspense that had hung upon our actions when we were half starved for meat and drink.

Still there were no signs of buffalo or Indians. Not a single wild horseman on the horizon since the great electric storm! When questioned, Shaw shook his tawny head ominously, but made no comment. I noticed that although he was always watchful he turned more often in his saddle to gaze long to the southward. Liligh scouted the idea that the buffalo had missed us. This broad track covering the western end of Nebraska and the eastern end of Wyoming had been the northern track of the buffalo for no one could tell how long, perhaps hundreds or thousands of years. "I'd feel safer if the main herd was past us," said the old plainsman.

There came another warm sultry day during which we

made unusually good progress. That evening we had a better camp fire than usual. We really did not need it because the air was much milder and without the usual nipping edge. It was a very quiet night too. I missed the coyotes. Across this barren stretch I had heard but few of the yelping choruses. We all sat around the glowing embers of our camp fire, not very talkative, which betokened that we were fatigued and would soon seek out bunks. In such infrequent intervals I was not able to resist the encroaching of a memory that seemed an endless time back in the past. And Shaw's sad face as he sat staring into the fire, beset by his own bitter recollections, was not conducive to my forgetting Kit Sunderlund. I did not forget her. Several times we had heard of Sunderlund's wagon-train somewhere to the west of us, but not very far, and the thought disrupted the rough tenor of my adventurous days. Not only was I haunted by the girl, but disquieted by the conviction that I would meet her again. How Shaw would enter into that picture, I did not permit myself to speculate.

All at once I observed Shaw turn his ear to the southward and become still as a stone. He must have been listening. I saw him do that often, but as often as I tried to hear something myself, I had to give up. The night was uncommonly still. There was some noise and murmur of voices from among the other wagons but outside and away from camp there was absolutely no sound that I could detect.

The cowboy got up and walked from us almost out of the circle of light. But I could discern him standing sideways, bending over a little, and surely strained in his listening.

"What the hell?" whispered Jack, sitting up and removing his cigarette.

"Vance must be hearin' somethin'," interposed Darnell, in the same low tone. "He shore is listenin'. What you think, Jack? Indians, mebbe?"

"Hell no!" ejaculated Lowden, standing up. "Vance never acts thet way when there's Indians around."

"What then?" I queried, quickly. But nobody answered. We maintained our stiff postures, the three of us intently watching Shaw. All at once he broke out of his motionless statue-like tensity and he ran back to us.

"Buffalo!" he announced, and his voice rang. "It's a stampede shore as God made little apples. We're right in line!"

"What!" I ejaculated. "Buffalo? Stampede?"

"Air you shore, pard?" queried Lowden.

"Shore as hell. I heard it long before I made shore we were in line."

"Wait! Let me listen. I ain't so pore," replied Lowden, and he walked out into the gloom.

We all waited with bated breath and I was aware that all of a sudden the very air had become charged with suspense. After a long period, fully several minutes, Lowden came tramping back to us, his spurs tinkling on the gravel.

"Pard, I cain't hear a damn thing," he said. "There ain't any wind. No air stirrin'. But I reckon if yo're shore we better not wait."

"Wait! I should smile not. Mebbe we haven't got time as it is. . . . Cameron, you run an' fetch Liligh. Jack, you an' Tom bring in the oxen. I'll rustle the hawses."

I ran off in search of Liligh, fully alarmed at the cowboy's look and curt voice and wondering what kind of danger we were up against. If the main herd of buffalo was stampeding and our camp lay in line with its travel, there certainly would ensue a serious situation. I found Liligh at his wagon, squatting with his crew around a little camp fire and I announced breathlessly, "Boss, come with me at once. Shaw wants you pronto."

"Me?" ejaculated the plainsman, making a wry face. "What does thet damn cowboy want me fer? What kind of trouble has he got a hunch about now?" But though he grunted and spoke complainingly he was quick to get up and let me lead him away. I dragged him along at such a rate that he swore and wanted to know what I was in such a hurry for.

"Boss, Shaw hears buffalo. He said it was a stampede and that our camp was right in line."

"Dernation!" exclaimed Liligh. "Thet is somethin'. I'd hoped thet main herd hed missed us."

In a very few moments we reached our wagon to find Shaw tethering the three horses to the wheels. When he saw us he said: "Liligh, I'm afeared I hear a hell's slue of buffalo in stampede. But thet very thing's been hauntin' me lately. Kinda loco about it, you know. I may be wrong. I hope to God I am. But you hustle out there away from camp an' turn yore ear south, an' Old Timer, be shore to stop yore breathin' an' yore heart's beatin' or you cain't hear it."

"Cowboy, how in the hell kin I stop my heart beatin'?" Liligh exclaimed, but he strode swiftly out into the darkness. I followed him, but to one side, and when I got out there alone in the dark I turned my ear to the south and tried to stop all the internal workings of my being to listen.

To my intense irritation, my heart beat like a trip hammer and I actually felt my blood racing through my veins. The great star-studded vault of the sky seemed to cover us watchfully; the silence and solitude were intense, magnified no doubt by my imagination; there was a soft almost indistinguishable breathing of nature or what might have been the low hum of insects; there was a melancholy in the great loneliness and mystery over all that dark prairie land. But listen though I might with all my power I could not hear anything unusual.

Presently when Liligh hurried back to the camp fire I ran to join him. Shaw looked up from his task and I saw his eyes glint reflections from the fire.

"Wal, how about it, boss?" he queried, sharply.

"Damn the luck!" burst out the foreman. "Right! When was you ever wrong, you dod-gasted Texas Injun? It's a stampede all right an' if I ain't fooled, thar air steen million buffs in thet herd."

"I reckon so. We just got time to make ready for them."

"Shaw, of course I've met with lots of stampedes," went on Liligh, hurriedly. "But you Texans might hev somethin' on us Northerners. What's yer idee? Spill it quick."

"Only one idee. Tell Creighton an' alarm the camp. Rustle up the oxen an' mules. Form the wagons in a wedge. Sharp point to the front. Haul two of the oldest wagons ahead. Have buckets of oil ready to throw on them. Send two men from each wagon to the front with rifles an' plenty of shells. Order two men left in each wagon to try to hold the stock. You know the rest. Rustle!"

Liligh ran away shouting. There soon followed a tremendous activity in camp, hoarse voices, tramp of boots, metallic rattle of harness, men running out on to the prairie with lanterns, yelling to each other, the advent of Lowden and Darnell with our oxen, the scrape and grind of wheels, and presently in what seemed to me record time the wagons were being moved, some hauled and pushed by a dozen men, others pulled by mules, and the encroachment on camp of many oxen. I helped in every way I could, running here and there, stingingly aware of the bustle around me.

Shaw presently yelled in my ear: "Grab yore rifle. Fill yore pockets with shells. Come with me. Jack an' Tom will try to hold our stock!"

The cowboy held a lighted lantern in one hand and a rifle in the other and he had two cartridge belts buckled around his waist and from the sag in his coat I knew he must have had more ammunition in his pockets. He gave some final instructions to Tom and Jack, then he whirled away with me at his heels. If pandemonium had not broken out in that camp, I did not know what the name implied.

Most of these men and the soldiers knew what a buffalo stampede meant; many of them had seen one. They worked with the desperation of men in peril. At the back of the wide wedge formed by the wagons they were leaving a deep space, evidently for the cattle and mules. A good many teams of oxen, however, had been hitched to the wagons. A crescent moon had appeared and it had visibly lightened the prairie. Oxen were being driven in from both sides. The few cattle which we still had were bawling, whch added to the confusion.

Men and soldiers armed with rifles and shotguns were forging to the front in twos and threes and all of them were talking in hoarsely excited voices. For all I could judge in the darkness, the wedge of wagons when it was completed would be at least a hundred yards long. At length we reached the front of the triangle. The point was two wagons wide and that arrangement held good for two lines back. Then the width was increased to three wagons and so on to four and more until the triangle spread wide at the far end. Fifty feet out from the point of the wedge stood two huge white canvas-covered wagons which were evidently intended to be sacrificed by fire. I saw men passing with buckets and I smelled kerosene.

There were fully fifty men and soldiers congregated at that point. They were loudly vociferous. Shaw did not have anything to say and I hesitated to question him. I did not run into Liligh up there but I noticed Wainwright, Widing, Nelson, Edney, and other Westerners with whom we worked. Their faces looked grim and determined. While they talked they all faced the prairie and no doubt they were all listening as keenly as I was. The commotion behind us was gradually diminishing, showing that as the wedge neared completion there was less need of shouting. However, the hum of excitement still continued. It looked to me as if there would be time to perfect the wedge before the onslaught of the buffalo.

Shaw indicated for me to follow him. We left the crowd of men and proceeded to the two wagons that were to be set on fire.

"Let's walk out in front a few steps so I can get a line on the buffs again," he said, close to my ear.

We walked ahead fifty steps and then stopped. The instant we froze in our tracks I heard a strange low incessant rumble somewhat resembling the rolling of distant thunder and for me, surely a heart-stopping sound.

"Hear thet?" queried Shaw, with that something in his voice that always made me quiver inside. "I shore miscalculated. Them buffalo were farther away an' a damn sight more in number than I figured. They're runnin' wild, stampedin' full tilt! Scared half to death! Funny how a herd of buffalo can get scared at nothin'. It's 'cause there's so many, I reckon, an' the craziness sweeps through the herd. Lay down an' put yore ear to the ground. Thet'll shore be somethin' new for you. I'll go back an tell the men to throw the oil on the wagons an' be ready to set fire pronto."

I did as the cowboy bade me, and removing my sombrero I laid my face close to the ground and pressed my ear to the sand. It seemed as if I had put my ear to a colossal sea shell, and was hearing that strange sound of the sea. It was like that yet different in many ways. I could hardly call it a roar but it resembled thunder—thunder not raised by the elements, but a thunder of life. Out there was inconceivable life on the rampage. It was an enormous beating without even an infinitesimal fraction between the beats.

I tried to concentrate my faculties to judge whether or not the sound was increasing and in a few seconds I decided that both volume and rumble were accelerating. Shaw returned and touched me with his boot, and when I arose, called in my ear:

"Pard, it won't be long now. I hope for the best but sometimes stampedes cain't be split any more than they can be stopped. Do what I do an' say yore prayers, thet's all."

As he turned back I looked out upon the vast prairie. Near at hand it was faintly moonlit and I imagined I could see distinctly at least half a mile. I made out telegraph poles standing like dark sentinels all of that distance but beyond that from where the growing sound came, it seemed opaque and ghostly. In my state of mind, imagination could conjure up anything; but I made stern effort to stem my agitation and be cool. Outwardly, no doubt, I succeeded.

When I turned back to follow Shaw the two oil-soaked wagons burst into flames and a great space all around us was brightly lighted. The faces of the men were no longer dark. Bare-headed and pale-faced, with burning eyes fixed on the prairie, they looked only in the one direction. Shaw herded them back even with the point of the wedge and lined them up on each side just in the lee of the two front wagons. If the herd split around these obstacles the buffalo would pass on each side of the men and of the wedge. If not—! Shaw lined me up beside him on the inside and he faced forward, rifle ready, with a shout that strangely sounded like a whisper:

"Shoot when I shoot an' keep on shootin!"

I knew, because his voice sounded so faintly, that the stampede was almost upon us, but I actually did not hear anything on the instant. When I took out my watch to make out the time by moonlight my hand trembled so that I could hardly discern the hands. It was eight-thirty. The next move I made was to peer ahead, transfixed with my feet riveted to the ground, sure that I was about to live the supreme moment of my life.

Then out there on the moonlit prairie I saw something. It moved. It was black. It was like the torrential flow of an ocean behind which there were unknown leagues of pushing waves. The fire, catching the top of the canvas wagons, flared up brighter. That oncoming wave swallowed up the moonlit space. Then I recognized the shaggy front of a buffalo herd in stampede. It had a straight front and extended as far as I could see on both sides, and surely for miles and miles.

I became aware that I was rocking on my feet. The ground had become unstable. It was shaking under me. On the moment, when I ceased to be aware of an engulfing tremendous pressure, I knew that it had been the roar of this avalanche and that I could no longer hear it. I was deafened. There was no sound. I knew there was no sound because when Shaw raised his rifle in a signal for us all to fire there was no report following the belching of red flame and smoke. Even reports of all the heavy guns in unison could not be heard.

Shaking as one with the palsy I imitated Shaw and rapidly emptied my rifle straight into the front of this rebounding black juggernaut with its myriad of shiny horns and fiery green eyes. But shaking though I was, unsteady on my pins, I could shoot and I could see.

And suddenly the center of that advancing line sustained a staggering shock and disintegrated, huge black shaggy forms hurdling high to fall and slide and others as if by magic taking their places until the augmenting pile encroached upon the burning wagons, bumping them to send aloft showers of sparks from the burning canvas.

My faculties, my blood, almost my heart itelf, had stopped with that first shot—the unbearable suspense— the suspension of thought until it became certain that the buffalo herd had split and the rolling black sea of the stampede was passing on to each side of us. I almost fainted then. This was a little too much for a tenderfoot.

Seeing Shaw reload his rifle, I did likewise with fingers that were all thumbs. His rifle was blazing flame before I had finished reloading. We were in the thick of something so supremely terrible that I became an automaton, reacting like a machine. I shot methodically, regulating my shooting and reloading to Shaw and the other men. My eyes were assailed by a fury of action, a maelstrom of churning buffalo, endless and boundless.

In time, coming to reload again, I fould all the ammunition in one pocket gone and had recourse to the other. One by one I inserted shells into my rifle with nervous fingers and shot ahead. The bright flare of the burning wagons had died down. There was not so much light. Only the wagon beds were blazing. A column of smoke rolled aloft a few yards to merge into the solid canopy of dust. My sight grew dim from exhaustion or terror or from the thickening of the atmosphere. For long I gazed through a haze with smarting eyes. The huge pile of buffalo on each side of the wagons grew apace to right and left, widening the barricade of dead bodies in front of our wedge.

Actually to hear once more seemed unreal and unbelievable. But my ears were filled with thundering din and it diminished to a roar. As my hearing returned I began to come out of the state under which I had labored. That trembling of the earth under my feet began to lessen. The men had ceased shooting. The dust clouds seemed thinner. I became aware of Shaw's arm under mine, probably supporting me. Again the great volume of thundering rumble was registered by my ears. It was receding. It was behind us. The hideous streaming black nightmare on each side of us had passed by, the earth between my feet ceased to rock and became solid again, the dust clouds roared away as if sucked into a vacuum created by the moving herd. The stampede was over. I heard voices again. In the pale moonlight Shaw's face was black from dust and powder stains. The faces of the other men were likewise.

Shaw's clutch of steel fingers was hard on my arm. "Wal, pard, it was kinda tough to have to weather a stampede like thet. Wust one thet I was ever in, but we split it! We're okay! I reckon yore eye-teeth are cut shore, this time. I'm proud of you, pard. You didn't see it but some of our men wilted under thet charge. Wal, there will be buffalo rump steak aplenty from now on."

Half an hour later the irrepressible among our workmen were broiling buffalo rump steaks over the burning remains of our two wagons. They made a sort of hilarious occasion of it.

But none of our party joined them. We returned to our wagon thinking that we would be ordered to break away from the wedge of wagons to form in the usual camp circle. No orders were given, however, and I dragged myself to bed, asleep before I got under the blanket. I didn't awaken or dream that night and Tom had to prod me the next morning to route me out. I smelled the savory rump steak and even that did not accelerate my motions. But once I got to moving and had a hearty buffalo breakfast, I was all right.

Immediately after eating I strode over to take a look at the scene of the battle. There was an enormous pile of the buffalo in front of the wagon wedge. Five or more deep in the center and sloping away to each side! It was apparent that neither the burning wagons nor the rifle fire would have been sufficient to split the herd without the insurmountable obstacle of the pile of dead buffalo.

What huge, magnificent beasts they were! Some of the great bulls were covered on shoulders and enormous heads and fronts with a long, thick, shaggy, black hair. The hind quarters were sort of tawny. Some of the workmen were taking advantage of the opportunity to obtain buffalo hides and I hired two men, who said they were butchering several corpses to take along with us, to get two fine hides for me.

"Wal, it looks sorta as if the buffs played hell with our telegraph poles," observed Lowden.

"More'n two days' job of repair, as far as I see," returned Shaw.

"I hope we are detailed to stay behind and put up those poles," I said.

"Ump-ummm," rejoined Shaw, shaking his head. "The boss will want us out in front."

"I see the telegraph wire is not only down but gone," remarked Darnell.

"Yes, an' it's over in Jericho by this time."

"You mean Wyomin', pard. It's fine an' clear this mawnin'. Thet Chimney Rock shore stands up fine. Wayne, how far is it away now?"

"Don't ask me," I returned. "Looks about five miles."

"Hell! It's farther away now than it was ten days ago," said Jack, facetiously.

Liligh left a crew of three wagons and a dozen men at that camp to make the repairs and catch up with us with the buffalo meat and hides. The rest of us were ordered to get ready to advance.

"Pard, somethin funny happened last night," said Darnell to me. "It happened after you fell asleep. We fellers all heard it an' were shore tickled. Creighton came over our way lookin' for Liligh an' when he found him he bellered: 'Liligh, take some men an' go out an' see how many telegraph poles are down.'

"Liligh was sittin' by the fire over there, dog-tired as anyone could see, an' at the boss' order he jumped as if somebody had stuck him.

" 'Boss, what the hell fer?' he yelled. 'Thar won't be any less poles down now than thar will be in the mornin' when mebbe thar'll be more.'

" 'I want to know how many,' roared the boss.

" 'Wal, Mr. Creighton, I just don't know how we're gonna find out to-night,' said Liligh, very quiet an' cool. 'Shore I wouldn't risk orderin' the men about to-night. It'd be much as my life is worth.'

" 'I hired you an' every last man of you to work any time or all night if necessary,' went on the chief, an' he shore was riled. 'When we get farther along this trail we won't have any rest atall, day or night.'

" 'Yes, thar will be, boss. Some of us will be restin' peaceful like in our graves on the lone praire.'

"That must have socked the boss where he lives 'cause he choked an' strangled an' glared like a wild man an' then went back to his wagon."

"Gosh, Tom, he sure is a slave-driver," I replied, emphatically. "But I suppose he has vision that is denied the rest of us. It must take such a man to do such a job as this."

"Aw, the boss is grand," returned Darnell.

By the time we were under way, wagon-trains stretched across the plain, all with work to do and doing it effectively. Scattered strings and groups of buffalo leisurely caught up with us, paying no particular attention to us and passing on their way. They were, no doubt, the stragglers from the main herd.

To watch these straggling buffalo was extremely interesting to me. Tom and I were in the last wagon, and while Tom drove on, stopping from post to post, I got out to drive the sharpened spikes into the telegraph poles. I had noted more than one buffalo bull sidle up to a pole and look at it curiously. And on more than one occasion when I saw a buffalo rub himself against one of our poles, I remembered the wagon-train left behind us to make repairs and I ceased to worry. I knew perfectly well from Shaw's mysterious air and Lowden's accompanying grin that we were yet to find out more about the buffalo.

Day by day the work progressed fairly well along this stretch and we began to approach Chimney Rock. All the time we were climbing the prairie, and now the ascent was perceptible. I spent many a moment gazing at the Oregon Trail and I thought of another and greater landmark, Independence Rock, somewhere along the trail in Wyoming, and I longed to get my first glimpse of the Rockies.

Straggling groups of buffalo passed us every day, some days more, some less. The storms had either ceased or let up for a spell and that favored our progress. The desert had taken on a fresh green color. There were flowers everywhere, most prominent among them bright sunflowers that had seemed to shoot up like magic. Water was still plentiful in the swales and hardly a day passed that we did not have to ford a stream. But the country remained unprolific of life except for the buffalo.

Toward evening at the close of a good day's progress Liligh halted us to make camp near a waterhole. As supper was not yet ready, I walked out a way to see what I could observe of the buffalo through my glasses. I was electrified to find them playing havoc with our telegraph poles. As I looked I saw the beasts level them as they lazily grazed and worked toward us.

Their favorite method of procedure appeared to be to lean against the pole and scratch their backs with the sharp spikes I had laboriously nailed into the poles for many weary miles and for days and weeks on end. A big shaggy bull would approach a standing telegraph pole and he would look up at it as if to say, "Well, I'll have to see about this thing!" and then he would rub against the pole. The sharp spikes would catch him in the back and that discovery settled it. The mud was thickly caked upon the back of these buffalo and that, entirely aside from any vermin they might well be infested with, made these sharp spikes simply a delight.

I could see the dust fly from their hides. When one big bull was having a great time another huge beast would take note of him and immediately proceed to scratch his back. The spikes were nailed all around the pole. So it was nothing unusual to see three shaggy beasts scratching and humping their backs with other buffalo waiting for their turn. And inevitably the poles would go down.

Soon the sharp-eyed Liligh took note of what was going on and the cursing that he vented upon those poor animals was something that made the very air lurid. He dispatched the cowboys, sending my field glass with them, to ride out five or ten miles and ascertain the extent of the damage. Then Liligh, dragging me along with him for no reason that I could figure except to sustain moral courage, took me to Creighton's wagon. We found the boss extremely busy with his telegraph operators.

"Boss, I'm sorry to disturb you," began Liligh, "but the buffalo air raisin' hell with our telegraph poles."

"Don't bother me. Can't you see I'm busy?" roared Creighton.

" 'Course I see," returned the foreman, tantalizingly, "an' we all air busier than hell too. The thing is, what air we gonna do?"

"Do! Man alive! What about?"

"Wal, I was talkin' about these pesky buffalo."

"Drive them away!"

We just stood there.

"Well, why don't you obey orders?" the chief snapped.

"Hell, we can't. Thar's only about ten thousand of 'em. We'll jest hev to let 'em mosy along and do their mischief, like they bin doin'."

"What mischief?" ashed Creighton.

"Why—they're pushin' over the telegraph poles."

At this juncture Shaw rode up.

"Come here, Shaw," Creighton demanded, "maybe you can talk straight. What about buffaloes and poles?"

"Wal, boss, I just rode in from scoutin' back along the line," returned the cowboy, laconically. Somehow I divined that Shaw was enjoying this. "There's about twenty-five miles of telegraph poles down."

"Twenty-five miles!" echoed our leader, incredulously. "Why wasn't I told? Talk, cowboy!"

"All right, boss, I will, if you'll let me get a word in edgeways. There was a good big bunch of buffs followin' us an' they passed us to-day. They laid the poles low an' they did it by scratchin' their backs on the spikes you ordered Cameron to nail in all our poles."

"Merciful heaven!" ejaculated Creighton. "That's a catastrophe. Buffalo scratching their backs? Who ever heard of the like? Spikes! Scratching their backs! Twenty-five miles of poles! . . . Good Lord, why wasn't I told?"

"You was told, boss. I just told you," returned the cowboy, with exceeding serenity and without a quiver of his smooth face.

Creighton stared. His face turned purple. He fell into a magnificent fury and first his raging was incoherent. He stamped to and fro and everybody got out of his way. Then his speech became clear enough for everybody to distinguish his meaning. "Twenty-five miles of poles down! Six days' work for the whole outfit! . . . All because—buffalo wanted to scratch their backs. All because I—*I* ordered the telegraph poles driven full of spikes. . . . *Haw! Haw! Haw!* I'm a fine engineer. I oughta be confined to digging post holes. . . . As if I had not suffered enough on this hellish job! This is the limit! This is the end! Twenty-five miles! Spikes! . . . And I was told—advised!" Then he turned fiercely to his shocked foreman and shouted hoarsely: "Liligh, kick me good and hard!"

And our chieftain, overcome by rage and grief and shame, turned his back to Liligh, who stood there, his jaw dropping.

"Boss! Yer—yer out of yer haid. I can't kick you."

"Somebody'll have to. . . . Somebody ought to do worse. . . . Shaw, get off that horse and kick me."

"Wal, I'll shore be glad to do thet," drawled Shaw with a smile that was ecstatic and beautiful.

He slipped out of the saddle and kicked our leader so hard that the blow sounded like a bass drum. Creighton plunged forward fully six feet and went sprawling to plow face and hands in the dirt.

I was in convulsions to which I was afraid to succumb. Darnell and Lowden were holding their sides as if about to explode. The rest of the men were stricken in mingled fright and mirth. Then Shaw lay down on the ground and rolled over and over and howled in a queer strangled voice. For a full long moment while we stood around paralyzed, Creighton scrambled to his feet. He was dirty from head to toe. He wiped the dust off his sweating face with a fierce gesture.

"You infernal devil of a cowboy!" he thundered. "I didn't order you to half kill me. You're fired."

Shaw sat up and after taking a moment to subdue himself, he said in a husky whisper, "Wal, boss, you told me to do it, an' it shore was comin' to you."

"You—you took advantage of my confusion and anger," fumed our leader, haltingly. He was coming to himself. It was evident that he was hedging.

Shaw slowly got to his feet. "All right, boss, I'm fired,"

he drawled, "an' thet means for the first time thet you've showed yella."

"*I!* Yellow?" choked Creighton.

"You shore are, boss. An' it's too bad, 'cause how in the hell are you goin' to finish this job without me?"

"All of you idiots get out of my sight," yelled our leader as if he could not bear to look at us longer. "All but you, Shaw! You come with me. We've got to talk!"

"Aw!" breathed the cowboy, with his slow infectious grin, "that's more like yourself. I shore don't mind if I do."

Wherewith Creighton put his arm around the cowboy's shoulder and led him away.

Chapter Eleven

THE LONG-looked-for Chimney Rock finally rose above us.

From a camp some five miles distant I saw the Rock at sunset standing grand and high, shining crimson aloft and gold at its base. After so many weeks, seemingly years, of flat barren prairie, there was something soul-freeing in the sight of this landmark.

The next morning before sunrise, in the transparent atmosphere of dawn, I saw it look like a great white sentinel beckoning the travelers to its shelter and to the pure water that it marked. That day we ran the five miles of telegraph poles in a state of mind that was in the nature of a celebration, with one day, at least, given over to a forgetfulness of bitter toil.

The conformation of Chimney Rock was still impressive even under its shadow. There was a volcanic-like cone of bare gray stone slanting to a sharp apex from which towered the high shaft of rock that gave the landmark its name. Not improbably the singular impressiveness to the fur traders and trappers and emigrants, the glory of Chimney Rock, was actually more in what it represented than in its splendor as a physical phenomenon. From afar when the west-bound travelers first sighted it, it meant an end of the ghastly barrens and the beginning of the long rolling steppes of rough country that led up to the Rockies.

We made camp in its shadow about mid-afternoon of a day that had been marked by clouded skies and pleasant weather. We were again a small camp and relatively few men at the hour. Creighton had gone off hunting with some of his men. This was actually the first time that I could remember his taking time off for recreation. Shaw and Lowden had ridden off on their own, no doubt to climb to the height and look the country over. Darnell was engaged in tasks around our wagon. He had grown somewhat quieter and more thoughtful since we approached the Wyoming uplands. I had long ceased to make mention of his self-imposed guardianship of me. It had irked me at first, but after he had saved me from catastrophe several times, I saw his regard in a different light. Liligh was in camp in charge together with Edney, Houser, Bob Wainwright, Hal Whiting, and Cliff Nelson. Another crew of men had started off with one wagon to unwind a coil of telegraph wire along the course of the trail.

I found myself inexplicably nervous and watchful and I attributed that to the absence of Shaw and Lowden and to the rather small company of men left in camp. It was because of that, no doubt, that I discovered a party of horsemen riding toward our camp up the trail.

I remembered Shaw telling me once that he could always tell a bunch of bad men at sight no matter if they were quite distant. It was not a coincidence that hard characters on the frontier affected dark horses and dark garb. There were eight horsemen in this group, driving several pack animals in front of them.

I did not like their looks but I hesitated to inform Liligh; and, by the time they had approached quite close to us, he discovered them and he stood stock still to favor them with a long scrutiny. Then he quietly told me to call Edney, Wainwright, and the other men in camp.

"I don't see Shaw and Lowden. Where are they?" he concluded.

"They rode off somewhere, boss," I replied.

"Shore. Why the hell air those cowboys always gone when I want them?" he complained. "I'll bet a stack of buffalo chips thet this gang of men don't mean us any good. Howsomever, whatever their game is, mine is to play fer time."

I had seen a good many hard characters since my sojourn on the frontier, but this was the worst-looking lot yet. They halted some dozen rods or so distant and some of them dismounted to hold back the pack animals. Then two of the riders approached us. One of them was a heavily built, darkly bearded man who wore a slouch sombrero pulled down over his face so that his eyes appeared to be only dark gleams in his visage. What struck me most about him was that he carried a rifle across his pommel and he wore two guns, one conspicuous on each side.

His companion was a younger man, a lean and rangy Westerner, sallow-faced and tawny-haired, a Texan if I had learned how to recognize one. The big man turned in his saddle and called back to the others in a loud, coarse voice, "Fellers, hyar's some of my timber left. They haven't used it all."

That speech amazed me and made Liligh curse under his breath. Wainwright and the other men came forward, curious and apparently not at all anxious because they were unarmed.

"Hey thar, Western Union men," boomed the heavily bearded leader, "whar's yore boss?"

"If you mean Creighton, he's away from camp jest at present," returned Liligh, coldly. "He'll be back pronto. While he's absent I'm in charge."

"Wal, we haven't any time to parley. I've trailed this outfit from Julesburg."

"Yas? Yu haven't trailed us very fast," returned Liligh caustically. "What'cha want?"

"I see you have five wagonloads of poles left an' you must have used twenty other loads. This timber was cut off of my homestead property back of Julesburg an' I'm gonna be paid for it."

"Say, man, air yu drunk or crazy?"

"I reckon you can see fer yourself, but it don't make no difference what we air. I'm callin' on you to be paid fer my timber."

"Thet's ridiculous," said Liligh, heatedly. "This timber was cut miles this side of Julesburg, but even if it hedn't been, nobody could charge us fer it. Why, thet's unheard of."

"Wal, you heared what I said," returned the other darkly. "I don't care what you think. I'm callin' on you to pay me fer my timber. An' I ain't gonna waste any more time about it."

"Ahuh. Then it's a holdup."

"Call it what you like, Mr. Superintendent."

"Ha! Ha! A new kind of holdup. Timber rustlers on the plains where thar ain't no property rights. Wal, thet's the limit."

The black-bearded man studied Liligh a moment with sharp eyes, that then shifted to us other men and then out around camp and beyond.

"Fork over five thousand dollars an' be quick about it," he ordered, harshly.

I thought Liligh would strangle trying to get rid of his tobacco quid and stutter and curse at the same time. He recognized the situation and it was a tough spot. The leader's companion had a rifle over the pommel and a swift glance ascertained that all the other men had also. There was not the slightest doubt that this hard outfit would not hesitate to enforce their demand by resorting to firearms.

It did not seem a question of Liligh's courage. He would fight at the drop of a hat, but it was certainly obvious that we were not only unarmed but outnumbered and that a fight was out of the question. Liligh had charge in the absence of Creighton and undoubtedly he knew where our leader kept his cash. Creighton would be one to yield to the demands of such a claim of robbers rather than have a single one of us injured. Money was the last thing considered in this construction of the Western

Union. Nevertheless, it was a bitter pill for Liligh to swallow.

"Yu ain't foolin' me none," he rasped. "I know damn shore yer a bandit. Yu hev no more claim on them sticks of timber than anybody else, much less us who took the trouble to cut an' haul 'em. Suppose I'm not willin' to pay yu the five thousand dollars?"

"Wal, thet wouldn't be very smart," returned the big man, with a grim laugh. "If you show fight we'll clean you out before you can do us much damage. Better pay up an' pronto. I reckon yore boss wouldn't wanta see those five loads of telegraph poles go up in smoke."

That decided Liligh. He appeared to sink. He sagged as if he had been kicked in the middle. He was fighting fury. There didn't seem to be anything that he could do about it, especially any way to prolong the argument. I had recovered from my own astonishment, and while prey to hot anger myself, I was revolving in mind some desperate chance to take. I determined if we were robbed and these men rode off I certainly would turn loose a rifle upon them.

But on the moment when Liligh surrendered, white in the face and frothing at the mouth, there came a swift thud of horses' hoofs behind our wagon and suddenly there were Shaw and Lowden dashing right up on us, and halting their swift horses to a sliding stop that scattered gravel all over.

I saw the lean rider give a violent start and call in a low sharp voice to the big man: "Bill, heah's yore old friend, Ranger Shaw. We cautioned you about this deal. Now, look out!"

Shaw's lightning gaze appeared to take in all in a single glance. "Liligh, what the hell is goin' on here?" he cut out, his voice thin and ice-edged.

"It's a holdup, Shaw. This feller claims we cut our telegraph poles from his homestead timber. He wants five thousand dollars. Says to produce the money pronto or fight. It's the damnedest, most bare-faced outrage I ever heared of."

Shaw's gaze was turned toward the mounted men and I could see only his profile, clean-cut and cold against the golden light, but I gauged his glance by the effect if had on these two robbers. They sat their horses motionless, tightly holding their rifles across the pommels, and facing something dire and terrible that might have appeared like a thunderbolt out of a clear sky.

"Howdy, Bill Peffer," called the cowboy, in a voice that put my teeth on edge. "They say you cain't teach an old dawg new tricks an' here you are rustlin' as always, only you must have forgot yore brand-burnin' tools."

"Shaw, that's my timber—an' I'm gonna be paid fer it."

"Shore as hell you air, but not with easy money, you damn cow thief."

Then followed a tense moment which seemed to me to be the deadly and potent lull before the storm. Lowden, who sat his horse a little behind Shaw, slipped out of his saddle. I noticed that out of the corner of my eye, for I couldn't take my glance from the two ringleaders in this sudden drama.

"Vance, do yu know this feller?" queried Liligh. "Yer talk is shore kinda familiar."

"Know him! I shore do," returned the cowboy, in bitter hardness. "Low-down hombre. I put him in jail in Brownsville for stealin' cattle. He broke jail an' killed our sheriff, an' here I run into him way up on the Wyomin' line."

"Hold! Wait a minute, cowboy," exclaimed Liligh, holding up his hand. "Creighton would rather I paid this man than risk some of us gettin' hurt."

But Shaw might never have heard this appeal, if the cold and menacing front with which he opposed the robber was any indication. "Peffer, thet's what I couldn't stand about the ranger service. Arrestin' low-down hombres instead of killin' them! I should have bored you when I had the chanct."

"Shaw—don't start anythin' hyar. We'll be on our way," returned Peffer harshly, his livid face dropping beads of sweat. He was shaking from head to foot and he crouched over his saddle. His action was that of an irresistible intention to jerk the gripped rifle over his pommel. It pointed in the wrong direction for him.

In a flash Shaw was out of his saddle and when he darted from behind his horse his gun was belching red flame and smoke. One of the two horsemen let out a mortal scream. I did not recognize which one. The big man lurched in his saddle throwing his rifle with upflung arms to pitch heavily to the ground where he began to flop.

The second rider had jerked into some kind of action which had been frozen by Shaw's fire and he slumped out of his saddle like an empty sack. His rifle fell on him. He never moved again. The horses plunged away clearly exposing the two men on the ground and on the instant the big man stretched out with his spurs digging the sand and then lay still.

Lowden appeared at Shaw's side and he ran forward, his two guns barking at the other horsemen. The distance was some rods and apparently his shot had no effect. But his intention and his wild yell put that group into furious action. They wheeled their horses and the three in the rear who had retained the halters of the pack animals, dragged them at a gallop.

It was all over so quickly that I could hardly realize it. Shaw, with his smoking gun in his hand, walked over to the two prostrate men, bestowing hardly a glance on the lean fellow; but in the case of the giant he pushed back the black sombrero from the dark face and took a long look. I wondered what was going on in Shaw's mind at the moment. Then, turning away, he flipped his gun, put it back in its sheath, and walked over toward his horse that had made no move at the gun shots.

"Boss," he said, addressing Liligh, "I reckon you ought've treated timber rustlers same as cattle thieves."

"Yeah," returned the foreman. "I see how yu Texans do it. Wal, by the Lord Harry, thet's okay with me, but I wish yu wouldn't leave this camp when I need yu. I been scairt plump out of a year's growth."

When we reached the higher country of Wyoming, I, for one, in my romantic way somehow anticipated a vastly different and more happy continuation of our labors. But the change to more picturesque country, the trees and birds and the wild animals and the colorful growths in the bottom lands along the streams, impelling contrasts to all that weary monotonous desert, did not change our work in the least. It was just as hard, on some days, as it ever had been. We had been driven to a point of physical and mental exhaustion. The telegraph line went up. Each stretch of country brought with it new kinds of obstacles. We had firewood in plenty and fresh meat to eat, but to offset this we had to stand guard for fear of other Indian attacks and again we had to find telegraph poles where they did not grow. Along here we had no company except the Pony Express riders coming from the west. What the Pony Express riders told us might better have been left untold. The threatened war between cattlemen and cowboys in the Sweetwater Valley had become a reality, and everything we heard about South Pass tended toward the conviction that the line would be harder to run through that place than anywhere in its whole length.

The Indians became bolder and we had several brushes with them. One night while I was in our wagon alone, when the cowboys had led a posse of men out after strayed or stolen oxen, I had a nightmare experience. After a day of more than usual labor, I finally fell asleep despite myself. I do not think I was awakened by noise, but something strange and terrible disrupted my slumber. It was full moon and the light shone through the canvas covering of our wagon. When I opened my eyes I was horrified and almost paralyzed to see the dark shadow of an Indian standing over my bunk with an upraised tomahawk. It was a wild and sinister image. Perhaps my violent start or jump was as much instinctive as anything else. At any rate when I rolled off my bunk that tomahawk descended on the pillow where my head had lain. As the next move in the midnight drama, I quickly grabbed my gun and shot the Indian.

As I dragged his warm limp body out of the wagon, shuddering at the hot blood that got on my hands, I commended my foresight in packing my gun when I went to bed. I was still too much of a tenderfoot to sleep any more after that. I waited up for the boys to return and hid under the wagon with my rifle in hand peering out through the spokes of the wheels and listening to the night's sounds.

Thus our days and nights were marked by incidents that had never been on the program of our construction work. While these things happened, the telegraph line went up day after day, week after week.

But on our arrival at the Laramie River, word passed from mouth to mouth that now we would be held up, for the Laramie was in flood. And while we made camp in the early cold twilight, some one of our men reported that a stage-coach and a number of freighters were halted on the other bank and that Sunderlund's wagon-train was stuck on this very side of the Laramie little more than a stone's throw from where we had halted.

That night I spent a long time pacing up and down in the starlight, listening to the roar of the flooded river and gradually succumbing to sweet hopes and fears that would not be denied now that I was in the vicinity of Kit Sunderlund again. Shaw and both the other boys left to go somewhere. As they did not come back, I thought I had better get to bed. And I did so, soon falling asleep despite my qualms.

Next morning we were called before sunrise. Our old devil driver, our great leader Creighton, had ordered that we cross the Laramie River. Liligh, who knew all about these northern rivers, threw up his hands and raged impotently. Although the men seemed grimly resigned to whatever might happen, I failed to see any opposition to our leader's command.

After breakfast, while Tom and Jack were bringing in the oxen and the horses Shaw went with me to take a look at the river. We had pulled up close to Sunderlund's camp and the bustle and activity over there intimated that Creighton's arrival with his soldiers and men had prompted Sunderlund to attempt the crossing also. His cattle train was not anything like as large as it had been, and the herd of Texas longhorns was only a patch on the original number.

Presently I stood on the banks of the Laramie River in flood. How high the stream might have been normally I could not judge, but the river was bank-full now, muddy and swift, eddying and gurgling, full of drift-wood and debris. It was narrower than I had imagined. Our shore took off at a jump into deep water and it looked as if, on the other side, some distance below, the stream widened and flowed over what must have been shallow bars, for there were snags and stranded logs and tufts of willow sticking out of the water. We could see columns of blue smoke and wagons on the other side, and oxen and mules grazing on the grass.

"She's on the rise," said Shaw, after a survey of the flooded stream, "an' I reckon we'll do well to cross pronto. Probably this river is one thet has a flood after every thunder-storm up at the haidwaters. In Texas I've seen a wall of water ten feet high come roarin' around a bend to nail us cowboys an' cattle before we could cross."

"Vance, I should think this crossing would be terribly dangerous," I said, ponderingly.

"Dangerous? Hell, yes. Shore it's dangerous. Ain't you got used to thet yet? But I never seen any mules or oxen that couldn't swim. Occasionally there's a cow or a steer that cain't an' just rolls under. The danger here is the swift current an' thet it might carry the wagons beyond thet point across there where it would be easy to wade out."

While we were studying the situation and talking, Liligh came out and joined us with Wainwright and Edney.

"What yu think, Vance?" asked the foreman.

"Wal, boss, we're just goin' across, thet's all," drawled Shaw. "But mebbe thet Sunderlund outfit will have some hell. I reckon he wants some help from us."

"Yes, he asked fer it an' Creighton bragged how we'd take his outfit across bag an' baggage with his longhorns to boot. Jest as if we wouldn't hev trouble enough on our own!"

"Aw, we'll make it, all right. I'm suggestin' thet we pull up river as far as the take-off is good so we can slant down an' hit this shallow place below here. I reckon Jack an' I will pile in heah on our hawses an' go across just to see how an' where the bottom is. Thet current is pretty swift. But whatever we do, we want to do it pronto an' advise Sunderlund to do the same."

In less than an hour the wagon-trains were rolling up river to a point some hundreds of yards above where Sunderlund had camped and they congregated there awaiting orders. When Tom and I drove up to join them we found ourselves in the thick of the caravan and some rods from the river bank.

It disturbed my equilibrium somewhat to discover that there were a good many Sunderlund wagons around us. But I resisted my inclination to look around and centered upon the river. Above where the wagons were congregated Sunderlund's cattle had been driven to the bank in a wedge shape with the sharp end forward.

Counting the riders on each side and those in the rear of the herd, there must have been a dozen of them mounted on horses, in addition to Shaw and Lowden who were at the extreme front end of the wedge. It was evident that our cowboys were going to lead the herd across. There was no hesitation about it and the cattle did not seem to be alarmed.

When the shooting and yelling began in the rear the mass of cattle moved forward and shoved the others into the river. They piled and slid off with great splashes and some of them went clear out of sight soon to emerge with noses out of the water. Lowden swam his horse above the point of the herd and Shaw moved at about the same distance below.

I stood up on the driver's seat the better to see. Used as I was to danger, I still could not control my agitation. Before the rear end of the herd had reached the river bank the first animals were halfway across and down river to a point below where I stood. The current swept them downward quite swiftly. The cowboys continued to shoot and yell and soon the whole herd was in the river strung out, disintegrated from its wedge formation, but valiantly stemming the flood.

It really was a beautiful sight. I saw a long line of wide horns sticking out of the water and I was amazed to notice how surprisingly easy it looked. Two hundred yards below my position Shaw and Lowden got out of deep water on to the bar and waded out with the animals close behind. There was hardly a doubt in my mind that the leaders of the herd followed the cowboys. They were used to crossing rivers that way.

In what seemed an astoundingly short time the cattle were wading out into the thicket on the opposite shore and when they were all out the cowboys rode up the opposite bank to a point as far as I could see, where they made ready to return.

The return crossing was a different proposition. Owing to the steepness of the bank on our side they had to hit the leveled-off place where the herd had been driven off the bank. It was exciting to watch and most satisfactory to see the return safely accomplished.

It developed that there was much more order and precision about the cattle crossing than there would be in the case of the wagons. Excitement and hurry, much jostling and noise complicated matters. The first wagons to make the attempt drove off with a rush, the huge prairie schooners careening and the double team of oxen dipping clear out of sight. The wagon beds sank a couple of feet, presently to rise buoyantly and with the oxen up and swimming and a man on each side mounted on a mule urging them on. They seemed to be having no difficulty.

"Say, pard," said Darnell, "I ain't so damn shore of two of my oxen. They gave me trouble before in the water an' I reckon you better fork my hoss an' ride upstream beside us so if my oxen stall or drown I can pile out of this here seat and grab my hoss' tail so you can drag me out. Don't look like that, Wayne. My hoss is grand in the water an' we don't stand to be in any danger, really. But we can't be shore of the oxen an' the wagon. Thet's Creighton's outlook an' we have only to do the best we can."

"Okay, Tom. I'm not blissful at the prospect but——"

I stepped back and untied the halter of Tom's horse and coiling it as I drew the horse up, I mounted from the wagon into the saddle, very much aware of the congestion in my breast and the high beating of my heart.

I had ridden this fine bay horse a number of times and had become accustomed to his spirited action and was grateful that he appeared to take a liking to me. He was big and strong and as far as he was concerned, I felt safe, but I feared a situation with which I would not know how to cope. Still, I thought that this was only another and different kind of adventure and that I'd come safely out of others far more dangerous and that all I needed was nerve and quick thinking to get through with this.

I followed Tom's wagon as he slowly drove up to the jumping-off place. It was a scene of confusion and noise. The fording of wagons had gotten under way. The many wheels and hoofs that had already gone over the bank had cut it down until the slant to the water did not seem at all precipitous.

As I took my place to the right of Tom there were three wagons ahead of us all in process of taking off, perhaps a dozen yards apart. Some of the oxen teams apparently did not have to be urged and there were others that had to be beaten.

When this trio finally started it was certainly something to see. The heavy wagons pushed the oxen into the river and, as in the first case, the front of the wagon up to the driver's seat went under water with a great splash. For a moment I held my breath. But again the oxen came up and the wagons were buoyant. The noses and horns of the animals were above the surface of the swirling current. The drivers stood up to the reins and ceased yelling. Then the swift current caught the wagons and they were carried down stream a good deal faster than they moved across.

Ahead of them and floating down in a long slant were other prairie schooners, some close together and others wide apart, all striving to reach the long shallow point. As far as I could see, they were not having any trouble.

Edney and Wainwright and Herb Lane had lined up beside Darnell. Herb Lane yelled to our men, "Follow me in single file, not too close. It won't do to get bunched. The river is rising and full of driftwood. Come on in!"

One by one the big wagons slid down the incline and took to the water. Darnell was last, not far from Wainwright, and I did not have to urge my horse. He stepped down to the water's edge at Tom's ringing call, and then he just plunged in, all but his nose going under and immersing me to above my waist. It was a shock to me, but the moment I felt him come up and breast the current, my trepidation changed to exhilaration. That horse liked the water and he certainly could swim. I had to hold him back to keep him from getting ahead of Tom.

"All you have to do is to look out for driftwood," yelled Tom. "If any runs into you, lean over and shove it aside. But if you watch carefully you can dodge the pieces."

In another moment we had passed the line of foliage on the near side and were out in the river. As far as we were concerned there did not seem to be anything to it. Darnell had been worried about his leading team of oxen but they seemed to me to do very well. I kept even with Tom about thirty feet up stream and now I felt quite safe on the horse. The three Creighton wagons were ahead of us, then there was an open space of water and then wagons scattered here and there on the way across.

Looking up stream, I noted that the current had apparently swelled and that there was more driftwood than before we started. Glancing backward, I saw that the wagons were hurriedly lining up, with drivers and soldiers on mules and men on foot shouting and gesticulating. There seemed to be more alarm than had been manifest before. That must have been because of the sudden rise in the river and I called to Tom about it. He shouted back that he was afraid the crest of the flood was reaching us and that those wagons which did not get across pronto might meet with a lot of trouble.

Creighton's loads of telegraph poles were lined up on the bank ready to start when they had a chance and behind them was a congested mass of oxen and wagons consisting of the soldiers' wagon-train, three or four of Creighton's, and the remainder and greater number belonging to Sunderlund's caravan.

"Look out for that floatin' tree!" yelled Tom. "Some of the branches will be under water an' if one of them catches you, it'll be Katy-bar-the-door!"

It was a small tree, apparently dead, for it did not have any leaves on the branches, rolling over and over in the current. It got pretty close to me, then stopped momentarily, one of its branches having caught the bottom; which was just long enough for Tom and me to get out of its path.

I began to worry that we might miss the shallow point which was now getting close. But when I saw Herb Lane ground and his oxen emerge to begin to wade I felt reassured. Wainwright followed close on his heels, and when Edney's wagon was halfway to shore across that shallow point, the foremost team on Tom's wagon struck bottom, strained and plunged, caught hold with their powerful hoofs and pulled the second team and the wagon out of deep water. My horse next found bottom and he announced the fact with a satisfied snort.

We waded out. Once out on dry land Darnell halted his oxen to give them a breathing spell and to look back up the river.

"Some sight, hey, Wayne?" he shouted. "If that mess of wagons come through all right, it'll be a miracle. I don't see how Sunderlund's drivers could still be green hands after their long drive up through Texas but evidently they are. Mebbe they didn't strike any flooded rivers, such as Shaw has told us about."

"Tom, it sure is a sight," I agreed, as I surveyed the scene. What struck me was the silence of the approaching wagons as contrasted with their take-off. Back there on the shore, however, where it seemed to me they were piling over the bank too swiftly and too close together, there was a babble of hoarse shouts that I could hear distinctly that long distance away.

"Wal, pard, I gotta be gettin' out of here," called Tom, taking up his reins. "That first wagon will be on top of me if I don't."

"I should smile it will, Tom. Get going," I yelled. "But what ought I do?"

"I reckon you better stay here jest a little below where we waded out. Mebbe you could help somebody. Don't worry none about Wingfoot. That hoss is some relation to a duck and he'll take care of you."

When Tom drove up the well-defined muddy road into the timber and the next wagon came wading out, I crossed the track to a point below and rode out on the sand bar until I was just at the edge of the swift current. I did not see what good I could do in case a wagon was swept beyond that point but I was keen to find out.

It was a good vantage point from which to watch the procession heading down the stream. Here I was able to note that the river had already risen a foot or two since we had started. The several logs of driftwood which had stranded on this shallow bar had floated away and the water was considerably farther up among the weeds and willows. Then there was more driftwood.

I could see one large tree, evidently a cottonwood to judge from its green foliage, rolling over in midcurrent way up the river beyond the taking-off place. Surely the drivers would have to avoid that dangerous piece. One by one the wagons came down straight as a bee-line, with their oxen striking the shallow water and heaving the wagons out on the hard bottom to wag up the gentle slope into the timber. Then they began to come in twos and threes, calculating their position so that they would hit above the shallow point.

In a very few moments it seemed the last of them had left the bank and there was a flotilla of white canvas tops gliding smoothly down the river. It was a remarkable sight. It brought into my mind the exploits of the early pioneers who had braved this unknown West without having any precedent to go by.

With the remaining wagons in the river, somewhere between thirty and forty, I calculated, the clamor and bustle that had marked our exodus had ceased. Only an occasional yell and pistol shot rang out. Above my position on the bank I noticed a group of spectators, some of them mounted Indians, all deeply interested in the crossing.

Facing the river again I saw the rolling green tree right in the midst of the wagons. It caught several of them, fortunately to slide off. Once a couple of soldiers swimming their mules laid hold of this piece of driftwood and pulled it or retarded it until the current slid it away from the wagon that it had imperiled. But this action endangered the prairie schooner behind and the one on the outside and farthest down stream. There were four oxen to this wagon and they did not appear to be breaking the current any too well.

Just at that minute there was a jam among the wagons behind and closer in shore, and the mounted soldiers and several other men on horses hurriedly got into the thick of the mêlée, no doubt to help the drivers extricate their oxen. The situation looked pretty bad but my calculation was that this tangle of wagons would drift upon the shallow bar whether they were able to untangle or not.

The small prairie schooner on the outside, however, could not avoid the green rolling tree which lodged squarely against the wheels. I saw the trunk of the cottonwood bob up behind the wagon, showing that it was quite long and that its weight would probably swing the tree around so that it would slide away from the wagon. But this did not happen. Already the wagon was out of line with the shallow point where I stood. In a few moments, if it did not get free of the tree, it would be carried beyond the point into the deep rough water around the bend.

I urged Wingfoot out into the river and waded him until he got beyond his depth. I had no idea what I should do except to get near the wagon and rescue the driver before the wagon was carried away. I was close enough now to make out the driver, who was a Negro and who was straining on his reins as if for dear life and bawling at his oxen. A fraction of a second later I made the astounding discovery that beside the Negro sat Kit Sunderlund with white face and wide dark eyes.

A hot gush of blood rushed all over me. My thoughts whirled over and over until for a moment I was absolutely helpless. Then she saw me and recognized me. She waved both hands frantically, and called out in a sweet high treble something that I could not distinguish except that it seemed a terrified appeal for help.

I spurred Wingfoot up stream and in a moment more he was even with the wagon and some fifty feet or more distant. I turned him then and we went down stream with the current, gradually approaching the wagon. The front team of oxen almost submerged and the second team could make no headway with that long tree lodged against the wheels.

I made the appalling observation then that only the noses of the second brace of oxen were above water and that the front of the wagon was sinking and the rear end lifting. In that position wagon and oxen drifted below the shallow point and headed around the curve.

The rough water with the big muddy waves extended from the middle to the opposite side of the river and, of course, if the wagon drifted among them it would be lost. But I believed that I could save the driver and the girl. The danger for me was in approaching too close to the tree lodged against the wagon and thus getting my horse tangled among the branches. So I forged ahead at the same time that I drew closer.

"Now, Sambo," I yelled, with all my might, "get off the wagon, take the girl—and swim till I can pick you up. I don't dare come any closer. One of these snags might catch the horse."

The Negro relinquished the reins and when he stood up to help the girl he was up to his knees in water. As he was about to help her the wagon gave a tremendous lurch, and the log bumped against it with a great splash, throwing him and the girl into the water.

They both went under. When they came up they were some feet apart and it was evident that the Negro was not an expert swimmer. Kit, however, could swim well enough to keep from drifting into the wagon or the oxen but there was great danger of her being struck by one of the branches that were thrashing about her. I realized that I had to get hold of her at once, so I spurred Wingfoot straight down stream.

As I was reaching for her one of the branches swung low, narrowly missing me and knocking the girl under water. But I got hold of her and reining the valiant animal away from the danger of colliding with the oxen and wagon, I dragged her out of harm's way. Wingfoot was making fast time when his progress was impeded. I thought one of the branches had caught us. I turned to discover that the Negro had caught the horse's tail and was hanging on to it. That was all right and as soon as I got the girl's head and shoulders up on my knee and we were headed shoreward, free from that wreck behind us I lost the icy grip of fright.

We made for the shore, even while we were being carried around the bend. I heard a loud splash and looking back saw that the tree that was obstructing the wagon had caught the current on its trunk end and was torn free from the wagon which righted itself with the second brace of oxen still swimming. They were drifting and floating out of the current.

Before I even hoped for such good fortune, Wingfoot found bottom and with a tremendous heave and snort he began wading and in short order brought us to safety. I slipped out of the saddle in water up to my waist and caught the girl in my arms. There was blood on her temple but she was conscious. I picked her up and waded ashore where I set her on her feet. Apparently she was not badly hurt for she could stand with my help. Wingfoot was following me and the Negro was rising to his feet, evidently none the worse for the accident.

Below us some distance the sturdy oxen were dragging their drowned companions and the wagon toward the shore. Then I noted that the animals had struck bottom for their shoulders and yokes heaved out and they plunged shoreward until the wagon with the front end submerged became stuck.

"Sambo, we've had luck," I said. "You can save that wagon. Run up the bank and fetch men to help you."

With that I started to walk up the sloping bank supporting the girl. "Well—that was a go!" I panted. "But we got out. . . . Are you all right—are you hurt?"

"I—I think I'm alive," she whispered, faintly, clinging to my arm. "I was stunned—by something. Then I swallowed—a lot—of that muddy water."

"Gosh, what good fortune that it's no worse!" I ejaculated. "Come, you're not walking very well."

"I—I'm afraid I'll—have to rest a little," she murmured, and she stumbled to her knees.

As I bent over her, supporting her, she let go of me and lay back on the grass. I knelt beside her, and, as I gazed down upon her into the darkly dilated eyes that were fastened with some intense inexplicable expression upon me, I was divided between fear that she might be hurt and an extraordinary sense of her beauty and helplessness, and the wonderful fact that I had saved her.

"Wayne Cameron, you—you—have saved my life again!" she whispered.

"So it seems," I replied, as lightly as I could. "Funny what a habit I have of hanging around when you get in trouble."

"Don't make light of it," she implored. "This—this second time is too much!"

"Oh, you're excited. You're upset, naturally. But don't let it worry you, darling."

"Darling?" Those great unfathomable eyes on me.

"Why, yes—of course. What else?" I replied, somewhat haltingly. "I'm one of these unfortunate people who, well, who never recover from——"

I did not know how to end the sentence, with her eyes fixed upon me. As a matter of fact, I was quite out of my head, but not so much that I did not begin to think of her condition.

"From what?" she asked, her voice stronger.

"Never mind what, Kit. I must get you away from here. You're all wet."

"Wayne? From what?"

"Well, if you insist, from the absolutely irresistible charm of a girl who thought bad things about me."

"Oh, forgive me—please," she implored. "Vance Shaw called on me last night. What he said to me—oh, I can never forget. It made me so small. . . . Forgive me, Wayne. Let me explain."

"Well, Kit Sunderlund, I will consider it," I replied, gravely, gazing down upon her. "But don't talk any more now. I must get up to the wagon-train. . . . Let's see, there's a cut and a bruise above your temple but it doesn't look bad and the scar won't show."

"As if my looks would ever make any difference again," she murmured.

"Lady, a thing of beauty is a joy forever. Don't underrate it. Now, let me help you up and on the horse."

I lifted her sideways into the saddle and ascertaining that she would be able to sit there and hold on I took up the bridle and led a zigzag way up through the willows and the cottonwoods, my heart painfully full.

Guided by the noise, I soon found my way to her wagon-train and eventually found Sunderlund who had safely crossed and who had been running around frantically in search of his daughter. I cut short his extravagant gratitude and directed him to where no doubt Sambo was already trying to extricate their wagon. Then I led Wingfoot off, glad to get away by myself.

When I reached the bank, the latter third of the wagon-train was still coming and evidently would make the crossing safely. To my great relief Creighton's four wagons full of telegraph poles had gained the shallow water. My first instinct was to slip away to find out where I was in regard to Kit Sunderlund. But I ran into Tom and Shaw. Tom whooped and made a grab for me and Shaw softly swore at me under his breath. Then Creighton burst upon me, wet, bedraggled, grimy, but beaming.

"Cameron, I've been hunting for you. Our telegraph poles are all across, thanks be, and that was my main worry. Nobody lost, but several men cut up bad, and you better get busy with your medicine kit."

It would have been much more pleasurable, not to say thrilling, for me to have stood on the bank to watch the wagons make their way across the river and safely up on the shore, than to have gone among those who had been injured in the crossing and minister to their needs. But I had my orders and even if I had not, I would have sacrificed my thirst for excitement for duty. Indeed, I was thankful that I was equipped to perform it.

It took me until sunset to care for all those that had been hurt. Only one man had been injured badly and it turned out that his injury was not too serious. Nearly all Creighton's wagon-train made the crossing without loss and Sunderlund's big caravan had not suffered in much greater degree.

Miss Sunderlund's wagon had been hauled out safely without any material damage to this little home of hers on wheels. Her Negro maid had been found in a faint upon the floor of the wagon. The forward team of oxen had drowned and it really was remarkable that under the circumstances the wagon had been saved.

When I finished my work I returned to see the telegraph line already stretched across the river and hooked on to a pole, and I asked Darnell how they managed to get it across. He told me Shaw had recrossed the river on his horse, taking Darnell's horse with him. On reaching the other side, he fastened one end of the wire to the saddle horn of his horse, spoke softly, mounted Darnell's horse and then plunged into the stream, his trained animal following. Creighton was so well pleased that the entire crossing was so successful that he raised one of his small American flags to the top of the first telegraph pole west of the Laramie, and called out in his stentorian voice, "On to Ft. Bridger!"

Chapter Twelve

I HAD started to walk away from our camp to look for Mr. Creighton when Vance Shaw caught up with me. He smiled and in his eyes was a look I had not seen for many a day.

"I saw you pull Kit Sunderlund out of the river today. Santa Maria, the luck of some people," he beamed.

"Luck? How do you call it luck unless you mean bad?"

"Wal, Wayne, comin' so quick after the little talk I had with the lady, it's just about too damn good to be true," drawled the cowboy. "Because thet haughty lady will be on her knees to you forever afterwards."

"Wonderful, from your point of view!"

"Wal, this has been comin' to Kit for a long time, pard, but outside of her just deserts, it just worked out grand. I found out just how terribly she is in love with you."

"Vance, don't give me that talk. What I want to know once and for all—are you in love with her?"

"Me! In love with her? Hell no," Vance said, and looked away into the distance. His eyes were seeing something beyond the horizon and they were sad.

There was a silence for a moment and I knew then I had been a blundering idiot and that it was not Kit Sunderlund that Shaw loved, but Ruby.

"Vance," I said, "tell me just what you said to Kit."

"Lord, I disremember, but I gave her hell," Vance said, looking back at me.

"All right, then, don't tell me. But don't you think at least that you owe some sort of an explanation to your tenderfoot friend?"

"Wal, Wayne, it's like this, and only Lowden knows: down in Texas I was so dawg-gone mad in love with Kit I couldn't see. Maybe she didn't lead me on and maybe she did. Damned if I know now. But each time you knew I went to see her, it was just on account of I made up my mind to butt right into yore affairs. You see, knowin' you and knowin' her, I just did the best I could figger to keep you two apart until I was damn sure that Kit felt about you the way you felt about her. And not the way she felt about me down in Texas. Pard, whatever anybody tells you as to why I left Texas, or whatever you heard me say, this is the truth—I left on account of her."

"That's all right, Vance," I said, trying to sound facetious, "but how about my finding her in your arms that night?"

"Wal, Yank, I see you still ain't learned too much. You ask too damn many questions. Howsomever, I'll give you the answer. Just a second before you came, I got through telling Kit that while you're no longer a tenderfoot as far as the West was concerned, you were still a damn tenderfoot in your heart. And loving you, she seemed to kinda like what I said, and that was her way of just sort of thankin' me for sayin' it. If I was you I'd look at thet full moon comin' up over the prairie an' I'd hunt Kit up pronto. 'Cause, my proud Yankee pard, you can have thet lovely girl in yore arms for the askin'!"

I plunged away from Shaw blindly. It might have been

fortunate for me that it took time for me to find Sunderlund's wagons. They were some distance from our camp up the river and located on the bank within the sound of the rushing water. There was a bright camp fire around which the Negroes were cleaning up and Sunderlund sat with the cattlemen partners, smoking and talking. His reception of me and that of his friends was most cordial.

"Well, Sunderlund, if you ask me, we were all mighty lucky," I replied. "According to Creighton that's just another ordinary incident past. But I called to ask after Miss Sunderlund."

"She's all right. You'd never guess she came near drownin'," returned Sunderlund, heartily.

"Mr. Cameron, why don't you come and see for yourself," called Kit from the wagon. And her voice was gay and carried a rich warm note.

I walked the few paces to the end of her wagon and there she sat in white with both the moonlight and the fire light shining in upon her. Notwithstanding my extravagant thoughts about her, she was a revelation to me. But, of course, I had never seen her dressed like that.

"Oh!" I exclaimed, "if you're able to—to make yourself look lovely like that, you must be all right after your fright."

"All right?" she questioned, archly. "That is relative. If you mean well—and quite happy—I am."

"I'm very glad. I thought you might have felt the worse for your accident. You had one knock I know of and then there must have been a shock——"

"Shock!" she exclaimed. "Indeed there was. I have been waiting here, hoping you would come to let me tell you about it. You know—you said you would consider."

"I will, if you'll put on a coat and walk with me a little. It's a lovely night, not so cold as usual, and almost as bright as day."

In another moment she emerged from the wagon clothed in a long dark coat with a hood around her head, and she took my arm and we walked away along the river bank. There was nothing lagging in her step. I ventured to think she was a strong girl to come through that ordeal with such composure and strength.

I felt pretty much embarrassed because she appeared like a stranger to me, and a tall lovely stranger at that, her clear pale profile exposed to the moonlight and strands of chestnut hair moving slightly in the breeze. I wished I could have burst out into speech but I could only be silent. I divined that this hour would be a crucial one in my life, and I had to stem my mad hopes with what rational thought I could summon.

Without a word we passed some distance up the bank and halted in a picturesque spot under the big cottonwood where a huge fallen log obstructed our path.

"Really, Kit, I should not let you walk too far," I said, earnestly. "This is a nice dry spot where you can sit down."

She made no move to seat herself and as I leaned against the log she stood in the moonlight facing me, still retaining her hold on my arm.

"I'm not so excited and therefore not so brave as I was down there on the river bank, after you rescued me," she said, a little haltingly.

"You don't have to be brave to tell me anything," I replied.

"It requires more courage than you think—for me," she resumed, with dark eyes studying my face. "We might have a great deal to say to each other, but in any event I have to tell you something—to explain, and again beg your forgiveness."

"All right, if you insist. I don't mind telling you that once I would have reveled in such a situation. But now there is nothing to forgive. I'm just happy to be with you."

"Don't heap coals of fire upon my head. There are two reasons—that will explain my weakness. I've been used to cowboys all my life. They are a lovable bad lot. Dad says Texas could not have been settled without cowboys. They are grand fighters as you well know by this time. But they haven't any morals. I became used to having them come to me after a rendezvous with some other girl and make love to me, swear unutterable devotion to me, and ask me to marry them. Vance Shaw did that often, but, in spite of the looseness of his character, I

202

liked him very, very much—almost loved him. Vance is chivalrous and fine but he just couldn't understand my point of view. Wayne, I hope you understand."

"Kit, I do understand you but I'm sure you have misjudged Shaw. But you go on and finish what you want to say."

"Anyway, that was one of my weaknesses. The other was something that I did not know very well I possessed. It is jealousy. At first sight, almost, I saw that you were the man for me. How I fell—all about it—I can confess later, if you want to hear it, but I was jealous. When just by chance I happened to look in your wagon and saw that big-eyed girl almost undressed—surely the prettiest thing that I ever saw—I was consumed with a burning terrible passion. I imagined you were in love with that pretty little dance-hall girl—to my everlasting shame, I confess I imagined even more. . . . Vance made me see last night not only my horrible mistake but what a shallow jealous cat I am. All the time it was Shaw who was in love with her. What a fool I was."

"Well, Kit, if it has relieved you, I'm glad. Of course he meant to marry Ruby. The singular thing about that girl is how her helpless plight appealed to the man in all of us. She had the youth and beauty and character which, coupled with an appallingly sad situation, touched us all. I would have done anything for Ruby. I can judge of Vance's heart only by this: since Ruby has been gone he is a changed man."

"Wayne, I hope you will champion me as you do him," she responded softly. "And now—am I to be forgiven?"

"Kit, you were forgiven before this," I replied, and I kissed her hand.

"Then what?"

I repeated her query. "I don't just understand you."

"What was it you called me back there on the river bank?"

"Oh! That was just a slip. It was natural, at the moment. Believe me, Kit, that was an overpowering situation for me."

"But if it was a slip—" she began.

"I don't mean it was a slip in sincerity. I think I should not have been so familiar in addressing the proud southern beauty."

"It has been used to me before many a time, but hardly with my consent and never with any of the feeling which it aroused in me when you used it."

"May I inquire just what that feeling was?" I asked, a little huskily, still trying to preserve my equanimity.

"Love."

The answer to that was spontaneous and irresistible. "You are a darling rebel!"

"If I *am* a rebel—I'm conquered."

And then as if of one mind, we were in each other's arms. For me her kisses were the epitome of all the beauty and wonder of this great West and for the time being I lost my sense of time and place, of the bright moon shining down upon the swirling river, the murmur of the flowing water, the wailing of the coyotes, and the wind in the cottonwoods. When we did emerge from that blissful unthinking state, I imagined from the rapt look upon Kit's beautiful face that it was the same to her as it was to me.

"Darling, I think we should be going back to the wagons, where I think it will be fitting for me to tell your father and ask his consent."

"Wayne, that will be granted," she said, with a low happy laugh. "He said that you were one Yankee he admired. But, after all, hadn't you better ask me first?"

"Kit, I thought *you* would take it for granted, from all I was saying—that I was *begging* you to marry me."

"No, dear, I didn't exactly. A girl—has to be asked. . . . I accept you, Wayne, and—and I'm unutterably happy. Oh, if you but knew the many miserable hours I lay awake at night torturing myself about you!"

"You could not possibly have suffered more than I. . . . Then, we are really engaged?"

"Indeed, sir, you are, and I will hold you to it. Have you a ring?"

"No, ma'am. I'm sorry to say I haven't and I wonder where in this uncivilized country I can get one?"

"Here, I have one," she said softly. "It was my

mother's. You wear it until you can get me one." And slipping the ring on my little finger where it fitted fairly well she continued, "Now, let us go back to camp. I will tell Dad. We have much to talk over. Soon we shall be in the Sweetwater Valley. Dear, when you are finished with the Western Union, come to me there."

Ft. Laramie occupied a commanding and picturesque site on the north bank of the Laramie River. It was a large structure, crudely but solidly built of heavy timbers, and had a high tower in front and bastions at two ends. In my first glance at the fort I saw the soldier sentries patrolling the platforms around these bastions, rifles on shoulders, on guard duty. Green hills ran down to the edge of the river, in marked and beautiful contrast to the monotonous prairie that we had traveled for so long. Back of the fort toward the slope of the hill was an encampment of Sioux, their high conical tents shining almost white in the sunlight. We made our camp well away from the fort; and Sunderlund, with his large caravan, camped still farther down the river.

This fort, the largest and most famous fort on the frontier, had been erected about 1841. It was a main stop on the Oregon Trail and still a meeting place for Indian tribes and trappers.

Later in the day when our work had been done and Ft. Laramie was brought into telegraphic communication with the East, the officers and soldiers made much of Creighton and his men and staged something of a celebration.

Barnes, the Pony Express rider, who had made friends with the cowboys and me, had arrived that day and took dinner with us.

"I got a lot to tell you, boys," he said, when we had repaired to our own camp fire and settled down. "South Pass is shore hummin' these days. You'll get the treat of yore life when you get that far. An' if you don't watch close an' stay away from town after dark an' out of the gamblin' dens, you'll get robbed of all you have an' probably knocked on the head in the bargain. I hear conflictin' reports about how the Western Union is regarded in South Pass. Most of the men I talked to think it is a grand idea an' will help settle the West. I heared it whispered, too, that there are some agin the telegraph, for reasons I can't imagine. Lord knows, yo're gonna have trouble enough gettin' up the Sweetwater an' over the Pass without havin' any opposition from white men. But I've a hunch you will have."

Other news imparted by Barnes, we received with heartfelt gladness. Brigham Young with his young Mormons was rapidly pushing the Western Union east toward Ft. Bridger. And the crew working east from Carson City toward Salt Lake City were progressing splendidly. It was a race to see who finished first.

"Let me tell you again, you cowboys, an' you too, Cameron, if what I hear about you is true," concluded Barnes, "the cattle business in western Wyomin' is goin' to be one grand bonanza. Shore there won't be gold to pick out of the streets like there is in South Pass, but there'll be a fortune for every one of you."

For several days out of Ft. Laramie I viewed the sylvan scenes of colorful beauty through a rosy haze. The amber light which seemed to hang like a transparent veil over the valleys, the lofty purple hills and the rugged gray bluffs, and the shining streams flowing between banks lined with golden and green cottonwoods—I imagined all this beauty to come from the first flush of the happy sequel to my love affair. But as we worked strenuously from daylight to dark up the river I realized at length that the beauty might have been heightened by my feeling, but it was there, and it increased as we worked west.

As we traveled higher and higher into this Wyoming hinterland the nights grew colder. There was frost in the early morning and that was what painted the leaves in gold and scarlet and brown, every day lending a more varied hue to the landscape. We used the last of our buffalo meat except that which had been made into *pemmican,* and we replaced it with venison and antelope meat and even with bear. I concluded that a rib from a young bear was just as tasty a morsel as the finest piece of buffalo rump steak.

It was on this stretch that we made our best time. Independence Rock, the most famous of the landmarks on the Oregon Trail, seemed to come upon us unawares. The Sweetwater came in here and we heralded sight of it with a loud clamor.

As we hauled up to make camp in a beautiful spot on the river near where the trail rounded the bold corner of the great rock, we were unexpectedly attacked by a band of Cheyennes. We fought from the cover of our wagons and the unerring marksmanship of our members, especially of the cowboys, soon gave that marauding band of Indians all they wanted. We maintained a double guard all night and were extremely vigilant. But the Cheyennes did not return.

Next morning at sunrise, as Liligh's scout assured us the Indians had gone, I climbed, accompanied by Tom, to the summit of Independence Rock. It was a gray granite pile looking as if it were a mosaic of separate rock irregularly joined together and towering at least a hundred feet above the ground. From here I had a wonderful view of the Sweetwater, a clear, amber stream winding away up the valley. This site furnished us an impressive view back over the rugged foothill country through which we had put up the telegraph line.

"Oh, Tom!" I ejaculated, breathing deeply. "It's grand."

"Wal, pard, it *is* pretty nifty, but you're lookin' in the wrong direction. Take a peep off here."

Following his pointing finger my gaze was directed to the northwest and upward to what I thought was the sky. The early morning atmosphere was extremely rare and transparent, and when I saw a magnificent ragged line of white run along the horizon to end in a wide break and then rise again, pure and sharp against the blue sky, I imagined that I was looking at a magnified line of clouds. I had never seen any clouds like these. Below that white ragged line, there was a zigzag belt of black and both the black and white lines ended at the dip in this strange formation to take it up again to the southward. I began to realize that this was not a cloud formation.

"Pard," said my companion, and his voice seemed to

come from far off, "you're takin' your first look at the Rockies. That's the Wind River Range of mountains, the finest range in the West. That break is the Pass you've heard so much about. The early trappers an' explorers went over there. South Pass, the minin' town, is down under this right-hand end. An' there you can see where the white peaks stick up again away to the southward."

So magnificent was the spectacle, so grand this upflinging of the main ridge of the Rocky Mountains that I could not speak. I dragged my gaze from the heights and looked down beneath the Rock to see the white wagontrains, the grazing mules and oxen, the blue columns of smoke trailing upward, the amber river shining between its banks of gold and scarlet. The Sweetwater Valley wound away between its purple hills into the colorful distance, to merge into a dark blue haze, out of which the two grand sawtooth sections of mountain ranges, divided by the pass between them, towered into the infinity of sky above.

Once down off that rock to the solid ground below I could hardly believe what I had seen. Tom showed me a further proof of the reality of the present and that I was actually standing in a place that would be forever historic, by directing my attention to the inscriptions cut in the smooth surfaces of the rock. Everywhere, in every place where a name or a date could be cut, there were inscriptions. Some were undoubtedly very old and a few were new. Every traveler who passed Independence Rock, and had the time, cut his name thereon.

Straightway I returned to the wagon and getting the ax and one of those discarded buffalo spikes, I cut my initials in the stone and those of my sweetheart. Then I added my comrades'. I laughed at myself as a sentimentalist but with the reservation that emotion enriched life's experiences.

Of all our camps, that was the hardest one to leave. Everybody I spoke to shared my opinion. Even Creighton said he hoped the rest of the camps would be like this one. But though travel up the Sweetwater seemed to be approaching paradise, the digging of post holes, the raising of poles and wires, the tamping down of rocks and earth into the holes, went relentlessly on and on and on. There had always been drive behind us, but now there was more. There was accomplishment—almost eight hundred miles of telegraph line raised and taking messages. I worked on, possessed by these inspiring thoughts, alternating with memory of the lovely girl I had won; and the days were as nothing.

I was so engrossed with dreams as I plodded on with my tasks that I failed to make a most thrilling discovery. Darnell brought it to my attention. The Sweetwater was full of trout, some of them as long as my arm. I loved to fish and every night when we knocked off work I chased grasshoppers over the level ground and pounced upon them with my sombrero to use them as bait for the big trout. It seemed another dream but it was nevertheless true that every time I cast one of these big juicy grasshoppers into the Sweetwater there would be a gleam of gold and red, a swirl on the water and I would be fast to a big wolf-jawed trout.

Of all the long trek, these days on the Sweetwater were ones that the hardest kind of labor could not spoil. To me they were unforgettable. The beauty, the color, the wild nature and wild life, the savages passing silhouetted over a ridge, the smoke signals, the never ending and always changing loveliness—these were rewards to me for far more than I had suffered, and were actual fulfillment of my dreams.

Chapter Thirteen

I, FOR one, did not compute the remaining distance on the Trail to Green River or Ft. Bridger where we expected to meet the Mormon telegraph builders working east. But I could not help but hear Liligh's men discussing it. Darnell became more silent and watchful as we neared the scene of his ruin and where certainly he could expect trouble. Yet his devotion to me never flagged. It was a different kind of friendship from that which the other cowboys had for me. I was afraid Tom had somehow made a hero out of me.

The Oregon Trail crept in a winding gradual ascent up this long slope to the continental divide. Therefore the erecting of telegraph poles and the raising of the wires took longer per mile. But to offset this our leader got us up in the white frosty dawn and made camp when darkness prohibited further work.

The days were growing shorter but the daylight hours afforded us the finest weather we had experienced. The sun was good and warm and really hot at noon.

But the sun went down early behind the silver-edged ragged line of peaks, and from then on it grew colder almost by the minute. We were getting up to high ground. Our great hope and purpose was to cross South Pass and get down off the backbone of the divide before winter caught us, and at the rate we were going we would succeed. As the days went on, we lost the rich thick amber light of the lower country. It was replaced by an austere light that had no color in it until sunset's wonderful transformation. After the gold had faded a clear cold darkness spread down the slope bringing with it the night wind through the canvas tops of our wagon. After dark, the vault of the sky was deeply blue, fired by white stars cold as ice. It was beautiful but I preferred lower altitudes.

We were less alone now in our work than at any time since we had started. Travel from Laramie and points east grew to be heavy. Only one wagon-train passed us and that was a small one. Every day, however, there were freighters, stage-coaches, mounted men with pack animals, and, of course, the Pony Express riders.

I thought the majority of my comrades directed their hopeful gaze over the Pass, but I was afraid my dreamy looking to the future was taken out in long steady gaze down the slope to the purple Sweetwater Valley with its winding ribbon of shining stream bordered by lines of gold. My heart was down there and I believed I would have wanted to make a home there even if Kit Sunderlund had never come into my life.

We slowly crawled up the slope like a gigantic snake, stretching the telegraph line. For some time we had seen the black and yellow smoke of the huge stamp mill marking the gold digging of South Pass. We were within a week's hard work of this objective when one morning Vance Shaw rode back to the caravan from his daily scouting trip ahead.

This time he dismounted beside our wagon where Tom and I were busy at our tasks and the other men were stretched out before and behind us.

"Bad news, pards, an' it's got me stumped," he said. "Jack, go after Liligh an' Herb Lane an' don't mention what I say. If the big boss should see you an' ask questions don't make anythin' strange of my ridin' in off the trail."

Darnell dropped his head and I saw a darker shade come to his face. I was burning to ply Vance with questions but I desisted. In short order Jack returned with our construction boss and the wagon-train leader, Herb Lane. Their eyes were questioning but their manner was not eager. It was not a hopeful sign to have the range rider from Texas summon them for an interview.

"Wal, men, gather around natural-like an' listen," began Shaw, and deliberately lighted his cigarette. "Funny how this mawnin' I was figurin' things had been workin' out too good for us. They shore have. But we've struck a snag. Mebbe it don't amount to a damn. Mebbe you fellers will make light of it. But it gave me one of my hunches an' I shore hate them, 'cause they always work out."

"All right, Shaw. Don't beat around the bush. Get it off yer chest," snapped Liligh.

"You seen me come in from ahaid on the trail. Wal, I was trackin' hawse tracks thet excited my suspicion behind us a ways. Early this mawnin' I rode back along the line. I found a telegraph pole down, not chopped but sawed clean through with a piece chipped out of the wire an' the insulator missin'. It struck me damn

211

funny. All along this nine thousand miles we've come there's never been a pole down in just thet way. Of course, it was white man's work.

"I saw boot tracks in the dust, made last night, in different sizes an' not hawseman's boots either. They was a big flat hobnail track new to me. Looked like two saddle hawses an' one pack animal. Wal, I tracked them at a trot five miles further back on the line an' found another pole cut just the same way. An' five miles further, more or less, I found a third. As the hawse tracks did not go any further east I reckoned there was no use ridin' any further back. The tracks came into the trail from up the slope an' I tracked them to a patch of timber a mile or so off, an' from there down into a little draw where two men with a pack animal had made camp last night, an' dug out early this mawnin'. They fed their hawses grain an' thet was shore peculiar to me.

"From ther I cut across an' took up the trail again past yore wagon-trains an' went on ahaid until I lost the track I'd been followin'. When the dew dried off the grass I found it very slow work to trail them any longer. Of course I *could* trail them, if I had plenty of time, 'cause trailin' tracks is my game. Now the whole damn thing has got me kinda stumped an' I reckon I'd like to know what you think about it."

"Hell," spat our Liligh. "That dovetails with somethin' I've suspected an' never told the boss. It kin mean only one thing. Some white man for some reason or other wants to block our telegraph messages back East."

"I figured out about the same thing," returned Shaw, blowing rings of smoke.

"Who in the world would want to hold Creighton up that way?" I asked.

"Tom, yo're familiar with this country. What's yore angle?" went on Shaw.

"Men, it sounds mighty like the underground doin's in South Pass."

"Wal, thet's tellin' us somethin', but it doesn't explain."

"It doesn't make a hell of a lot of difference now," went on Liligh. "Creighton hasn't any telegraph operator just now an' he says thet while he could make a stab at sendin' messages, they wouldn't be accurate. But any day now he's expectin' an operator to ketch up with us by stage, an' then, if the telegraph line is cut an' the important messages stopped, it'll make a tough situation."

Herb Lane put in quietly: "Mebbe we better not make too much of it until we see whether this work is followed up to-night or to-morrow."

"Thet's the ticket," agreed Liligh. "It's hopin' against hope. Meanwhile I'll send a wagon back along the line unbeknownst to Creighton to repair those breaks."

"I agree it would be wiser not to tell the chief if we can help it," I put in, earnestly. "He'd call it only a flea-bite, only another incident of construction work, but a lot of flea-bites can make a man sick and a thousand incidents more or less can put him down. I'm sure you've all noticed how strained and thin Creighton has become. He's lost more weight than any of us. He has had the physical work the same as all of us, but he has had also the mental and moral responsibility. He's been marvelous to stick it out as he has done, but he's not superhuman. I suggest that we keep this from him."

"Right," agreed Liligh. "Now, Shaw, you an' the cowboys an' yu too, Cameron, scout back along the line at night an' see what yu kin find out. If anythin', report to me."

The construction work went on just as before with our chieftain ignorant of the new depredation. That night at midnight Tom awakened me and on foot, bundled in our heavy coats and packing rifles, we scouted back along the line of five miles or more without seeing or hearing anything to excite our suspicion. Returning to camp we awoke Shaw and Lowden. They brought in their horses, padded their hoofs, and made ready for their scout.

"Fellers, it wants a couple of hours before it begins to get gray," said Shaw. "Now, we'll walk our hawses back along the trail a matter of ten miles or so. Lookin' an' listenin' at night is our long suit. But if we're dealin' with slick outdoor men, we're up against a hard job."

They rode away into the cold melancholy night without a sound of hoofs. Tom and I huddled over the little fire for a while, warming our hands and feet and then we went to bed. It was sunny and bright when we awakened, and the grassy slope and the bunches of sage and the boulders were glistening white with hoar frost.

While we were at breakfast the cowboys returned to camp, taking the precaution to ride in from the west, and each of them had the carcass of an antelope across his saddle. The meat was surely welcome but no doubt it was their intention to give the impression that they had been hunting. They unpacked and unsaddled, and had their breakfast without comment. Just afterward Liligh and Lane and Bob Wainwright, who had been given the job of repairing the line the day before, sought us in eager anticipation.

"Wal, yu lean-faced Injun. What hev yu got to report?" demanded Liligh.

"Same thing, only wuss, I reckon," drawled Shaw, getting ready for a smoke.

"Wuss! How wuss? It couldn't be no wuss."

"Wal, boss, our pards Wayne an' Tom walked out last night, miles back of camp. They didn't come on anythin'. Then Jack an' I rode out with our hawses, hoofs muffled, an' we walked them slow an' easy, often stoppin' to listen, back about fifteen miles. We never seen nor heared anythin'. When we come back about five miles it got daylight an' we found three poles down with the wires cut an' insulators missin', same as the mawnin' before. These places were miles apart. After the last break the hawse tracks led off the trail to the north. Trackin' was shore a slow business. It'd take a Comanche tracker a long time to work out those tracks. Besides I reckon it wouldn't be smart of us to show ourselves followin' them. These wire cutters are cute. Shore they'd be watchin' from some hidin' place."

"Three poles down an' wires cut in three places!" exclaimed Liligh, sarcastically. "Is thet all? I reckoned all the poles would be down."

"Don't lose your temper, Liligh," quietly interposed Lane. "Bob, what you think about it?"

"Wal, I reckon I think yer makin' a mountain out of a molehill," replied Wainwright. "What's a few telegraph poles cut down every night in our young lives?"

"It's a hell of a lot," snapped Liligh. "It took yu eight hours yestiddy to hang back thar an' make those repairs, an' to-day it'll take longer. Purty soon the chief will wanta send messages an' how the hell is he gonna do it? Particularly when we don't want him to find out."

"Wal, boss, I reckon we cain't help it," replied Shaw. "But we'll shore try hard. Jack an' I are liable to run foul of those hombres to-night, or soon anyway, an' we'll shore make it kinda hot for them."

But the odds were largely against the cowboys. Every night for three more nights they stalked the trail, while Tom and I went out on foot for half the night, all to no avail. And every night or early in the morning there were more telegraph poles cut down. The marauders added one pole on each successive night. During this period we progressed fifteen miles nearer to the mining district and camped the fourth night just this side of the hill beyond which lay the first gold diggings, Atlantic by name, which was a branch of South Pass a few miles farther on. Incredible to believe, we were within a day or two of another of our great objectives. It was none the less stirring also to think we were about to pass through the most famous and bloody and fabulously rich of all gold diggings.

By this time almost all the men connected with the wagon-train were aware of the depredations on the telegraph line, except our chieftain Creighton. By some miracle we had been able to keep it from him. He was so happy that none of us had the heart or the courage to tell him that for four days the great Western Union would not have transmitted messages, even if we had had a telegraph operator.

That night Shaw and Lowden, as they reported to us in the morning, rode out early and scouted along the rough terrain north of the trail, and in extremely heavy timber they espied a tiny camp-fire blaze. They stole upon it like Indians. They tried to hold up the two men whom they found there, as they wanted to discover who was behind this cutting of the telegraph line. But a fight resulted in which one of the men was killed and the other escaped into the woods.

When the cowboys went on further and returned along the telegraph line, they found three more poles had been cut and the wires down, presumably by another crew of men whose tracks, the daylight disclosed, were not the same as those of the earlier party. We were filled by consternation at this news and the cowboys were deadly angry. Shaw said it was no longer a petty matter, prompted by a few treacherous men to further their own needs, but that there was something big behind it.

That day we ran the telegraph line over the hill almost as far as Atlantic and camped at the side of the trail on the ridge top. It had been a short day's work with only three miles of telegraph line laid. That gave me time to interest myself in this gold digging.

Viewed from the top of the hill where the trail went over, this place was a remarkable one to see and wholly different from anything I had pictured. I faced a deep, wide gulch down the side of which the trail wound, crossed a roaring stream, and zigzagged steeply up the other side. Here and there were patches of fir trees. Halfway down the slope began a cluster of innumerable, queer, unsightly, patchwork shacks, with tents interspersed between them. They led the eye down and down to bigger huts and finally large, crude, board buildings, all facing down hill.

Parallel with the rushing white torrent and the trees which lined it ran an enormous ditch extending all the way up the gulch to the base of the mountain, and in this ditch and on its banks and everywhere around were active moving men, so many and so colorful in their red shirts, and so apparently frenzied that they resembled an army of ants. This, then, was a forerunner of the South Pass gold digging.

It made me catch my breath to gaze down there. To think that that place was only ten miles from the Sweetwater Valley and Kit Sunderlund's ranch! Then I saw the road, about which I had been told, that followed the stream all the way through the gulch and out at the lower end.

I made my way back to our wagon and burst upon my three comrades in excited raving about the gold diggings. I was trying to tell them what it looked like when Darnell, exclaiming, pointed out the arrival of the Pony Express rider. It was our friend Barnes and he was dismounting to deliver mail and dispatches into Creighton's hands. They conversed a few moments. Then Barnes left him and came running to us.

"Now what the hell is the matter with thet gazabo?" queried Shaw, as he rose to his feet. "I've seen too many fellers look like thet."

"Pard, he shore looks excited, but I'll bet my spurs he's not got bad news," replied Jack.

"Hyar, you cowboys, get your heads together with me," said Barnes, as he came up to me. "I've got to go right away an' I've no time to say anythin' over twice. Shaw, I don't know if this concerns you more than Cameron or any of you, but listen. On my last trip west through South Pass, three, four days ago, I seen that girl Ruby that one or another of you was sweet on."

The cowboys seemed stricken dumb and I burst out with a loud exclamation.

"Wal," went on Barnes, his sharp gaze on Shaw. "I knowed her before you fellers did back in Grand Island. She was a nice kid an' shore to be pitied. I seen her in South Pass an' she seen me. What's more, she recognized me. Her face lit up an' she waved, then somebody jerked her away from the winder, an' I'll say he jerked her! . . . Don't look like that, cowboy. There's absolutely no doubt. I saw her plain an' besides Ruby *knew* me."

Strangely enough it was to me that Shaw turned in this poignant moment. No doubt it was due to my intense sympathy with him in regard to this girl. His eyes were closed and tears were seeping from under his tight eyelids. His face was working convulsively and his clutch upon my arm was like a steel vise.

"Barnes," spoke up Lowden, tersely, "I knowed you

had good news an' it shore was welcome. You come damn near savin' this outfit. But, listen—*whar* did you see Ruby?"

"I don't know exact, Lowden. That's the hell of it," returned the express rider. "I was makin' tracks an' I like to show off in town an' I seen her just as I flashed by. I tried to remember just where. It was about half-way down the road from the express station in that row of houses all tucked together on the side of the street where the brook runs. It was upstairs, don't forget that. Comin' back to-day I looked sharp all along from the big gamblin' hall with the decorated upstairs porch an' I seen half a dozen winders, any one of which could be where I seen Ruby. Anyway I *seen* her. An' it's up to you fellers to find her. Good luck an' good-by."

In a moment or two Shaw pulled himself together. This was the first time the cowboy had ever betrayed any strong feeling in front of me and I gauged his reception of Barnes' news about Ruby by the way he had shown it.

"Pard, I reckon we'll have to forget about telegraph wires for a spell," he said, curtly. "Jack, get the hawses an' saddle up."

In the few moments during which I tried to collect my thoughts Vance and Jack were away down the hill toward the diggings at a brisk lope.

"Gosh, Tom!" I exclaimed. "We can't just sit here. What'll we do?"

"I reckon we ought to follow them," he replied. "It don't worry me none. With this beard I'm growin' I wouldn't be recognized in South Pass. I'll get my hoss. You can ride an' I'll walk."

"No. We'll both walk if we can't find some other way to get over there," I returned.

"There's wagons to and fro between the two camps every little bit. You can see 'em now climbin' the hill. Mebbe it's better we can't get over there fast. It'll give us time to think."

"You're right, Tom. I am so overjoyed about knowing where Ruby is that I can't think clearly. Come on. Let's rustle."

"Okay. But buckle on your gun. If my hunch is right you're gonna need it. Put a handful of shells in your left coat pocket."

We began the descent of the canyon just as Shaw and Lowden had reached the summit of the opposite slope and were riding on top, darkly silhouetted against the cloud of yellow smoke that rose from the mill. Its huge red mass could be seen topping the horizon.

"Pard, you've seen some action so far on the frontier," Darnell was saying, "but what we're liable to get up against here may be different. Keep your head about you. Listen to me or watch me."

"I certainly do not recollect ever being in such a state of mind," I returned. "I'm not scared or excited or loco as you fellows call it. I feel a swelling inside. I feel buoyant."

"Wal, pard, if that buoyant means floatin' around in the air, you come down to earth."

Darnell's remark jarred me back to the realization that we were embarked on stern business. We climbed rapidly down the slope and soon reached the line of shacks. Some of the little houses were hardly large enough for a man to turn around inside. They all had stovepipe chimneys sticking out of their makeshift roofs.

Passing through a broad belt of these huts, we came to a fairly wide street on the uphill side of which began the larger and more commodious edifices. For every shop and store there were several saloons and they all bore rude fantastic signs nailed up or painted above the doors.

Farther down where this street made a turn to cross the bridges over the ditch and the stream, there were still bigger houses, some of them painted and quite pretentious. One bore the name Miner's Rest, and the adjoining one, much larger, was named Gold Strike. The last building on that side appeared to be a good-sized merchandise store.

There were men in sight, a few of them miners, but the horde that we had seen from the hilltop were in the gold diggings. It occurred to me to step into the store and make an inquiry.

"I'd rather stay outside an' look people over," said Darnell.

I went in and accosted a middle-aged man of rather important bearing, evidently the merchant:

"I'd like to inquire if you know anything of a Colonel Sunderlund who just recently located in the Sweetwater Valley on a ranch not far from here?"

"Yes," came the ready reply. "I'm glad to inform you that Sunderlund has been here several times, the last time only yesterday."

"Does this road go to his ranch?"

"Straight as a bee-line. You can't miss it. The ranch is in plain sight from where the road opens out into the valley. It's high up above the river partly surrounded by pine trees. Prettiest place in the valley."

"Thanks very much. And about how much of a drive?"

"Well, Sunderlund drives it in less than an hour, but that black team of his is a fast-stepping one."

I returned to Tom, tingling all over with the thought that I was that close to Kit, and that if chance afforded, I could see her in short order. We talked a few moments, taking opportunity to look about us and not missing anything. Presently an empty wagon came along. We hailed the driver and he cheerfully bade us pile in. We did so and I found a seat on some bags while Tom leaned against the driver's seat and plied him with questions.

It was about mid-afternoon and the sloping sun was losing its warmth. The ascent on that side of the gulch was less precipitous and at times our view downhill was intercepted by clumps of pine trees. When we got to the top, however, we could see that all along the stream as far up as our sight would carry were miners working like beavers. There was not an open space along the stream where there were not two or three men on each side standing in the water. It made me shiver to look at them. When we surmounted the top of the hill, we found the road led across a level space for a mile or so to another gulch, and apparently a much larger one.

The big gold mill at once claimed our undivided attention. It belched huge clouds of yellow and black smoke. It resembled nothing that I had ever seen in mills or blasting furnaces, and appeared to be a jumbled-up mass of stacks and shafts and huge round tanks and square buildings with pipes both large and small running in every direction. Long before we reached it we heard the roar of machinery and presently we espied many workmen passing to and fro.

Below the mill the road sloped down and curved to the left around a spur of hill on which were numerous shacks such as we had passed in Atlantic. To the right opened up a large triangular-shaped valley, literally covered with the habitations of miners. Some of them were bizarre, others funny, others rickety, but all of them make-shift shelters. Beyond them a goodly distance was another stream which swarmed with toiling men.

When we turned the curve the driver informed us that here was South Pass. And it burst upon my bewildered sight like nothing more than a comic opera scene on a grand scale. There was one wide street as far as we could see and two lines of buildings of every imaginable color, some of them even being blue or pink. The road and the narrow board sidewalks were congested with moving forms. On one side there were vehicles all the way down. I noted many gaudy sign boards but was not yet close enough to read the letters.

"Here's a livery stable, if you gents want to hire rigs," the driver informed us. "That gray stone building up the hill a ways is the bank. The big frame house on the left is the general store where you can buy anything, and across from it on the corner is the best hotel. This road turns off there and it's the same old Oregon Trail. Crosses the brook and winds out on top. . . . I suppose you young gents will buck the tiger?"

"We probably will if we can find any place that's running a small enough game to fit our pocketbooks."

"Well, there's all kinds of games and I'm giving you a hunch most of them are crooked. Stay out of the dens 'way down the road. The fine-looking ones are bad enough."

We thanked the driver and descended in front of the

big store. The wide steps running around this building afforded us a better vantage place than the hotel across the street and we chose that for our first stop. We were all eyes to get a glimpse of Shaw and Lowden. There was a motley stream of humanity passing up and down the street, for the most part miners in rough colorful garb. But we noted many different types of people and, to our surprise, a number of women.

The store behind us was well patronized. I looked at each pedestrian with a quick glance that did not register anything. I was in a hurry for something to happen, just what I knew not. I did not believe it was agitation. But it didn't help any to have my imagination picture Shaw standing in the middle of that crowded street with his gun spitting fire and smoke. I could even conjure up a picture of him running down the street with Ruby in his arms followed by Lowden with two guns keeping off the pursuers.

The instant I saw a brunette girl standing in the doorway of the store and gazing at me with startled dark eyes, I knew that whatever I had anticipated was now beginning.

The girl recognized me. She started impulsively out of the doorway and then halted, nervously gazing all around as if she feared to be seen. It was the same dance-hall girl, Flo, that I had met in Gothenburg and with whom I had danced.

"Look, Tom. There's that girl, Flo," I whispered, nudging Darnell.

"That's correct, Pard. It is Flo, who was friendly to Ruby. I guess mebbe our hunch wasn't a slick one."

I hurried to the girl's side and Tom followed me. Addressing her eagerly, I said, "Hello, Flo. Of course you remember us."

"Yes, you're Mr. Cameron and I recognize your cowboy friend too," she replied, hurriedly. "I've been looking for you boys to come through this place for weeks."

"Thank goodness, Flo. That must mean you're still our friend. The Pony Express rider, Barnes, told us he had seen Ruby here in South Pass. Shaw and Lowden are in town looking for her and so are we."

"Come inside the store. It'd be all my life is worth if I was caught talking to you," she said, swiftly, and let us just inside the door where there was a small space between the counter and piles of merchandise that offered a little seclusion. We faced her there and took our cue from her look of apprehension and her husky whisper. There was paint on her face but her pallor showed through it. She appeared older, and not so pretty as when I had seen her before.

"Listen," she began. "Ruby was carried off from Julesburg the night of the Indian raid by Red Pierce and his men, and brought west to South Pass in a wagontrain. She was here in town until a few days ago. Then Pierce moved her over to Atlantic. She is now kept in that new saloon and gambling hell called the Gold Nugget. The first saloon on the left as you cross the bridge."

"Is she being held prisoner there?" I asked, in a tense whisper.

"It amounts to that. She has tried to leave several times. Pierce has her guarded jealously."

"Does he mistreat her?"

"Yes, he has beaten her but she holds out against him. She told me she knew you cowboys would get here eventually and rescue her. Pierce finally fell in love with her and she was at her wit's end to keep him off. I told her to work on him—anything for the time, and so far, she has done it."

"But Ruby wrote she was married. I thought it might have been to Pierce," I interrupted.

"No, Ruby ain't married. The reason she left that note for Shaw the time of the Indian raid was 'cause a member of Red Pierce's gang Shaw didn't know, forced her. He trailed Ruby for Pierce and swore he'd shoot Shaw in the back while Shaw was shooting Indians if she didn't write that note. He told her what to say 'cause he overheard both of them talk about getting married that day."

"Then, pard, we're just in time," muttered Darnell. "But, Flo, tell us a few more things. You are shore an answer to our prayer."

"Has Pierce got a place in this town too?" I asked.

"I'll say he has. The Four Aces saloon and gambling place is next to the biggest one. It used to be run by Emery who was hanged out here in the Sweetwater Valley recently."

"Tell us more," I went on hurriedly. "Is Pierce here now?"

"He is. Sitting in a private gambling game but only his own men know him under the name of Red Pierce here. He's known as Bill Howard."

"Then it's the same old game, saloon and gambling hall and girls?" I queried.

"Don't fool yourself, Cameron. This saloon and gambling hall stuff is poor potatoes for Pierce. He has bigger ideas than that. Only last night I heard him talking to men, one of them his right-hand man, Black Thornton. They've got a big deal here but just what it is, I don't know. I think it's a bank robbing job and maybe a wholesale robbery of the miners. They want to make a clean sweep and then go on west to the California diggings. Pierce must be a big man in his field. He's a robber and a murderer or if he doesn't murder men outright himself, he hires his tools to do it."

"Tom, we're on the right track," I whispered. "Big deal! Clean sweep! . . . Flo, could by any chance Pierce be mixed up with this systematic cutting of the telegraph line that we've been up against for days?"

"Ahuh. And what for, Flo?" queried Darnell, grinding his teeth.

"Simple as A B C. I can answer that one. I've heard them talk. Pierce said he didn't mind the telegraph line coming through here eventually, but he wants to stall it off until he can pull his big deal."

"And for why?" Darnell shot at her, and I echoed his query, although we already knew the answer.

"Pierce doesn't want any messages sent back over that wire to Ft. Laramie to get the soldiers here. Some of the big men here are trying to have a sheriff to bring law and order."

"That's the answer, Tom," I returned, hurriedly. "Flo, bless your heart. You are a friend in need. We won't forget it."

"Pard, you're wastin' time. Flo, tell us once more how we can find Ruby," concluded Darnell.

"I know exactly where she is. There's a big loft over that Gold Nugget saloon and gambling hall and it has been partitioned off into rooms. I was never there but one of our girls has been and she told me. There's a door and a stairway to the right when you enter the saloon. You go up that stair to a narrow hall with rooms on each side, and I suspect that Ruby's is the farthest on the left, because this girl Jo said Ruby could lie on her bed and reach up and touch the eaves of the roof. Anyway, you can find her easily enough. Good luck to you. And . . . don't forget me."

"I shore won't!" was Darnell's surprising reply.

We stalked out of the store. By tacit consent we faced up the street toward Atlantic. Darnell's mind worked more quickly than mine. He said the first thing we'd need would be a buckboard and a team of horses. We must not waste time in trying to find Shaw.

We hired a vehicle from the boarded livery stable man and with Darnell at the reins we were trotting up the hill in short order. There was a buffalo robe on the second seat and I got that and spread it over my knees. The sun had tipped the mountain range and the air was chill.

We drove down the slope into the town, across the bridge, passed the big store, up to the hitching rail in front of the Gold Nugget. There were discordant music inside, the hum of a roulette wheel, the clink of glasses and loud laughter.

"One last word, pard," Darnell whispered in my ear. "We're in luck 'cause there don't seem to be many people. Follow me inside an' take your cue from what I do. I've a hunch there'll be shootin' before we get out."

When we entered the wide door of the saloon, we saw a large, gaudy, newly furnished room with a string of miners lined up at the bar and a few gamblers at the wheel. Otherwise the hall was empty. We sauntered in and no one paid any attention to us. There was the doorway to the right and I caught a glimpse of steep stairs. In a moment we were climbing them. There was light above somewhere because it was not dark. We reached the corridor and tiptoed all the way down to the last door on the left. My heart was in my throat when, at a sign from Tom, I knocked on this door. We heard something yet could not distinguish what it was.

"Ruby," I called, in a low tone, unable to keep it from shaking, "are you there?"

We heard a rustle, soft feet thud on the floor, then an answering voice which sent the blood away from my heart. "Yes, I'm Ruby and I'm here. Who are you?"

"It's Cameron, and Darnell is with me," I called back, my lips at the keyhole. "We've come to take you away. Flo told us."

The first incoherent cry that followed my words, muted though it was, attested to an almost overwhelming joy. "Oh, Wayne—Wayne—I knew you boys would find me, but I'm locked in—a prisoner! I can't get out!"

"Stand back to one side—away from the door!"

I braced myself against the opposite wall and flung all my weight powerfully against the door. It was a flimsy affair and the lock was not strong. My first onslaught almost did the trick. At my second plunge the door flew off the lock and hinges and went smashing to the floor of a tiny room. My impetus carried me into the room while Tom guarded the door. Then I saw Ruby. Her face was as white as a sheet and her big eyes seemed bottomless gulfs. I picked her up and carried her out into the corridor.

"Pard, we gotta rustle," whispered Darnell, his gun out. "They heard that crash below an' we can look for trouble. Keep behind me."

He ran to the top of the stairway and as I came up to him I saw a dark man bounding up the stairs. He and Tom began to shoot at the same instant. I heard bullets strike flesh. Above the red flash of gunfire below us, I recognized Black Thornton's face. He let out a mortal yell, and flinging his gun which banged on the landing below, he tried to hold to the wall but Darnell, stepping down, kicked him loose and he plunged down the stairs to alight with a thud that jarred the house.

I kept at Tom's heels. There were shouts from the saloon. I heard heavy footfalls. When Darnell stepped over the prostrate body of the dead man, I saw that he was unsteady on his feet. He had been hit. But keeping in front of me, he reached back with his left hand and dragged me over the dead man out into the saloon. The heavy footfalls belonged to a man I knew, the one I had fought in the saloon at Gothenburg. He had a gun in his hand and on his dark face there was a look of surprise.

"None of that," he bawled, and he fired an instant after Darnell's gun exploded. But Darnell was sagging and his shot went low. He let go of me to hang on to the door and he kept deliberately in front of me using his body as a shield to protect Ruby. This second assailant kept firing again and again. The bullets made a sickening thud as they struck Darnell.

"Bore him, pard," he called, in a strangled voice.

I had shifted the girl to my left arm and had drawn my gun. I was quick to lean away from Darnell and shoot the man. His gun dropped to the floor, and both his hands went to his middle. Uttering an awful cry, he plunged face downward in front of us. And the next instant Darnell also fell, his gun clattering and his last choking gasp was: *"Rustle!"*

I ran out of the saloon, lifted Ruby into the front seat and tearing the reins free, I leaped in beside her and pulled that team away from the rail and turned it into the road that ran down the gulch. We had not gotten many rods before there came shouts and shots from the saloon door but the bullets sped harmlessly by, kicking up the dust around us, and in another moment we were speeding out of sight behind the bank.

Chapter Fourteen

THE ROAD led straight down the gulch for what appeared to be miles without another vehicle in sight. The team of bays were fresh, and, as I held them back, they settled into a swift pace that drew the buckboard rapidly along. With almost anything on wheels I saw that I could hold my lead, but saddle horses might be available at once near the Gold Nugget and they, of course, could overhaul me before I got to the valley. In the event that I was pursued by mounted men I grimly planned to fight it out with them while in flight. A thought burst upon me too late—I should have taken Ruby up to the construction camp; but the Sunderlund ranch as a refuge for the girl had lodged in my mind.

The road was fairly good, hard-packed with only occasional dips or bumps. When the buckboard presently went over a bump with a jar, the unconscious girl slid off the seat to the floor. As I glanced down upon her she showed signs of returning consciousness. Holding the reins tight with my right hand, with my left I covered her with the buffalo robe. It was fortunate that I was in the buckboard because the cutting wind was cold. I looked back up the road, aware of that hard constriction in my throat. But no one was following.

The team was flying down the road. I had to hold back hard to keep them to an even pace. In the event of pursuit, of course I would have pushed them to swifter gait. That would be risking accident which I wanted to avoid if possible. Not for an interval that seemed endless did I turn around again to look back. Still no one in sight! I had traveled five miles or more from the gold diggings and the turn of the road was close. As I made it I saw another long straight stretch. Its end was marked by a widening and flattening of the sides of the gulch and a void which I knew must be the valley.

Twice more in the next few miles I turned to see if I was pursued. When I saw that I was not, there came a sudden change in my feelings. The thought of Darnell sacrificing his life for Ruby, the deliberate way in which he kept her from being struck by bullets, returned to me with agonizing vividness. At that moment Ruby stirred at my feet and called out my name. I replied, bending over to assure her in forceful tone that we had escaped, and that we were almost certain to be safe presently.

"But, Tom—what of him?" she cried.

"Don't think about that, Ruby," I replied, unsteadily.

"Where is Vance?"

"He and Jack are in South Pass searching for you. It was Barnes who told us that he had seen you in a window. I ran into Flo. She told me about you—where to find you. Tom and I didn't dare to wait for the boys so we rushed to Atlantic alone."

"Wayne, where are you taking me?"

"To the Sunderlund ranch down here in the valley. You'll be taken care of there until we can come after you. . . . Ruby, are you all right?"

"Yes, I guess—so. I feel sort of stunned. Can you cover my feet? They're freezing."

I reached down and tucked the heavy buffalo robe around her feet and then under and around her head. She was better off lying there, especially in the event of pursuers attacking me. She did not speak again. I directed all my attention to driving the mettlesome team.

Several times I could not resist the temptation to look down upon Ruby, to see her white face and wide dark eyes and bright hair against the buffalo robe. Once she smiled at me. It was such a tender, such a pitiful little smile, with its gratitude and hope, that I dared not look again. But I did look back. No vehicle—no horsemen! I had almost reached the valley without any-one on my trail. And again the thought of Tom Darnell assailed me, and again I fought it off. It was creeping, insidious, strength-taking.

The road made another turn and then opened into the wide Sweetwater Valley. I was not in the mood conducive to appreciation of beautiful scenery, but the prospect struck me, though without emotion. A couple of miles or more out in the valley, which was level and purple in hue, the river was marked by a heavy line of willows and cottonwoods. Their tips and the high bluff above, crowned by a white house, were reflecting the last golden rays of the setting sun. Beyond the hill all was still bright in the sunlight, leading afar to the bold walls of the valley standing out in red and gold.

As I neared the river I made out a log bridge spanning it and the curve of the road as it wound to the left up the slope to the back of the bluff. Soon I drove across this bridge, to find the Sweetwater somewhat smaller, and clearer in its amber hue than I remembered it many miles below. Halfway up the slope I noted horses and cattle grazing out in the sage, but I could not see the ranch house until I surmounted the bluff. I had crossed one road leading north and south before taking to the slope.

Some distance ahead there was a signpost too far for me to discern what was written upon it. As I drove up to the house it was with tremendous relief that I saw saddle horses standing with bridles down, and a buckboard with a team very like the one I was driving. There were several men gathered there who suddenly became keenly interested in my approach. One of these was Colonel Sunderlund.

As I pulled the team to a quick halt, Sunderlund, recognizing me, stepped forward exclaiming:

"Why, if it isn't Cameron! What in the world brings you heah? Ah! Yo're pale and——"

"Hello, Colonel," I replied. "Don't be startled. I'm all right. I have a girl here in the buckboard. You will remember—my pard Shaw's sweetheart. There was a fight. Darnell was killed, I'm afraid. Will you call your daughter? I want to beg her to look after Ruby until Shaw comes for her."

"Darnell killed? Thet fine young cowboy? Too bad!

You are certainly welcome, Cameron. Kit will be glad indeed to receive the girl. Fetch her in."

I leaped out of the buckboard, and raising Ruby from her position half under the seat, I wrapped her more securely in the buffalo robe and lifted her out. As I turned I heard Sunderlund calling his daughter. Then I faced the house and saw that a porch ran the whole length, showing several doors. Sunderlund stopped before the last one which immediately opened to disclose Kit. I mounted the porch then and made my way toward her with my burden. I heard Sunderlund talking rapidly and Kit's wondering exclamations. Then I confronted her.

"Kit, there's been the devil to pay," I said. "You remember Vance's girl, Ruby? Well, here she is, and I want you to take her in and look after her until I can find Shaw and we can get back."

The gladness in Kit's expression was greater than her amazement, but her fine blue eyes shot arrowy lightnings at me as she said, "Wayne Cameron! Always rescuing some girl! If you are not the gallant—a regular knight of the West. And this time it's your little friend Ruby."

There was a little note of sarcasm in her rich voice, a hint of pride and jealousy in her darkening eyes.

"Kit!" I expostulated. "Darnell was killed. He sacrificed his life for Ruby, and Shaw is running amuck in South Pass. I've got to get back."

"Oh, Wayne!" she cried, impetuously, with a lovely warm smile that changed everything. "I was only shocked. You know me—how—how funny I am. . . . Bring Ruby in. I shall be only too happy to take care of her."

I carried the girl into a room that blazed at me with its bright lights and colors and I laid her down upon a couch. Sunderlund came in and stood solicitously beside his daughter as we all gazed down upon the white-faced Ruby.

"Ruby, you're all right now," I said, earnestly. "I must hurry back to South Pass—to find Shaw and Jack and tell them you are safe."

"Thanks—Wayne," faltered Ruby, almost unable to

speak. "Tell Vance—that I've waited for him—that I've been faithful."

"Of course, Ruby. Flo told me why you wrote that note. I'll tell Vance everything," I interrupted, turning away from her.

Kit detained me at the door a moment. I kissed her warmly, held her tight a second, telling her I would come back soon, possibly before the construction work was finished. Then I tore myself free and hurried away with Sunderlund tagging at my heels.

"Colonel, is there any way I can get to South Pass without going back to Atlantic?"

"Yes. Take the road to the left just across the bridge. It's only four miles farther and it's a much better road. But take my man Wilson with you. He'll drive and you can make better time. I'll pick him up to-morrow in South Pass and I'll see you too. I shore want to be in thet gold diggings when Creighton gets there with his wire."

From the buckboard as we turned away I glanced back at the house and a pleasant surprise interrupted my grim mood at sight of Kit standing in the doorway of her room with her arm around Ruby. Kit threw me a kiss and Ruby waved, then the driver sped us away.

During that swift ride in the cold piercing wind I plied Sunderlund's cowboy with innumerable questions, more to escape from my own feeling than to get actual news of the valley and South Pass. But I learned more in that ride than I possibly could in any other way in so short a time.

As we drove down the long descent leading into South Pass and crossed the bridge, I instructed Wilson to drive to the livery stable.

"Maybe I can learn something there."

The grizzled livery stable man greeted me with much more effusion and acclaim than I thought was due me, even if he had learned about the fight over at the Gold Nugget. His first words proved to me that he not only knew about Darnell but also about Shaw and Lowden.

"Them cowboys rode up the hill just about dark," he said. "An' they left this town split wide open. South Pass, tough as it is, never had many visitors like Shaw and

Lowden. I was down town when the big rumpus came off, but I missed the first part of their act when they played lightning and thunder in half the dens in town. Those cowboys' deal was to make these gamblers and houseowners talk—tell them where some man named Red Pierce had hidden some girl. But they never found her.

"The man they called Red Pierce turned out to be Bill Howard. I've knowed him pretty well for weeks, ever since he started running a big place in town. I was in the Four Aces when it happened. Howard or Pierce had got hold of the biggest hall in town—I never heared such a row in my life. Men yellin', guns crackin', chairs and tables and poker chips and coins clashing! I ran in there to find a crowd of gamesters spillin' away from the two fire-eyed cowboys who had Howard on the floor. Two of his men were dead, but Howard was still alive. He had been all shot up. Arms, legs, and I don't know where else!

"Shaw was orderin' him to tell where he kept that girl. Howard swore she was at his place, the Gold Nugget over in Atlantic. I heared afterward that he had persisted in tellin' Shaw that ever since he had been first shot. But Shaw didn't believe him. That cowboy was the coldest, fiercest proposition that ever stepped into a hall in South Pass. And, believe me, all the bad men in the West have done that. And just after I butted in there I heard Shaw tell Howard he'd let him off if he'd tell the truth, and Howard, gaspin' and pantin', half sittin' there in his blood with both arms broke and hangin' limp, told the same story.

"I don't know if Shaw believed him even then but he an' the other one left. When I got out of the Four Aces with the crowd an' came here, the cowboys were mountin' their horses. They had left them with me to feed and water. They rode off, then, up the hill and that's all I know."

"We'll go on to Atlantic and the construction camp," I decided. The livery man's shocking story had affected me with relief more than horror, and showed me that I must not lose any time in finding Shaw.

"I reckon I'll ride over with you, if you don't mind,"

said our informant, and, upon being assured that we would be glad to have him, he clambered into the back seat.

"Wilson, take it easy up this steep hill, but push the horses when we get on top," he directed.

When we got down into the gulch and across the bridge we saw a crowd of men in front of the Gold Nugget. They had their heads together and were so interested they did not even notice our approach. I bade Wilson stop outside the circle of light, and, getting out of the buckboard, I said I would hold the horses while they went in to see if they could find out any more news. In case of drastic action of any kind I wanted to be on my feet in the dark. Wilson and the livery stable man were gone what seemed a very few moments. When they returned we all got in the buckboard and resumed our journey.

"Shaw and Lowden were here early in the evening," said Wilson. "They threw guns on the gang in there but didn't do any shooting. They found out pronto that the girl had been taken away and the body of your dead pard was laying outside. The cowboys lifted him over a saddle and went off up the road."

The certainty of Darnell's death at last broke down my resistance and I sat there in my buffalo robe, shivering with grief and regret. I had only partially recovered when we reached the construction camp. There were bright camp fires burning and men sitting in groups all around. Liligh was the one who met me and he held to my arm while he told me that the cowboys had just buried Darnell over beyond the edge of the trail.

"Did Creighton hear about this awful thing?" I queried.

"Yes. Shore he heard. But, at thet, he was about the last one. It spread like wildfire."

"And what did the chief say? I'm afraid—I hope he won't fire us."

"Fire yu? Good Lord, yu haven't learned to know our boss yet. He roared like a bull, but it was in praise of all of yu."

"Then he had been told about the cutting of the poles

lately—that Red Pierce's gang was doing that to hold the telegraph messages back?"

"I reckon thet was what made Creighton so mad, an' shore an' sartain was the reason of his great appreciation fer yu fellars. An' he's gonna hev a stone cut to mark Darnell's grave."

I sought out Wilson, and, giving him messages for Sunderlund and Kit and Ruby, I told him to go back to South Pass, as the Colonel had directed. Then I hurriedly strode over to our wagon and to the little camp fire around which the two cowboys were sitting smoking. They got up to greet me and at first it was a silent welcome, the simplicity of which was emphasized by the powerful grip of their hands.

"Vance, I took Ruby—over to Sunderlund's—for Kit to take care of her," I began, with my unsteady voice breaking huskily. "Ruby was all right. She'll be well cared for there until you go after her." And then I gave him Ruby's message.

"Pard, I reckon I never thanked God for my good luck," he replied, quietly. "But I'm goin' to begin now an' be grateful for such a pard as you. Tell us now all about the fight you had when Tom got his everlastin'."

Stirred to my depths I related that story in detail.

"It's just too bad me an' Jack wasn't with you," was the cowboy's comment. "We'd have beat those two hombres to a gun an' you know by now thet when a man is bored even as he throws his gun he ain't goin' to shoot very straight."

A little later I stood out of the circle of the camp-fire light by the freshly made mound which was Tom Darnell's grave. It was alongside the old Oregon Trail, on a high barren ridge where it was lonely and desolate and the wind mourned through the shrubs and sage and the great black mountain frowned down, and the white stars blinked pitilessly.

I could not, at the moment, fully appreciate the devastating truth that Tom Darnell had laid down his life for Ruby, a dance-hall girl—and me! But I already felt that it was a great and glorious act and would somehow ennoble my life. These wild, fiery-spirited cowboys had never been understood by Easterners. There must have been something in their hard lonely life on the ranges that made for greatness. From the very first Darnell had attached himself to me, had borne the brunt of many hardships for me, and now he was gone, leaving me to remember forever that greater love hath no man . . .

The next morning Creighton came over when we were having breakfast and said abruptly, "Shaw, I want you and Cameron to take the day off."

Shaw looked at me and said, "Wal, Wayne, cain't you understand your orders? You an' me are ridin' pronto over to the Sunderlund ranch."

And so off we went, having much to talk about concerning the future of each of us and the girls we loved.

On arriving, Kit ran up to me and Ruby ran up to Shaw, but somehow Kit and I did not embrace. We stood aside sort of half embarrassed, both of us feeling that this moment belonged to the reunion of Shaw and Ruby.

After giving Ruby more than a hearty kiss, Shaw turned to me:

"Wayne, you old tenderfoot, don't you realize we have to get back to Creighton and our telegraph line?"

"What's your hurry, Vance? You haven't seen Ruby in Lord knows when."

"As sure as God made little apples, I guess I'll have to keep figuring things out for you the rest of my life. The sooner we get back on the job, the sooner that piece of iron wire will reach Ft. Bridger, and the sooner you and I will be married."

"And you were the one who was talking about obeying orders," I laughed.

That same day the Western Union crossed the gulch where the Atlantic miners cheered as it passed, went up the hill and down into South Pass.

That night I tramped the single indescribable street of South Pass for hours on end but I did not enter one of the saloons or gambling hells or do anything but look.

I met Flo on the street. She was sorrowful over Tom Darnell's death, but the killing of Red Pierce and his minions had liberated her as it had Ruby. She told me there was a young miner who wanted her to marry him.

He was an honest fellow and had done well in the diggings.

"I'm not good enough for Jim," Flo confessed. "And I know it. But he doesn't think so."

Next morning Creighton and his wagon-trains rolled out of South Pass bound on the last lap of their journey. I drove our wagon. The sky was overcast and the wind that whipped from the peaks was piercing and cold. We were caught by a blinding snowstorm before we could cross the high flat of the pass.

Perhaps it was the irony of fate that a big wagonload of Creighton's telegraph poles was instrumental in averting a tragedy. We built a bonfire of those logs and kept it burning all night while the storm raged.

The gale blew out by morning and the snow ceased and the sun rose dazzlingly upon a changed white world.

We forged on and the next day reached the purple sage country where rapid progress with the line could once more be made.

We had beaten the winter. We covered the last one hundred fifty miles of our telegraph trek in sixteen days, including the crossing of the Green River.

At last, historic old Ft. Bridger appeared before us, with its stone walls almost hidden among the grove of cottonwoods and its meandering branches of the Black River running before and behind the fort, where we already knew the Mormons were to meet us.

We spent four restless days in Ft. Bridger waiting for the Mormons to complete their end of the Western Union. Shaw and I were the most restless of the lot. We could hardly wait to embark for the Sweetwater and all it would mean.

It seemed ages from the time when we saw the first pole of the western division of the telegraph construction pop up on the horizon until the Mormons had run the wire down into the valley. Creighton's big hands trembled as he climbed aloft our last telegraph pole and connected the wires. The expression on our chieftain's face beggared description. What a moment for him! His part of it was done.

Yet there was another delay before Creighton could

rejoice—before Western Union had spanned the continent. The crew working east from Sacramento toward Salt Lake City had been held up.

We waited four more interminable days, Shaw and I champing at the bit, so to speak, to be on our way. In the meantime a temporary shelter had been erected and our telegraph operator sat hour by hour at his little table before his instrument waiting for the final word. At last this came late in the afternoon. We all stood motionless and silent as Creighton awaited to intercept, en route, the first official transcontinental telegraph message from Stephen J. Field, Chief Justice of California.

While he waited, Creighton sent a message to his wife in Omaha. His face lighted up as the operator transposed his anxiously written words into code. He handed the message to Shaw to read, and as the cowboy spoke, I felt a lump in my throat:

Ft. Bridger, October 17, 1861
To Mrs. Edward Creighton, Omaha, Nebraska
This being the first message over the new line since it is completed to Salt Lake, allow me to greet you. In a few days two oceans will be united.
(Signed) Edward Creighton

Finally the long-awaited telegram passed through Ft. Bridger. The operator wrote it down and handed it to our chieftain. Or task was finally done. Creighton trembled as he read the message aloud to us:

"To Abraham Lincoln, President of the United States: In the temporary absence of the Governor of the State, I am requested to send you the first message which will be transmitted over the wires of the telegraph line which connects the Pacific with the Atlantic States. The people of California desire to congratulate you upon the completion of the great work. They believe that it will be the means of strengthening the attachment which binds both the East and the West to the Union, and they desire in this—the first message across the continent—to express their loyalty to the Union and their determination to stand by its Government on this its day of trial. They regard that Government with affection and will adhere to it under all fortunes. (Signed) Stephen J. Field, Chief Justice of California."

Creighton's voice did not break, but it sounded several times as though it might.

Almost immediately another message came through from Mayor Teschermacher, San Francisco, to Mayor Wood, New York City: "The Pacific to the Atlantic sends greetings, and may both oceans be dry before a foot of all the land that lies between them shall belong to any other than our united country."

"You know," whispered Shaw to me, "this damn silence is a hell of a sight louder than any stampede I've ever heard . . . and a damn sight more pleasing to my ears."

During this elevating and all-satisfying moment, I could not have found my voice even if I had created something fitting to say. Suddenly a hand touched my shoulder and I turned around to see Kit ·Sunderlund's father.

"Gentlemen," he said to Shaw and me, "I shore drove a long way to get here in time for this little ceremony. I'd have missed had it not been for your eight-day wait. However, I don't suppose either of you wants to listen to the prattlings of an old man like me. But say, now that this is all through, I wonder if you'll both come over to the fort? There's somethin' I want to show you."

Shaw and I went with him mechanically. For a reason I cannot define we did not feel surprise at Colonel Sunderlund's being there in Ft. Bridger. We had no expectation of what it meant.

We followed the Colonel into the fort. Despite its being so late in the year, the enclosure was carpeted with yellow flowers. The air had a tang but the sunlight seemed mellow like Indian summer back home.

Standing by the well were two figures. Shaw halted in his tracks as if he had been shot. I looked but did not believe my eyes.

The two figures ran toward us, enveloped us. They were Kit and Ruby.

"Oh, Wayne, we wanted to see the joining of the wires but we wanted to surprise you too," Kit said.

I heard incoherent mumblings beside us, some of which sounded like Vance and some like Ruby, except that his voice held something I had never before heard in it.

"I just can't believe this," I managed to breathe.

"Dad didn't want us to make the long trip because of storms, but we just wouldn't stay home," Kit went on.

Suddenly Creighton appeared, his voice booming ahead of him.

"Wayne! Vance! I've been looking all over for you. Congratulations!" He shook hands all around.

Then he went on: "Now that this telegraph job is finished, mark my words, the railroad will be next. But according to my good friend the Colonel here, you boys will be mighty busy raising cattle. I'm going in for that myself and Colonel Sunderlund is going to handle them for me. With Vance and you on the job, I won't be worrying." And with that he walked away.

"Wal, ain't thet just like Edward Creighton," Vance drawled. "Telegraph, railroad, cattle! His work ain't never done."

"Look, boys," Kit broke in. She was pointing toward the long row of telegraph poles with the wire and the sun shining on it, diminishing in the distance.

"Just look as far as you can see," I said to all of them and to myself too, "and then remember the many torturous miles beyond and all the tremendous difficulties we encountered in order that what happened to-day could happen."

"Yes," drawled Vance, "shootin' an' fires an' thunder an' stampedes an' Indians an' all, just to bring a little piece of iron wire to meet another little piece of iron wire."